Mary & Bright

A Maple Falls Novel

SHANNON GRAUPMAN

Mary & Bright

ISBN 978-0-9982151-2-9

The characters and events of this book are fictional, and any resemblance to actual persons or event is coincidental.

Cover by Paper and Sage Design

Printed in the United States of America

To my Mom and Dad

You mean the world to me

Other Books by Shannon Graupman

Maple Falls Series

Bake My Day

Falling For You

Chapter
One

Mary Bradford's heart raced as she sat on the edge of her king size bed — her gaze affixed on the single white sheet of paper resting on the nightstand. She brushed her hands along the top of her thighs, wiping the sweat that began to pool in the creases of her palms. She reached for the paper, the sunlight catching the reflection of the silver glitter-covered edges. She gently ran her finger along the bottom edge, causing a glitter snowstorm on her lap. She was there the night it happened, making a special trip home just for the occasion, so it shouldn't have upset her as much as it did. Physically holding the wedding invitation in her hands, reading the fancy script font, she finally came to the realization that it was actually going to happen. Her worst fear was staring her in the face, literally in black and white. She was officially the last sister to get married.

She always assumed Susie would be the first to get married since she's the oldest. She started dating Grant her sophomore year in high school and had her whole life planned out on a clipboard of fun. But when Ali, her *younger* sister, got engaged, Mary couldn't help but feel a knot form in the pit of her stomach. She was happy Ali and Zach found each other, but she couldn't help the overwhelming feeling of jealousy that consumed her. Mary knew that birth order was no guarantee in determining who would be married first, or who would have children first, but being the only one left without either, she couldn't help but feel a heaviness in her heart.

Two years ago, Mary left the only life she'd ever known to move halfway across the country with Alex. They had been dating for two years before this, so making the cross country move to continue their relationship didn't seem that crazy. One night his old college roommate, Brian, called him and offered him a partnership in his new real estate brokerage that he recently opened out east. Talk about a life changing phone call!

Mary assumed they would live in Maple Falls forever, get married in the same church as her parents, send their children to the same school she attended, and drop them off at the same after-school hangouts she used to frequent. Never had it crossed her mind that she wouldn't raise her family there.

To be honest, at almost thirty-five years old, she never

imagined herself still being unmarried and childless. She and Alex weren't even officially engaged yet, and lately, it seemed as though her life wasn't moving in that direction any time soon. People were constantly asking her if they were married, or even more embarrassing, people would assume they were and address her as Mrs. Dawson. Alex always ignored it, so she would be left in the awkward position to correct them. The correction was almost always followed from others by the inevitable *why?* She would then recite her generic answer that they were happy with how their lives were at the moment and in no hurry to get married. While that may have been true for him, it was far from the truth in her heart.

Even though it appeared to everyone else that she was happy, she felt an emptiness — something was missing from their relationship. Alex's priorities seemed to have changed direction over the past six months, and they talked about marriage less and less. Mary never wanted to be one of those women who gave their boyfriend an ultimatum, but she also didn't want to be one of those women who were naive enough to stay in a dead end relationship too long, waking up one morning at the age of forty to the sound of five cats purring in her ear.

The last time Mary brought up the topic, Alex told her it wasn't a good time to be getting engaged. He and Brian were about to sign a deal on a new condo development and he would be the main listing agent assigned with the task of selling over two-hundred units. He told her he'd be working late nights and most weekends and he'd be unable to give her much of his time to help with the wedding plans. She wasn't convinced it was an acceptable reason though — more of an excuse, really. She knew full well that typically the woman was the one who did most of the planning anyway. Mary brought that up in their discussion, but he wasn't sold on her theory.

After that particularly heated talk, she began to wonder if there would ever be the perfect time in his mind. She was no real estate expert, but she knew enough to know that it would take years to sell all of the condos. She started questioning in her mind whether or not she was willing to wait that long. And who's to say another big project wouldn't come up again, postponing the engagement yet again. If they still lived in Maple Falls, that would be one thing, but being so far from her family and friends, she wondered if it was all worth it.

She placed Ali's wedding invitation back on the nightstand as Alex stomped down the hall towards their bedroom. She hurried to the closet, pulling a couple last minute outfits off hangers to add to her suitcase.

"Aren't you ready yet?" Alex demanded, checking his watch. "I have a meeting across town in forty-five minutes, and I can't be late." He strolled over to the full length mirror standing in the corner of the room, straightening his tie. Turning side to side, he gave himself an approving nod.

"Almost," Mary replied. "I was just deciding on a few last minute things I thought I might need." She folded one more sweater against her chest as she walked across the room.

Alex paused from admiring himself in the mirror, glancing over at her suitcase resting at the end of the bed. "I hope its nothing more than an extra pair of underwear," he said, "because nothing bigger could possibly fit in that thing." He checked his tie one last time in the mirror and stomped back to the doorway, checking his watch again.

"They'll fit," Mary argued. "It's only a couple of sweaters." She looked at her suitcase, noticing her clothes were already stacked nearly six inches over the side zipper. Crossing her arms, she took a step back. "Maybe you're right," she said, pulling one sweater off the stack, placing it back on the hanger.

Alex sighed. "I'm going down to the garage to warm the car. You have five minutes to get down there; otherwise, you'll have to call a cab. I can't miss this meeting." His voice trailed off down the hall.

Before Mary had a chance to reply, the front door slammed. After two more sprints to the closet and three more sweater changes, she was satisfied with her selection. She flipped the suitcase flap over and carefully slid it down the side of the bed to the floor. Taking a deep breath, she placed both knees on top of her suitcase and pulled the zipper, shifting her weight as she went around. She clapped her hands together, proud of herself for actually getting it to close.

Her cell phone vibrated across the counter, startling her. Two missed calls and a *hurry up* text from Alex. Assuming she had less than a minute to get down to the car, she tossed her phone in her purse, zipped up her leather boots, and locked the door handle on her way out. She whipped her wool scarf around her neck as she dashed down the hall, catching the elevator just as the door was closing.

Linda flipped the switch on the coffee grinder, startling several customers sitting at a nearby table, as the wonderful scent of freshly ground coffee beans filled the Maple Falls Coffee Shop. She slid the container of freshly ground beans out and poured them into a fresh coffee filter. The pot began to grumble as it forced hot water through the spout, filling the air with an even more awakening aroma.

"Linda, did the shipment I ordered last week come in yet?" Roger asked, standing in the office doorway, his pen tapping impatiently against the stack of papers in his hand. "I'm waiting on the new holiday blend and wanted to have it out on the shelves by today."

"Not yet, dear, but I'm sure they'll be here shortly," Linda assured him. "Carla stopped by and said she saw the delivery truck down the street a few minutes ago. I think she's waiting on a delivery, too. I'll let you know as soon as Will arrives with it." She carried a fresh tray of pastries to the front that Cora had dropped off earlier that morning. Grabbing them one by one, she slid them down the trays in the front display, replenishing the empty case.

The bell overhead on the door jingled as Will pushed it open, the cloud from his breath following him inside. "Whatever you have there smells delicious," Will said. "I'd never be able to work here. I'd either have constant jitters from sampling too much coffee, or a sugar high from eating all of the sweets," he joked, pulling in a cart full of boxes.

"Good morning, Will. Would you like one?" Linda offered. "Cora baked them fresh this morning." She raised her eyebrows trying to tempt him.

"No, thank you. I'm trying to watch my figure," he said, standing up tall. "Where would you like me to unload these? I can bring them back to the office if you'd like." Will enjoyed helping Roger and Linda when he could. In the last few years, he noticed them having a harder time moving the heavy deliveries.

"You can bring them right back," Roger responded. "I need to unpack them right away," he said, popping his head out of the office, disappearing just as quickly.

Will leaned his cart back and pivoted around the counters to the back. "You seem pretty excited about what's in these boxes," he said. "Another new product?" He lifted each box and lined them up on the floor.

"Yes," Roger replied, "I'm hoping this is the new Christmas blend I ordered last week. It was on backorder, but they emailed me yesterday saying it would be arriving today." Roger grabbed the utility knife off his desk and cut open the first box. "Yes," he whispered, grabbing a bag out and tossing it to Will.

"Peppermint spice coffee sounds very fitting for the holiday season," said Will as he pressed his nose to the bag, breathing in deep. "I'll bet you sell out before the week is over. I may have to come back after my shift tonight and pick one up for myself."

"You may have to wait until tomorrow," Roger said, checking each bag off of his inventory list. "We're closing early today."

"Early?" Will questioned. "You never close early. Is everything alright?"

"Oh, yes, everything is more than alright." Roger stacked the bags on top of his desk and opened another box. "Mary is flying home today, and we're all going to the airport to surprise her."

The smile on Roger's face was priceless.

Will's stomach began to flip flop. "Mary is flying home *today?* I thought she wasn't coming home until the wedding." His hands started to clam up and his mouth felt as if he'd been stranded in the desert for days. He tried to clear his throat, but it wasn't helping.

"She wasn't going to, but since she still hasn't found a job, she decided to come home early and help out for the holidays," Roger said, filling his arms with inventory. "She also wants to be here to help Ali with all of the last minute things that women do before weddings, whatever that is," he said, carrying the bags to the front.

Will grabbed his cart and followed behind him. He hadn't seen Mary since last year at Ali's engagement party. Part of him still regrets not going up to her that night. It would have been the perfect time to tell her, but by the time his courage finally came, she'd already caught her flight home. He glanced at his watch.

"I better get going, my truck is stuffed today," he told Roger. "The weatherman said we may have snow possibly later this week, so I don't want to fall behind. Have a safe drive to the airport, and I'll be back tomorrow for a bag of that coffee." The bell jingled again as he opened the door and left.

"Have a nice day, Will," Linda shouted from the back, "and don't forget to stop by and say hello to Mary."

Will's cheeks were so flushed that he could barely feel the cold wind blowing against his face. *Stop by and say hello to Mary,* he thought. If only he'd had the guts to do it last year, or even better, before she moved away. It was something he wrestled with often, but she'd made her choice, and he had to respect that. Securing his cart, he climbed back into the cab of his truck and drove around the corner to his next delivery.

Chapter
Two

The drive to the airport with Alex was quiet, but not a nice, calming quiet. It was more of a tense, uncomfortable quiet, and Mary wasn't sure that breaking the silence was the best idea.

"What do you have planned while I'm gone?" she asked him, deciding to take the risk. "I wish you weren't so busy with work so you could come home with me. You haven't been back since we moved two years ago, and I know a lot of people who would love to see you."

The traffic was heavy, horns honking all around them, and no one was getting anywhere fast. She watched the expression on Alex's face as he concentrated on the road. Stopping at the red light, he turned on his blinker and waited impatiently for the light to turn.

He exhaled loudly, disgusted with everyone traveling around them and grunted back at her, "I have four meetings this afternoon, I'm showing houses all day tomorrow to an out of town buyer, and my office holiday party is the night after that."

The light turned green as Alex merged onto the freeway entrance. Traffic was so backed up they only made it two car lengths before coming to a stop. Several cars behind them were in just as much of a hurry as Alex, not paying attention and were stuck in the middle of the intersection.

"The party should be fun," Mary said, trying to lighten the mood, "but I'm sad I'll miss it. Hopefully you won't be the only one there without a date."

Alex drummed his hands against the steering wheel in frustration. He looked down below at the freeway and saw little to no movement, just the bright glow of red tail lights as far as the eye could see. Mary held her breath, unsure if he was going to have a complete meltdown or not.

"I knew we should have left earlier," Alex scoffed. "There's no way I'll make it to my meeting on time." He let out another sigh, fogging up the driver's side window.

"I'm sorry the traffic is so terrible," Mary said apologetically, "but I really appreciate you driving me to the airport so we can spend a little extra time together." She looked over to him. "I hope you won't miss me too much while I'm gone." He hadn't heard a word she said.

"Finally!" he shouted, merging onto the freeway. "The

gas pedal is on the right, people. Let's get moving. Not all of us get holidays off. Some of us have important meetings to get to."

Alex constantly shouted at other cars while driving, thinking they could actually hear him. If anything, he just drew more attention to himself with his crazy hand gestures. She noticed an increase in that behavior since they moved to the city, but letting her drive was typically not an option.

She sat back in her seat quietly for the remainder of the drive, concluding that breaking the silence, in fact, was a bad idea.

A steady mist began to fall from the low hanging clouds, the fog spreading lower along the skyline. Mary turned her seat warmer on, sliding her hands underneath her legs to warm them faster. As they approached the airport exit, she watched out the window to catch an airplane flying overhead as it peeked in and out of the drooping clouds. The roaring sound of the jet engines shook the car as it passed over the freeway.

Mary had been fascinated with airplanes ever since she was a little girl. Her father used to take her to every air show that came to Maple Falls to watch them fly in their formations. Whenever she drove near the airport, she would adjust the speed of her car perfectly so the airplane would fly directly over her. Alex hated when she did that. Maybe that's one of the reasons why he insisted on doing most of the driving.

The traffic halted again as they merged into the airport

exit lanes. Alex gripped the steering wheel in annoyance, his knuckles turning white.

"Awe, come on!" he hollered. He reached down and pulled the center console up and fished around for his phone to call the office.

Ten minutes later, they finally arrived at the curbside drop-off. Mary sat still for a moment, afraid to interrupt his phone call. The car behind them started honking. She carefully tapped him on the shoulder to get his attention, clearly ignoring the angry man behind them.

"My luggage is in the trunk," she whispered, pointing to the back of the car.

Without acknowledging her, he leaned forward and pushed the release button, opening the trunk. The wind gusts nearly blew the door right out of her hand as she pushed it open. The mist had turned into tiny granules of ice, causing the sidewalk to become a skating rink.

Mary stood at the back of the car, waiting for him to hang up his phone call and help her with her over-sized suitcase. She peered at him through the back window. Based on his wild hand gestures, he was still on the phone and had no intention of helping her unload her suitcase.

The ice pellets were really coming down now, piling up rapidly on the ground making it hard to keep her balance. She should have rethought her choice in boots this morning. Although they were toasty warm on her feet, the traction on the bottom didn't exist. After nearly falling on her butt twice, she finally got it out of the trunk, slamming the door back down hard.

Mary wheeled her luggage around to the driver's side door, tucking a strand of hair behind her ear as it fought against the wind. Alex was still on the phone, not even noticing her standing there. She slid off her glove and tapped the window with her fingernail, as he pressed the automatic window button.

"I think I have everything," she said, taking a step back to allow him space to climb out.

"Okay, great. Call me when you land if you want," Alex said, holding the phone away from his ear. "I really have to get going to my meeting. I'm not sure how long it will last, so you'll probably just have to leave a message." He gave her a half smile and rolled the window back up. He pulled away from the curb, leaving her alone in the middle of the street.

Mary stood there for a moment, trying to process what just happened. It was a far cry from the romantic curbside good-bye she had in mind. "That's all I get?" she said to herself. Taking a step forward, her boot caught a large patch of ice as she fell flat on her butt. The welled up tears she tried to blink back were now pouring down her cheeks. The piercing air made her cheeks burn, and her hair was now covered in ice pellets. She wiped the tears away with the back of her hand and slid her glove back on, pulling herself up off the ground. The only way things could have been worse is if someone had run her over with their car. The way people were weaving in and out of lanes, it wouldn't surprise her if it had happened.

She checked in her luggage with the attendant at the

curb and hurried inside to attempt to warm up and dry off before her flight. She was in desperate need of a cup of hot coffee and a bathroom hand dryer to de-ice her head.

After thawing out her hair and touching up her makeup in the airport bathroom, she wanted nothing more than to get home to Maple Falls again. She thought about the last time she'd been there, celebrating her little sister's engagement. She missed being with her family so much that it hurt. As she thought about how fun that night of the engagement party was, her mind immediately flashed to Will.

Grabbing a quick coffee, Mary rushed through the terminal and waited by her gate for them to announce loading the plane. She found the last empty seat next to a sleeping man by the check-in desk. Pulling out her phone, she scrolled through her contacts, finding Will's name at the very bottom. She created a new text to him, letting him know that she was flying home today and would love to see him. Who was she kidding? Why would he even care? If he wanted to talk to her, he had every opportunity to do so when she was home last. She stared at the text for a moment, her thumb hovering over the send button.

This is so stupid, she thought to herself. Just as she was about to delete it, the sleeping guy next to her stirred with a loud snore, making her jump, and she accidentally hit the send button.

The boarding of Mary's row was being called overhead before she could figure out a way to get the text back. Panicked, she tossed her phone in her purse and met the airline employee at the check-in counter. She'd just have to try again when she boarded the plane.

As the afternoon was coming to a close, Will's body began to ache from the constant cold exposure, thawing in between deliveries in the toasty warm shops along his route. He made his last delivery to Nancy down at the hotel by the lake, finishing a lot earlier than he planned. These days, he was never in a great hurry to get home. Though he loved where he lived, it was so quiet and empty since Lauren left. It was such a beautiful log cabin he bought on the outer limits of town, a place he hoped to begin his life with her. Since Lauren left, the air seemed colder, and the creaks seemed louder. Although she didn't live with him long, he was getting used to her being there, waiting for him every night. Coming home after a long, hard day at work, to a warm meal and someone to share it with was simple, but that's what Will Roberts was, a simple man.

He drove by the coffee shop one more time on the way to return his truck for the day, the windows all dark. He knew she wouldn't be there, but he thought it was worth a look. Most of the other drivers were still out on their routes. He backed his truck into his parking space and sat there, staring out the windshield as tiny snowflakes landed on the glass, melting instantly from the defrosters. Will exhaled heavily, fogging up the side window, breathing out his annoyance. Lauren had made her intentions clear to him, but his heart had apparently missed the memo.

It would have been one thing if he had seen it coming, or if their relationship had been floating on troubled waters, but it wasn't. Nothing Lauren said to him that day made sense. He played it over and over again in his mind, seeming to change slightly each time, forgetting exactly how it played out all those months ago. But to him, the pain was still there like it was yesterday. He tried to stay as far away from the restaurant Lauren worked at, not needing the daily reminder that she'd clearly moved on. Now being one of the most senior drivers, he was able to pass off some of the deliveries he would rather not make on to other people. The restaurant was one of them.

Back at the truck terminal, he gathered his things from his truck and punched out on the time clock, ready to go home for the day. The town seemed to have begun to slow down as he made one last pass through in his vehicle. Though he wouldn't normally go the route he took, he couldn't make his car turn off Main Street.

Still dark at the coffee shop.

The road leading to his house was long, tall pines surrounding both sides, blanketed in white snow from the previous storm. The branches were heavy, sagging low as they bounced in the wind.

Upon arriving home, Will went inside and changed into comfortable attire, hanging his uniform neatly on hangers for the next day. He grabbed a few fresh logs from the bundle he kept in the living room and started a fire, his toes still frozen from the long day. The logs began to crackle as the flames came to life, the orange glow filling the stone fireplace. He kicked his feet up on the coffee table, facing them towards the fire — something Lauren hated that he did — almost making him want to keep them there all the more.

He leaned back, studying the mantel. He hadn't brought himself to take down their photos yet. He remembers the day she stood there, right in front of those photos, the tension in the room as tight as guitar strings. He knew something was wrong, but neither said a word for several minutes. What came next was not at all what he was expecting. The words cut through him like a serrated knife. In that moment, he couldn't think of a single word to say. Now, after all this time, he finally knew what he would have said — word for word; not that it would have made a difference. She made the decision and had made up his mind for him, and he had no choice but to accept it, although he still wasn't sure he had.

Chapter
Three

The plane was nearly full by the time Mary finally boarded, the overhead bins packed to capacity and then some. Having checked her bags at the curb, she only had a small carry-on left that fit nicely between her feet on the floor.

Every time she flew alone, which was every time she went home, she requested a window seat. She loved being able to look out at the world below, seeing giant corn fields and tiny houses placed haphazardly around the earth. She was able to lose herself in her thoughts, keeping her mind busy among a plane full of strangers.

The flight attendants were preparing to close the airplane door as the last few passengers boarded and took their seats. The remaining seats in her row were still empty, something that rarely happens this time of year. Flights tended to be overbooked rather than under. As the last two people — a couple — made their way down the aisle, they paused next to her, double checking the seat numbers with their tickets.

"I think we're your neighbors today," the woman said politely, shuffling into the seat next to her. The woman looked over to the man she was with, and said, "You have longer legs than I do, so you can have the aisle seat."

Mary pulled her bag closer to the side of the plane, trying to give the woman a little more leg room to fit her carry-on. The overhead storage was all filled up, so she was out of luck. The woman's clunky sorrel boots took up even more space, but that's what came along with traveling in the winter.

The seatbelt sign chimed overhead as the plane began backing away from the gate. They were told there were three planes ahead of them before they could take off, so they sat on the tarmac and waited. It seemed like forever, but at least they were getting on their way.

Three sodas and two bags of peanuts later, their flight was finally starting it's descent into Maple Falls. With winter here, the days were getting shorter, and the sun had already set on the horizon. Looking below from the plane as it descended, Mary could see the faint glowing of the town's Christmas lights in the residential areas near the Maple Falls airport as they flew over. They were beautiful, as more and more appeared with the sun sinking lower in the sky.

Mary looked over to the woman sitting next to her. "I'm not sure if you've ever seen Christmas lights from an airplane before," she said, "but they are really beautiful tonight. Would you like to take a look?" Mary leaned back in her seat, allowing the woman to look out her window.

The woman smiled and leaned toward Mary, glancing down at the sight below. As her gaze met the ground, moving quickly below in their descent, she jerked back to her seat, frantically searching for something in the seat pouch in front of her. Without any warning, the woman began to vomit in the airsick bag. Never before had Mary been so thankful she had grabbed a pillow while boarding the flight. She shoved her head into the frame of the window, attempting to move as far away from the woman as she could. Covering the other side of her face with the pillow, she was able to minimize the sound, and more importantly, the smell. Never in her life had she regretted taking the window seat — until now that is.

When the plane landed and they finally arrived at the gate, Mary felt safe enough to finally uncover her face. She ran her hand along her cheek, feeling the faint imprints of the pillow fibers on her skin. The couple sat silent for the remainder of the landing, appearing more uncomfortable than she was. Before the seatbelt sign was turned off, they had all of their bags loaded over their shoulders, ready to disembark the plane as quickly as they could.

Mary stepped off the plane into the tunnel, the cold air hitting her face hard, still wind burned from the incident outside the airport earlier. She weaved through the waiting passengers at the gate and made her way down the escalator to the lower level to the baggage claim area.

The area was extremely loud, passengers running around trying to find the correct luggage carousel for their flight. The automated glass doors kept opening and closing with the rush of people passing by them. Departures and delays were being announced over the loud speaker, making a crackling sound every time they turned the speaker on. She found the cluster of flight monitors near the middle of the large room and scrolled her eyes to the very bottom where her luggage carousel number was. As her luck would have it, it was the one located at the very end, nearly the opposite side of the airport from where she was.

Squeezing through the crowd that was gathered tightly around her, a woman in a business suit and shiny black heels nearly knocked her down. It was amazing Mary hadn't seen the woman coming. Her very blond hair was ratted a mile high and sprayed with the contents of one giant can of aerosol hairspray to keep it that way. The woman let out a grunt as she stomped by Mary, turning a dirty look at her as she trampled past a few more travelers on her way out the door.

"Merry Christmas," Mary yelled after her. Unfortunately, that is what you find these days around the holidays. People were either kind and generous toward others, or they were rude and should have the word "Scrooge" tattooed on their forehead, pushing people down to get where they needed to go with little consideration for others.

Mary finally reached carousel fifteen, seemingly the last person to get there from her flight. She zigzagged through the crowd, trying to get as close as she could to the ramp that lowered the bags down. A man to her left, who was talking on his phone, kept bumping into her, pushing her further and further away from the ramp. Three rounds later, she got close enough to grab her luggage before it passed by her again. Flustered by the elbowing people, she pulled the handle with a jerk, nearly falling backwards. She quickly pulled out the extending handle and got out of there as quickly as she could. Reaching the outside edge of chaos, she froze.

"What are you doing here?" she said, still frozen in her steps.

Standing directly in front of her was her entire family. Not just her parents, but her sisters, her niece and nephew, everyone shouting her name. Her eyes began to well up again, completely overwhelmed. After her miserable day of travel, this was exactly what she needed.

"I know you said that you'd just take a cab to the house, but we couldn't let you do that," her mother, Linda, said.

"I don't know about the rest of you, but I couldn't wait to see you," her sister, Ali, said. "I called mom last night and asked if we should come and surprise you. I bet you can guess how little convincing that took."

"I'm glad you made it safely, but too bad Alex couldn't join you," her mother, Linda said.

Mary wasn't sure if her mother really liked Alex or not. She'd never come straight out and said she didn't, but part of Mary always thought that. He was, after all, the one who took her away from them.

"He has a busy week of meetings and a few closings to sneak in before year end," Mary explained. "It was just too much to pass on to another agent to cover for him." As soon as she saw her family, she'd forgotten all about him. Their warm greeting was the kind everyone hopes for. She wished her send off from Alex would have been even a fraction of what she was feeling with them.

She shook him out of her head for the moment, ready to focus on those who were around her, suggesting they finish this at home away from the craziness of the airport. She was finally home.

The air inside her parents' home was warm and inviting, with the fresh sweet smell of something baking in the oven. When she walked in the door, it smelled of cranberries and homemade apple pie. Her father, Roger, walked over and lit a fire, sending tiny embers floating up the chimney. The house was so very festive with the Christmas tree resting perfectly centered in the front window, decorations everywhere, and felt Christmas stockings with each of their names on them adorned with sequins hanging from the mantel, arranged in order of their age.

She breathed in the scents of home. *Home,* she thought. A place she never knew she could miss so much.

"Mary, I'll bring your bags up to your old room," her father, Roger said, wheeling her luggage to the bottom of the stairs.

"Thanks, dad," Mary said.

Now *this* is how Mary remembered Christmas being, a far cry from what her apartment looked like. Other than a tiny tree she kept on an end table, there wasn't much for decorations. Alex wasn't one for clutter, decorations being part of that category, so she was reluctant to put much out. Even if she had, nothing could ever compare to going home for Christmas.

Ten minutes later, the rest of the family arrived, pushing through the front door to get out of the cold. The calm, relaxing environment immediately disappeared, replaced with noise and chaos. Mary wouldn't have it any other way. This was how her family was, and she missed the chaos of it all. Being home alone most days, the silence in her apartment had become deafening. She found herself always having the television on, or tuning into a new radio station, something to fill the void. But when she was home, no supplementary noise was needed. She just needed home!

Alex was an only child growing up, so whenever her

family got together, it seemed to bother him. His family was small, just he and his parents, so her family was a bit overwhelming for him. The last Christmas they spent together in Maple Falls, he made up a reason to have to run to the office quick, but never managed to find his way back. Mary knew it was a lie, but let him go anyway. Something she'd forgotten about until just now. Maybe his scheduled meetings for the week were pre-planned to avoid coming home on purpose.

Everyone piled into the living room, making themselves at home. It was something her parents insisted upon for anyone who may have walked through their door. Mary squeezed herself in between her sisters on the couch, wriggling back and forth to fit.

"So, Ali, give me all the wedding details. I want to know everything since I missed the planning stages." Mary stared at her, eagerly waiting for her to speak.

Ali reached up and swiped her finger along Mary's cheek. "You have a bunch of glitter on your face. Were you crafting on the plane?" Ali joked.

Mary rubbed her hands on her cheeks, hoping to remove any more that was there. It must have clung to her earlier that morning when she sat in her room, sulking over her baby sister getting married. Looking at how happy she was, sitting right in front of her, it all seemed so silly and unnecessary.

Mary changed the subject. "Tell me what the dresses looks like."

Ali didn't happen to notice. "The bridesmaid dresses

are dark crimson red with a cream-colored sash across the bodice, tying down the back in long tails. They are floor length, so any shoes you want to wear are fine."

Mary smiled. "That sounds perfect for a holiday themed wedding," she said. "What are the decorations?"

There was so much information to catch Mary up on; Ali didn't know where to start. "The ballroom will be filled with white Christmas lights, just like the ones Zach used for our proposal," said Ali. "We ordered poinsettia plants and mirrors for our center pieces, with four tea light candles floating in glass cups on the corners of the mirror."

Ali went on and on about every last detail, down to the place settings they chose. Mary was getting the guilty feeling back in her stomach, the same one that haunted her at their engagement party. She never wanted to miss planning her sister's wedding, but she'd missed every moment of it. She tried to help from far away, but most phone calls warranted an in-person meeting, one that she wouldn't be able to attend.

"Don't forget about the Christmas tree that'll be set up near the dance floor," their sister, Susie, chimed in.

"Yes! That's one of my favorite parts," Ali said. "Zach and I designed a Christmas ornament together and will hang them all over the tree; one for each of our guests to bring home with them. We thought it would be a special way for them to remember being at our special day." She smiled over at Zach.

"That is such a cute idea; I can't wait to see them." Mary hoped next year she and Alex would have a full-size tree to hang it on. She stood from the couch, stretching her back and legs from her flight. "Before dinner is ready, I'm going to run upstairs and get settled a little and call Alex to let him know I arrived safe and sound. Let me know when everything is ready."

Mary wasn't usually one to shy away from helping in the kitchen, but she was beyond exhausted and had to muster up any energy she had left for her conversation with Alex. She paused on the landing of the stairs, turning around to look down at her family, thankful they could all be together under one roof again.

When she moved out of her parents' house, her room was converted into a guest room, even though she was technically the only guest to ever stay in there. Gone were the vibes of a teenager, completely removed and replaced with a lace dust ruffle and sheer curtains. The paint color was still the same, and if Mary looked closely, she could still see the faint outline of the toothpaste marks left behind from hanging her crush's poster on the wall from the latest teen magazine.

She found her suitcase on the bed. As much as she didn't want to unpack it, she didn't want to call Alex even more. She pulled her cell phone out of her back pocket and dialed his number.

The phone rang four times before he answered. "Hello?"

"Hi, it's me. I only have a minute to chat before dinner," she claimed. She knew that wasn't the whole truth, but throwing it out there right away gave her an out if needed. "I'm just unpacking and thought I'd check in with you. How was your meeting?" She could hear the wind howling in the background, assuming he was either walking or driving.

"The meeting was fine. Brian covered for me until I got there since I was late." He made sure to throw that out one more time, apparently. "We're just about finished with the condo deal. Once it's finalized, hopefully next week, we'll be working pretty much non-stop for the next eighteen to twenty-four months." His phone was cutting in and out. "The plan is a minimum of two-hundred units, but depending on how quickly they sell, the builder will consider adding more, fifty units at a time." Alex spoke with such excitement in his voice, more than she'd heard in a long time.

"That's great, Alex, I'm excited for you." She wasn't sure how she really felt about it, but now wasn't the time to get into the details of it all. He already worked well over forty hours a week, so the thought of him being gone even more, didn't really thrill her.

"Thanks," he said, "we have another meeting next week with the builder to go over more of the fine print."

Mary was thankful she was away on vacation during all of this. She didn't want to have to deal with the stress of him, waiting for the next meeting to come, and her having to walk on eggshells until the ink was dry. "I'm sure everything will turn out the way it's meant to," she said, trying to sound upbeat. "What are you doing for the rest of tonight?"

"I'm on my way home now to change into a fresh shirt," he said, "then I'm going to Sunset's for drinks with some of the agents from the office. They all want to hear about the deal Brian and I have been working on, so we're going to fill them in on all the details."

Mary heard Ali yell up the stairs that dinner was ready, the perfect excuse to end the call.

"I'd better run, dinner is ready, and I don't want to keep my family waiting."

"Okay, talk to you later," Alex said, and with that, he hung up the phone.

She guessed he was in as much of a hurry to get off the phone as she was.

Chapter
Four

Will woke up on the couch a few hours later, not realizing how tired he was from the day. He pulled his socks off his feet, now damp from sweating in front of the fire for so long. The house was dark and quiet; something he should be used to by now, but still felt unsettling. His stomach growled, breaking the silence that filled the room. His sister stopped by the night before to bring him leftovers. He tossed a plate in the microwave and went back to the living room to turn on the television.

He wasn't a huge fan of watching the news, but since his job involved being out in the elements, he turned it on to watch the weather. The top stories aired just as he turned it on, nothing he was interested in, but noise filler nonetheless. The microwave beeped, and he carried his plate back to the couch, his eating place of choice as of late. He kicked his feet back up and rested his plate on his lap. He shoveled in the first bite as his phone buzzed on the coffee table.

A text from Mary.

Will's stomach fluttered as his heart began beating harder. *Why would she be texting me,* he thought. A million questions rolled through his mind as he stared at her name on the screen. He held his breath and opened the text. *"She'd love to see me,"* he read aloud to himself, checking her words three times to make sure he read it right.

More questions flooded his mind, hardly being able to hold them all and process the message. He glanced back at his previous sent texts, wondering if he sent one to her by mistake, but there was nothing there. Nothing to warrant the text she sent. Maybe she sent it to him by mistake and was meant for someone else. He looked at the time she sent it.

Three hours ago.

It must have come in when he was passed out on the couch. Now the big question — does he reply to it? He stood from the couch and paced the room. Maybe it was sent by mistake. Maybe she would be upset that it took him so long to reply. Maybe he should act like he never got it and not reply. He made another lap around the room, suddenly too worked up to eat his dinner.

He placed his phone down on the coffee table again, still unsure of what to do. He walked to the kitchen to fill a glass of water and slammed the whole thing down, hoping it would calm him, or at least take his mind off the text temporarily.

He heard his phone buzz again from the kitchen. Taking a deep breath, he walked back in the living room to see if it was Mary again.

It wasn't.

It was Lauren.

Mary sat back in her chair and crossed her arms across her stomach. "Dinner was amazing, mom," she said. "I think I ate enough food to feed me for a week." She took a deep breath, hoping for her stomach to settle.

"I'm glad you enjoyed it," Linda said as she started to clear the table. "I had to make a lot to feed all of you. It's been so long since we've all been together under one roof — a cause for celebration if you ask me."

"Sit back down and relax, mom," Mary said, "you've done enough for one day. We'll clean up for you." Susie, Ali, and Mary peeled their over-stuffed selves out of their chairs and gathered the plates and silverware. Grant and Zach started grabbing the leftover food and carried it to the kitchen to be divided among each family. That was the one perk of having a big family get together…leftovers!

Linda had brought out the fancy china for dinner, the set that was not allowed to go in the dishwasher. Mary and her sisters learned that lesson many years ago, and needless to say, they'd never make that mistake again. This time, they'd actually enjoy spending time together doing the dishes.

"Would you mind putting on a pot of coffee while you're in there?" Linda asked.

"Sure, I'll bring it out when it's ready," Susie replied. "Black, right?"

Linda never put cream or sugar in her coffee. She always said if your coffee doesn't taste good enough black, then you're drinking cheap coffee. In a sense, she had a point.

"Always, dear," Linda shouted from the dining room.

"There's a woman that's set in her ways, that's for sure," Ali joked.

"Do you want to wash, rinse, or put away?" Susie asked her sisters. They flashed back to when they were kids. The dishes had always been one of their chores, and Susie always volunteered to wash. Not that it was easy, as it was probably the hardest job, but that way she would finish first and get to the television remote before her sisters. When the fancy dishes were used, they always voted for Susie to wash anyway, being that she was the oldest and should have to be the one to take on that responsibility.

"Since I'm pretty much the expert on putting the dishes away, having been volunteered for that task all these years so I finish last, I guess I'll take that job. But only under one condition — you don't ditch me before I'm finished," Ali demanded, throwing the sponge at Susie.

Susie poured soap on the sponge and waited for the water to warm as Mary took her place between the two of them.

"Zach seems to be fitting in around here pretty well. I think you've trained him well for our family dinners," Mary teased.

"He's great, it's like he's always had to endure them," Ali said. "We have a lot of fun together. Every day with him is an adventure, someone I can be silly with. Definitely someone I pictured myself marrying someday." Ali's face lit up as she talked about him, her feet almost gliding across the floor to the cupboard.

Mary thought about Alex, trying to remember the last time they'd been silly together or had an adventure. As hard as she tried, she couldn't think of one. She swallowed hard. "I'm so jealous of that," she said. "Having someone to spend your time with, watch your favorite shows with, someone to eat dinner with every night." Mary swished another plate through the water.

"What are you talking about," Susie questioned. "You live with Alex. Isn't he home with you at night?"

Mary could see the puzzled looks on her sisters' faces. "Not exactly," she explained. "He works a lot of nights and is now working on a new construction deal, building and selling about two-hundred condos." She rinsed another plate, moving her hands side to side through the warm water.

"Mary, that's fantastic," Susie said. "I bet he's been crazy trying to get everything lined up. Will he still work late nights after the deal is done, or just until they sign the papers?"

"When I called him before dinner," Mary said, "he told me that once they break ground, he'll be working non-stop for the next two years." She kept her glare down at the soapy water, not wanting to see the look she knew her sisters were giving her — the faces she couldn't lie to, and who knew when she was. Bracing herself, she waited for their questions.

"So he'll just never be around?" Ali asked. "What are you going to do?"

Mary lifted her head slowly to face them.

"Are you happy out there?" Susie wasn't going to ask, but she needed to know.

There it was. The question she knew was coming, but didn't want to answer. In her mind, yes. The area was beautiful, and they had a great place to live, close to the parks and shopping. But in her heart, not at all. She missed her sisters and ached for home.

"Girls," Roger said, breaking the silence, "did you have to go to the field and pick your own beans? What's taking so long?" He was always joking with them, lightening the mood at just the right moment. He once again came to the rescue, just as Mary was praying for someone to change the subject.

"Sorry, dad, you know how we are when we get together," Susie explained. "We get wrapped up in conversation, and time gets away from us. I'll put it on a tray and bring it right out." She opened the cupboard and placed the mugs on the wooden serving tray. "Just so you know, this conversation isn't over," she said to Mary as she walked out of the kitchen.

Two pots of coffee, an entire cake, and a major caffeine buzz later, they started wrapping up their night. Ali and Susie live a few miles away on the other side of town. Mary stood from the table, wondering how many of these family dinners they'd had since she left. How many meals she'd missed, how many funny stories, how many milestones of her niece and nephew. Everyone was good at calling her and keeping her up to date on things, but how many things were missed? How many stories got lost along the way that she would have loved to hear?

Susie's husband, Grant, stood from the couch, still trying to recover from the meal. "I'm going to go outside and warm the car for the kids."

Before the adults settled into the living room earlier, Susie had tucked Molly and Jack into her parents' bed with a movie to wind down. Within a few minutes of it starting, they were sound asleep.

"Now for the fun part," Susie said, "waking them up and bringing them out in the cold, half asleep. Care to help a sister out?" She looked at both Ali and Mary.

"I'd love to," Mary said, jumping up. "I never get to snuggle sleeping kids." She helped gather their coats and boots from the front closet and followed Susie into the bedroom.

"I'm not sure how cuddly they'll be, but I admire your optimism," Susie laughed.

The two of them managed to bundle both of the kids up without too much fuss. Sweet little Jack curled right up into Mary's arms, resting his head in the curve of her neck as she carried him out to the car. Mary breathed him in and held him close. It was one of those auntie moments she lived for. She buckled him into his car seat while Grant assisted Susie with buckling Molly. She closed his door and waved good-bye as they backed out of the driveway. Ali and Zach crossed paths with Mary on her way back inside, hugging them good-bye as well.

"I'm going to my office to check on my orders that are arriving tomorrow," Roger said. "I'll leave you ladies alone for some girl talk, or whatever it is you do when us men aren't around." He kissed them both on the cheek and walked down the hall to his office. The house was still, not a sound to be heard.

"I think they left the front door open too long," Mary complained, "because it's freezing in here. I can't possibly do any more coffee, but is there a blanket I can cover up with?" She looked around the room.

"There's a quilt draped along the back of the couch," Linda said. "Go cover yourself up, and I'll boil some water and make you a nice warm cup of tea." She disappeared into the kitchen, leaving Mary alone by the crackling fire with her thoughts.

Mary wanted to talk to her mother about Alex, but she

wasn't sure where to start. Her biggest fear since the day she moved away, has been hearing someone say "I told you so." Those are the four words she did not want to live by. She was sure no one would intentionally try to hurt her by saying those words, but if she even thought someone was thinking that, it would make her feel like a failure.

She knew that if she didn't move away with Alex, she would have always wondered, *what if?* To her, what if was almost worse than failing. But, what if the cards would have fallen the other way and she did stay? Where would she be now? Would she still be working for her parents? Would she be dating someone else? It had only been two years since she left, but to think of what could be different in that amount of time was overwhelming. Would she have ever had a chance with Will, or would he still be with Lauren. Maybe he was still with her, for all she knew. She felt so indecisive about her life at the moment; she felt like it could all spiral out of control at any minute.

Linda returned from the kitchen with a small tray in hand. "Here is a cup of chamomile tea, dear," Linda offered. "It should help warm you up and help you relax. You look tired tonight, a lot of travel time I suppose."

Mary admired the crochet cozy that was wrapped around the mug. "Thank you, mom. Did you make this?" she asked, admiring the stitching.

"Yes," Linda said, "as a matter of fact I did. I took a crochet class at the new yarn shop that opened this past summer in town. Connie, the owner, comes in for coffee every morning and had been asking me to take one of her classes for weeks."

"That sounds like fun," Mary said, wrapping her cold hands around the mug.

"When that project came up," Linda added, "I decided it was a small enough project to start with, so I gave it a try. I just signed up for another one next week to learn how to make a cowl. Maybe you'd want to take it with me." She poured herself a cup of tea and joined Mary.

"That sounds like fun, mom, but isn't that one of those classes where I'll be twenty years junior to the other students? I don't want to feel like an old lady," Mary teased.

Linda wrinkled her brow. "Watch the old lady comments; I'm not that old, yet."

Mary laughed. "You know what I mean. I just don't want to end up an old spinster, crocheting alone in my rocking chair while my dozen or so cats play with the balls of yarn." She tried not to picture it, but it was coming in crystal clear. "Ali getting engaged this past year has really opened my eyes to where my life is going — or not going for that matter. It's made me realize how old I am: single, no kids, and still no job." She didn't want to admit to her mother how many jobs she'd actually applied for in the past two years.

"You're always welcome to come back to the coffee shop, dear," her mother said. "There will always be a job there with your name on it." Linda wasn't sure if making that offer made Mary feel better or worse.

Roger and Linda bought the coffee shop when Mary

was young. Once each of the girls reached the age of fifteen, they were allowed to start working there part-time after school and on weekends. They would cross-train each of the girls on all positions on the off chance someone was out ill. When Mary decided to move two years ago, she was practically running the place. She still held a lot of guilt for that, knowing they were looking to retire soon and wanted to leave it to one of their children. Keeping the business in the family had been their vision since day one.

"There's just one problem with that, mom," Mary said with a sad expression on her face. "I don't live here anymore, remember?" She took a slow sip of her tea.

"I know that," Linda said, "but if you and Alex ever decide to move back here, I would be happy to give you your job back. How is his new business venture going anyway?" Linda hardly brought him up in conversations they had on the phone. She'd always been a good mind reader when it came to her children, but over the phone, Mary was able to hide it a little better.

"He's doing well — very well, actually," Mary told her. "I called him before dinner tonight and he was telling me about a new construction deal he and Brian are working on. He sounded pretty excited about it. They have their final meeting about it next week to sign all the papers."

"That's wonderful dear," her mother said, looking at Mary with a puzzled face, "but you don't seem very excited about it." There was no fooling her mother. On the phone was one thing, but in person, she was an expert at facial expressions and body language.

"I *am* excited, just not about all the extra hours he'll have to work." She wasn't trying to sound ungrateful, but she wasn't used to being so secluded. He works so hard for the two of them, but she wanted to contribute, too. "I knew he'd be busy when we first moved there, getting his business up and running, but I thought it would have slowed down by now." She stared into the fireplace.

Linda was trying to read her, but it was hard with her face turned to the side. "How long will the new project take to finish?" her mother wondered. "Certainly Brian will be there to help him, allowing him a few days off here and there, right? He can't possibly work seven days a week."

Mary took a deep breath, trying to hold herself together. "I'm sure it will all work itself out. We'll know more after the meeting next week. Maybe he'll be able to hire a few more agents so he doesn't have to work so much." She forced a smile. "Maybe I just feel a little lonely because I'm still not working."

"I'm sure you'll find something soon, dear," Linda assured her. "The right job is out there waiting for you; don't give up hope." Her mother has always been the optimist in the family. No matter what the problem was, she would always put a positive spin on it, or at least turn the situation into a positive lesson learned. When she and her sisters were younger, they'd often pause during her pep-talks, waiting for the sappy music to start playing in the background like all the family sitcoms used to.

"I know," said Mary reassuringly. "I just wish I would

get called for an interview. The rejection letters in the mail are becoming depressing." She hadn't applied for anything new in the past two weeks, knowing she wouldn't be in town. With the holidays so close, she figured no one would be conducting interviews anyway.

Linda tilted her head to the side. "Why doesn't Alex hire you? I'm sure with this new project he has coming, he could surely use an administrative assistant to help out around the office, return his phone calls."

Mary huffed. "I actually suggested that to him a while ago, but since all I know how to do is make coffee — his words, not mine — I wouldn't be of any help around the office." She knew she probably shouldn't have told her mother that, but to this day, that comment still bothered her.

"That's the most ridiculous thing I've ever heard," Linda argued. "Doesn't he know you were practically running our business before you left? He'd be lucky to have a hard worker like you around the office."

Mary agreed, but he'd already made up his mind. "I guess not," she said in a somewhat grumpy tone. Her brain was becoming exhausted, talking about Alex and the stresses that were waiting for her when she returned. "So tell me, what's new around the shop?" she asked, slyly changing the subject. "Still the same regulars from before?"

"Yes, ma'am, and they all ask about you daily." Linda knew everyone in town, and being the only coffee shop in Maple Falls, everyone knew her family.

"So what do you tell them? That I'm lonely, homesick, and desperate for a job?" she said sarcastically. Mary tried to laugh at herself, but it came off a little more pathetic than planned.

"Don't be silly," her mother assured her. "I tell them how wonderful you are and that we miss you every day."

"I don't feel very wonderful, but thanks for the vote of confidence." Mary sighed.

Linda set down her mug and sat straight up. "I forgot to tell you; guess who came by the shop this morning asking about you?" She stared at Mary, her hands cupped together.

"I have no idea," Mary said. "Who?" There were hundreds of people who came into the shop on any given day.

"Will Roberts. He was asking if you were coming home for Christmas," Linda told her. "I said that you were flying in today and would be around the shop helping out during the holidays. He said he'd be sure to stop back and say hello." Linda tried to hide her excitement, but was failing terribly. Mary knew she always liked Will more than Alex.

Mary's heart stopped briefly, fluttering back into rhythm. The mere mention of his name made her mind begin to whirl. She placed her empty mug back on the tray. "Nice," she replied. "The tea really helped me, thank you. It's been a long day, so I'm going to head up to bed. Tell dad goodnight for me when you see him." She climbed the stairs to her room, hoping her mind would slow long enough for her to fall asleep.

Chapter
Five

Roger and his daughter, Mary, left the house in a rush and arrived at the coffee shop in the morning to find a front parking spot near the entrance, a rare occurrence this time of day. The flower boxes under the front windows were adorned with bright red poinsettias, mixed with sprigs of greenery throughout. A large wreath with a bright red bow hung on the door, no doubt it was purchased from a child fund-raising for their school. Through the frosted windows, Mary recognized a few regulars right away.

The aroma of fresh ground beans rushed at her as she pushed the door open, the bell ringing overhead. "Wow, who needs to actually buy coffee in here?" Mary said. "Just a few deep breaths of the air, and you'll be awake for a week." She smiled as the customers noticed her walk through the door.

"Mary!" several of them called out.

"Welcome home, dear," Helen said, a daily visitor from as far back as Mary could remember. "You look great — how have you been?"

Mary embraced her frail frame. "Good morning, Helen," she said. "I'm great. It feels wonderful to be home, especially during the holidays. I see that the shop hasn't changed one bit." She looked around the room, appearing the same as though she'd only left yesterday. The seasonal display of their holiday blends stood next to the register, the same as it had every year.

"Mary, come on back, and I'll hang your coat for you," Linda shouted from the office. "I need your help in the back with a few things."

"I better run — duty calls." Mary said good-bye to Helen and hurried back to the office.

The hours moved quickly as she fell right back into her old role, noticing the tasks that had been neglected. Roger put her in charge of inventory checks, deliveries, grinding fresh bags of beans, and placing a few orders. Everything was flowing as well as it did two years ago. She worked straight through the morning, familiar faces popping in and out periodically.

She made a lot of progress, cleaning around things that hadn't been done for some time, placing larger orders of supplies to get them through the end of the year. She felt like her main job, among the many hats she wore around there, was to make things easier for her parents. They loved owning their shop, but there was a lot of pressure on them to do it all. Ali still popped in to help out, but the wedding has taken so much of her time over the past year, that they struggled to stay afloat with just the two of them.

When Mary went to the office, she saw the list of daily things she used to do around there hanging on the wall. She wasn't trying to get credit for all she did, but to help them out with what they needed to keep up on. Their vision of slowing down and dropping down to a couple days a week vanished the day she moved away. Not that Mary's vision was to run a coffee shop her whole life. She enjoyed it then, and still now that she was back to help out, but her ultimate plan was to stay home and raise a family. Alex made plenty of money on his own to support a family on his own, so she planned on hiring help and checking in once a week or so.

"Mary, would you mind checking the stock on the holiday blends?" Linda called out, snapping her back to reality. "They've been flying out the door this morning." Linda usually did most of the restocking, while Roger focused on the ordering, but Mary was taking on as much as she could while she was home and did both.

Mary walked around the counter to find the display nearly empty. "Is there more in back? The dark roast is completely out of stock."

"No, everything is out on the floor. But not to worry, your father ordered a bunch more, and it should be here later this afternoon." Linda paused and looked out the front window. "Well speak of the devil...look who just pulled up."

For a split second, Mary's breath suspended as she joined Linda's glance, spotting the large brown boxy delivery truck parked right outside. She watched as Will jumped out of the front seat and walked to the back to load the boxes. She squinted, trying to focus on his face, but the frosted windows prevented it. She felt her body freeze as he got closer to the front door, her feet heavy as cinder blocks as she took a few steps closer to the door.

Will pushed the door open, like many times before, and met Mary's gaze instantly. He looked as surprised to see her as she was of him. Her feet still couldn't move as she pivoted her body toward him. Trying to find the words, any words, so the staring contest would end, but it was broken up by a loud shriek.

"Mary!" was all she could hear as a woman with long blond hair moved side to side behind Will, trying to pass him in the doorway.

Mary's eyes widened. "Grace! What are you doing here? I thought you couldn't make it home for Christmas?"

Will dropped his head and bypassed Mary. Roger was waiting eagerly in the doorway of the office, clipboard in hand.

"I rearranged my meetings, shuffled around a few clients, and booked a flight out early this morning," Grace said, hardly taking a breath. "I knew you were already home so I came straight from the airport."

Mary and Grace have been friends since the summer

before fourth grade. Her family moved across the street from them, and they spent almost every day together. Grace didn't have any siblings, so Mary's family took her in as an honorary fourth daughter. Linda always wanted four children, so Grace filled that dream for her in a way.

"I can't believe you didn't tell me," Mary said, still in shock. "Come back and put your luggage in the office. I'll pour us a coffee, and we can catch up."

Mary led the way back to the office, careful not to make eye contact with Will who was standing just inside the door. She popped out of there as quickly as she popped in, hoping to go unnoticed, and poured them each a coffee. Grace chose one of the high-tops in the corner near the window.

"I still can't believe you're here, sitting in front of me," Mary said, nearly breathless. "How was your flight? Do you love your new job?" Questions were flying out of her mouth as Grace sat there, unsure of which one to answer first.

"Crazy, isn't it?" Grace squealed. "My parents didn't know either until I called them from the airport. Luckily, they aren't spontaneous travelers, or I'd have to bunk with you," Grace laughed. "I'll probably be making payments on my ticket for the next six months, but this moment, right here, is totally worth every penny."

Mary never realized how much she would miss Grace when they moved in separate directions of the country. Flying home to visit family and not having your best friend home at the same time was hard. She loved both of her sisters dearly, but there is something to be said about a best friend. No one can compare.

"What are your plans tonight?" Mary asked. "Are your parents having a big welcome home dinner for you?"

Grace shook her head, saying "I have no idea; I haven't even been home yet. I'm sure nothing fancy as I only sprung it on them a few hours ago. I think they both volunteered to help set up for the Christmas services coming up at church, so I'll probably just relax at home."

Linda came out of the back with a fresh tray of muffins. "Grace, is that you? You look wonderful, dear," she said, speeding across the room. "What a nice surprise."

"Would you mind if she and I went out for a bit tonight?" Mary asked. "Her parents already have plans, and I would hate for her to sit home alone all night." Mary looked up at her mother with the same eyes she used as a child to get what she wanted.

"Of course not," Linda said, "take the rest of the afternoon off, and go hang out at the mall, or whatever it is you girls do these days."

Mary giggled. "Thanks, mom. I'll be home later tonight." She rushed to the back to get Grace's luggage, now that the coast was clear.

"Bundle up girls, the wind is really starting to pick up." Linda crossed her arms.

"We will," they shouted as they ran out the door.

The wind howled, blowing patches of fresh fallen snow across the sidewalk. Grace started the car quickly, cranking up the heat before the engine was even warm. It didn't take long to forget how cold Maple Falls can get in the winter. When the weather never drops below seventy degrees where you live, a cold winter can slap you in the face, quickly bringing you back to reality.

"I hope I still have a hat and mittens stashed somewhere at my parents' house," Grace said shivering. "My body is definitely going to take some time to adjust to this weather."

Grace pulled away from the curb and started heading out of town. She pulled up to the stop sign at the end of block, and Mary spotted Will's delivery truck parked outside of Cora's bakery. As Grace let off the brake, Will came outside and looked directly at them. Mary's stomach began doing flip flops again as she watched him in the side mirrors as they passed by.

"Was that Will Roberts?" shrieked Grace.

"I'm not sure — I think, maybe," Mary stuttered, leaning her head back against the headrest.

"I do believe you are blushing, Ms. Bradford. Maybe we have more to catch up on than I thought," Grace teased.

Mary could feel the heat radiating from her cheeks. "No, it's just windburn from walking outside is all." She tried to tell her cheeks to calm down, but it wasn't working.

Grace just smiled and sat silent for the rest of the drive, wondering what her best friend was hiding.

The bakery smelled of fresh baked bread and cupcakes as Will pushed through the door, his senses awakening. Lily ran out from behind the counter at her fastest speed to greet him at the door.

"Good morning, Lily," chimed Will. "Have you already gotten into the sweets today, or did you just sleep really good last night?" Will couldn't help but laugh at her energy.

"Good morning, Will," Cora said. "I'm glad to see you. Would you mind rolling the boxes to the back? I'll join you just as soon as I finish unloading this tray of muffins." She placed each flavor in its own row, restocking for the late morning rush.

"What did you bring us today?" Lily asked, falling in step behind Will. "Sugar? Flour? Oh, I know, more frosting!" She ran circles around him as he unloaded the boxes onto the counter.

"I'm not sure what's inside them," he said. "I just deliver them. But if I had to guess, I would bet it's very important ingredients you need for baking." Will winked at her.

Cora met them both in the back, weaving around Lily as she continued running her circles. She checked the order and signed the packing slip. "I wish I had her energy some days," Cora joked. "It's pretty cold out there this morning; can I send you with a fresh cup of coffee to stay warm? I'm happy to throw in a sweet treat if you'd like, too." She raised her eyebrows, knowing how hard it was for him to resist.

"I'd love some," Will said. "I think that's exactly what I need to keep me going on my route. I normally don't hit a wall until later in the day. Must be the cold weather, I guess."

Cora poured him a cup of coffee and bagged him a fresh muffin straight out of the oven. "Did you hear about the woodworking expo at the hotel tonight?" she asked. "I saw a flyer yesterday and thought of you. Maybe it's something worth checking out."

Will balanced the coffee and muffin as he tipped his cart back. "I haven't seen anything about it. It's at the hotel?"

"Yeah," Cora said, "I think it said it was in the conference room. It looked to me like there were a bunch of big companies from around the country coming into town looking for local woodworkers. Might be worth stopping in to check it out." Cora carried the boxes into the supply closet off the kitchen.

"I think I will, thanks for letting me know," Will replied. "I have a delivery on the truck for Nancy, so I'll ask her about it when I'm down there later. I'd love to have someone look at my work, even though it's just a hobby at this point." He walked toward the door, saying, "See you later, Lily." He waved to both of them as he went back out in the cold, thankful for the hot coffee.

Chapter
Six

Later that night, Grace and Mary drove back into town to grab some dinner. The sky was getting dark, illuminating the beautiful Christmas light displays along the way. Living in a condo in the big city, Mary missed being able to drive down the street and see so many houses fully decorated. Nearly every house in Maple Falls gets decorated.

A committee formed a few years ago, and members of that committee go door to door the weekend after Thanksgiving asking if folks need help hanging lights. While many residents decorate together as a family tradition, there are still quite a few who use the committee's services. Many of the elderly folks around town look forward to their visit every year from the members and sit in the front window and watch the lights come to life.

"The lights are so beautiful this year," Mary stated. "It makes my condo look so boring compared to these. I suppose I could have hung a strand or two out on our balcony railing, but it's just not the same." They drove by a lot of their old friends' houses; many of their parents still lived there.

"I know what you mean," Grace said. "My apartment doesn't even have a balcony. I bought a two foot tree to place on the end table. At least you get snow where you live. Christmas in California is pretty lame in the weather department."

Grace moved to California when she finished college, taking a job she was offered at a popular public relations firm. She is head of the party planning department and loves every minute of it. When a celebrity books her for their party, Mary is always her first call to talk about it. If Grace could, she would stealth a quick snapshot with her phone when they weren't looking to send Mary, too.

"No snow at Christmas would be hard," Mary admitted. "Alex let me put up a small tree, but it still didn't feel like Christmas to me when I was there. I've always been a big tree kind of girl — tall and full, packed with as many colored lights as I can find, silver garland, and enough ornaments to make the tree sag a bit. My mom still hangs the ornaments I made in elementary school on hers. I can't believe they haven't disintegrated yet. That salt dough must be pretty durable."

"Hey now, we aren't that old," Grace laughed.

There were no visible parking spots as they neared the restaurant. After circling the block twice, a car finally left. Grace put her parallel parking skills to work; something that Mary would never have been able to do. Had she drove instead, they'd still be circling the block.

"Wow, you can tell it's a Friday night," said Grace. Looks like the whole town decided to eat out tonight. But then again, what else is there to do around here?" Being used to living in Los Angeles, this crowd was nothing for Grace.

"I think a hot beverage is in my future tonight after this walk," Mary said. They climbed out of the car, walking almost two blocks, the packed down snow crunching under their feet.

A handsome man approached the door a few seconds before they did; pulling it open and letting them go in first.

"That's not something you see much in California. Thank you," Grace said to the man. "People out there will budge right in front of you, slamming the door in your face if it means getting on "the list" sooner than you."

The thought of living around people like that made Mary's stomach hurt. "Ugh, I don't think I could live there. I'm a small town girl all day long," she admitted. "Maybe that's why I stay home so much where I live now. The city life intimidates me a bit."

"You get used to it after a while," Grace said. "I just ignore those kinds of people when I'm out and about.

Besides, most of the places I go, I created *the list*."

The restaurant was dimly lit, teetering on the border of too dark. White lights strung around the side walls gave off a shadowed glow, not quite bright enough to make out anyone's face. Mary squinted to read the specials etched on the chalkboard hanging near the front.

"I have to run to the restroom quick," Grace said. "Would you mind putting our name on the list?" Grace squeezed her way through the crowd, disappearing quickly behind the many diners sipping their drinks while they waited for a table in the bar area.

Reluctantly, Mary joined the back of the line for the hostess behind a large man, making it impossible to see around. She overheard the hostess tell him that it would be a fifteen minute wait, which didn't seem too bad, considering the amount of people in there. She often wondered what they based that time on. How did they know how long people would stay, even after paying their bill? The hostess activated a buzzer and handed it to the man in front of her, motioning for him to move to the side for the next person in line.

Without looking up, the hostess asked how many were in Mary's party.

"Just two of us," Mary replied, noticing something familiar about her. As the hostess raised her head to ask for a name, Mary's heart stopped.

It was Lauren.

And it wasn't "nice Lauren" she used to know many years ago. It was Will's ex-girlfriend Lauren, who Mary was fairly certain, hated her.

"Mary," Lauren said, caught completely off guard.

"Hi, Lauren," Mary replied, shifting her weight from side to side.

Grace pushed her way back through the crowd. "Did you get our name on the list?"

Mary half smiled, motioning with her eyes in Lauren's direction, trying to get Grace to look at her without being too obvious. Finally, she looked over.

"Lauren!" she gasped.

"Grace," Lauren said, her fake smile fading. She walked over to the buzzers and held one out; unsure of whom she wanted to interact with less. "When the buzzer sounds, bring it to the front and someone will seat you. Feel free to wait over in the bar area." She stood there awkwardly, waiting for them to get out of the line and as far away from her podium as possible.

They each thanked Lauren, and Mary followed Grace into the bar area. "Could that have been any more awkward? That definitely calls for a drink."

"Well, on the bright side," Grace stated, "at least she's the hostess and not our waitress. Less chance of ending up with spit in your food."

Mary wasn't sure if that was much of a bright side, but she agreed. They waved down the bartender, ordering two vodka tonics. The bar was packed, only standing room left. They stood near a high-top table that the chairs had been removed from, placing their drinks on a paper napkin.

Grace scanned the room, trying to keep an eye on

Lauren's whereabouts. "This drink tastes heavenly; just what I needed after a long day of travel."

Mary sipped her drink, following Grace's glare. "I didn't think she hated me that much. It's not like I broke her and Will up; she did that all on her own. At least that's what I heard. You know how rumors are in this town." She rolled her eyes and took another sip, realizing her glass was already half empty. "They really shouldn't put so much ice in these drinks." She shook her glass back and forth.

"Is she and Will back together or something?" Grace asked. "Have you even talked to him since you've been back?" Grace clearly wasn't the most observant person, completely forgetting about seeing Will only a few hours ago at the coffee shop.

"He walked through the door literally two seconds before you did today," Mary said. "Don't you remember the man in a brown uniform you nearly plowed down in the doorway? That was Will." She laughed, not at all surprised.

"That was Will? Why didn't you tell me? Why was he there?" Grace whacked Mary in the arm.

"He was delivering our coffee," Mary pointed out. "What was I supposed to say? Please hold on Grace, my best friend I haven't seen in years, a guy I have a crush on just walked in. Um, I don't think so."

Grace held her hand up. "Wait a minute," she paused. "Did you say *had* a crush or *have* a crush?" She knew what she heard, but wanted to hear Mary say it again.

The buzzer began vibrating across the table.

Mary slammed down the rest of her drink. "We better get up there so we don't lose our table. That is, if Lauren didn't erase my name off the waiting list." She grabbed the buzzer off the table and walked to the front, saying a silent prayer in her head that Lauren was on break.

Her prayer was answered. Lauren was nowhere in sight. Mary handed the buzzer to the other hostess and followed quickly behind her before Lauren came back.

She placed the menus on the table, motioning them into the booth. "Your waitress, Ashley, will be right with you. Can I get you another drink while you wait?"

"Yes!" Mary blurted out.

"We'll have two more vodka tonics, please," Grace said calmly. "Would you relax, Mary? For all we know, she's off for the night and has probably left already."

Mary hadn't thought of that and tried to relax her shoulders. "Why does she make me so crazy? I haven't seen her in years, and I didn't even do anything to her to make her hate me."

"Don't let her ruin our night," Grace said. "Let's talk about something else. How is everything with your new place? Does Alex like his new job?"

Mary glanced into her empty glass, stirring the ice cube around with her straw in hopes of sipping a little more vodka out of it. "Things are good — just different," she said. She continued to stare down at her glass. "He works a lot more hours than he did when we lived here, but because I don't have any friends or family out there, it seems like more than it probably is."

Grace stared at Mary, who was undeniably avoiding eye contact with her. "Are you happy there?"

There was that question again, Mary thought. She sat still for a long second, wondering if she should give her the sugar-coated version she had been giving everyone else, or get straight to the point. If there was anyone who could fully understand how she was feeling without any judgment, it would be Grace.

"I hope you know I can tell when you're lying," Grace claimed, "so you might as well just tell me the truth. Are you happy?" She stared at her hard, not breaking.

Mary knew she had to come straight with somebody or it would eat her alive. "No."

Their impeccably timed waitress arrived right at that moment with their drinks. She quickly took their orders and disappeared to wait on another table.

"I knew you weren't," Grace shouted, "I think I just needed to hear you say it."

Mary felt relieved. "I think I needed to hear myself say it, too. You're the first person I've actually admitted it to."

Grace slowly shook her head. "Are you unhappy with where you're living or who you're living with?"

Mary sunk lower in her chair. "Both," she admitted. "Everything really. I committed to moving out there with him and support his new job so we could have a wonderful new life there together, but it isn't wonderful. It's miserable. I don't know what to do about it, and I feel like I can't talk to my family about it without hearing the words *I told you so* come out of one of their mouths." She spun her straw around, moving her ice in circles around her glass.

"That's great that you wanted to support his choice and make a life out there," chimed Grace, "but if it isn't the life you want to live, then why are you still doing it?" Grace reached across the table and placed her hand on top of Mary's. "Is he as supportive with your job as you are with his? Those kind of things have to go both ways, you know."

Mary paused. "Well, sort of. I haven't found a job yet, so I haven't given him a chance to be supportive." She wasn't sure she wanted to tell her that he wasn't supportive at all when she suggested working for him. It still bothered her all this time later. "I also haven't made any friends out there, so when he's gone working his long hours, I have no one to hang out with to fill that time. I feel like I lost a big part of myself when I moved, and I don't know how to get it back."

There, she said it. She finally put it all out there to someone else, freeing her mind a little. It wasn't to the person it probably should have been, but it was a start. Grace had always been there for her, and she wasn't sure what took her so long to tell her. Just being with her in person made all the difference.

Grace's face softened. "Maybe you need to move back for a while. No one will say *I told you so,* and I truly believe that the missing piece you are looking for is here in Maple Falls," she said. "You never wanted to leave our town —

you already had your kids, teachers and activities all planned out here — the same things you did as a kid. Have you ever thought of the other side?"

Mary wrinkled her brow.

Grace continued, "Have you ever thought about how many people would be ecstatic if you moved back? Your parents, your sisters," she paused, "Will."

"Oh, you're so funny, Grace," said Mary. "For all I know, he's still with crazy Lauren." Mary scanned the restaurant again, hoping she wasn't lurking nearby to hear her. "Until I hear it officially from him, I'm not going to assume anything."

"There's only one way to find out," Grace smirked. "Are there anymore deliveries coming this weekend?"

Chapter
Seven

The morning air was brisk, setting off a chain of wind gusts that were blowing patches of snow across the parking lot. The intermittent rays of sunshine that peeked through the thickening clouds caught the sequined white gowns on display in the front window of the bridal shop. Ali pushed against the door, the wind forcing her inside.

"Good morning, ladies," a woman greeted. "What can I help you with today?" She was very well put together — a solid peach colored pant suit and her hair pulled back in a tight ponytail.

"Good morning, I'm Ali and these are my bridesmaids and my mother." Ali pointed to the women standing next to her. "We have an appointment this morning for our final dress fittings," she said, smiling ear to ear.

"Wonderful," she replied. "I'm Cheryl, the shop owner. It's so nice to meet you all. Your dresses are hanging in the back room. Please make yourselves comfortable, and I'll be right back with them." She walked behind a shimmery, floor length curtain that separated the back room from the rest of the shop.

A few minutes later, Cheryl returned with a large rolling rack filled with dark crimson red dresses on the front and Ali's white gown hanging on the back of the rack. Cheryl pulled one dress off the rack at a time, starting with the shortest one, and placed each one in its own dressing room. "These two, I'd guess, are for you lovely young ladies," she said, leaning down to Lily and Molly. "Once all of you are dressed, I'll call our alterations person up to the front to have a look at each of you."

"Thank you so much," Ali said as they each made their way to their own dressing rooms.

Linda came with to support Ali and to soak up every moment she could as mother of the bride. It was a moment she dreamed about since the moment each of her daughters were born, knowing she wouldn't miss this moment for the world. While her plan was to sit back and admire all of the beautiful girls, she soon gained the title of dress zipper, as one by one they came out of their dressing rooms holding the bust of their dresses and turning for assistance.

One at a time, they began gathering near the front of the shop, lining up the bridal party in order in front of the wall of mirrors, waiting impatiently for Ali to come join them. Cheryl was in assisting her, lacing up the back of her dress one loop at a time. As Cheryl pulled the curtain back, she stepped to the side for Ali to make her entrance.

Each of them held their breath as Ali made her grand entrance as the beautiful bride.

Most of them had already seen her dress, having been with her when she found 'the one.' But for Mary, this was the first time seeing Ali wearing it in person. The earlier cell phone photos that were sent to her didn't do it justice compared to actually seeing her in person. To say Mary was choked up was an understatement.

Holding her dress up in the front, Ali made her way to the mirrors, placing herself in the middle of the women — two to her right, and two to her left. The bright white satin with metallic sequins covering the bodice popped among the dark crimson red dresses. Multiple layers of tulle gathered underneath the gown gave it just the right amount of flare. A white satin cording crisscrossed down her back, tying near the bottom and draping down the gown, adding to the already stunning bride.

"Ali, you look so beautiful," Mary said. "This dress was made for you," she said, unable to take her eyes off her sister.

"Thank you, Mary," Ali said. "I wish you could have been here to help me choose the right one, but I'm glad you were able to come home for the most important part of it all — the final fitting."

Mary's stomach fluttered. She still hated that she

missed so much of the preparation. Had Mary been able to predict the future, she would have just continued to live in Maple Falls for the past year. It wasn't like she had made any forward progress in her new life during all that time. If only she'd known.

Ali looked down the line in both directions. "You all look so amazing." She looked each girl up and down then turned to face Linda. "So, mom, what do you think?"

Linda was already on her third raid of the Kleenex box before Ali even came out of her dressing room. She'd been an emotional wreck all morning. At this point, her pockets were bulging from tear-filled tissues.

"All three of my beautiful girls together again, and two of their good friends alongside them," Linda said. "And you two little princesses couldn't be cuter. I don't think anything could make me happier. You all look absolutely stunning." She dabbed the corners of her eyes again.

"What about Mary getting married," Ali joked. "Wouldn't that make you happier?" Mary whacked her sister in the arm. "Easy now," squealed Ali, "you don't want to bruise the bride before her wedding. This *is* a sleeveless dress, you know." Ali rubbed her arm up and down, spinning in circles to admire her dress. "I can't believe this is already our final fitting. It feels like it was so long ago when we were picking out these dresses. I thought this day would never come."

They all posed for a quick photo as the seamstress came out to the front. One by one, Cheryl lined them up as the seamstress checked the length and fitting of each of their dresses. Mary had been panicked all week about how her dress would fit, especially after a big dinner and drinks with her friend Grace last night.

Cora was the last bridesmaid to get checked. She stepped down off the riser while the seamstress finished up her notes. "Wait," Cora said, holding her hands up in the air. "Before we change out of our dresses, there is one more thing we have to check."

Cheryl, and the seamstress, looked puzzled as Cora ran over to the radio on a corner shelf and turned it on.

"We all know we look great in our dresses," Cora announced, "but can we dance in them?" She turned the volume up as high as it would go and shimmied across the room, returning to the other girls.

They all burst out in laughter, even Linda, as they broke it down and began to dance. Katie, the other bridesmaid, tested out her limbo skills under an empty clothes rack nearby.

"Oh yeah," Ali clapped, watching Katie make it all the way. "These dresses were made for dancing."

They all joined hands and spun in a circle, singing along with the song at the top of their lungs. Molly and Lily didn't know the words, but the moves they were making made up for the lack of lyrics. Linda joined in, dabbing more tears as they flowed down her cheeks — this time from laughing so hard. Ali smiled at them all, taking in the moment with her favorite women in the whole world, so thankful to have them all by her side.

The men were gathered a few blocks away, going through the same motions as the women were, making sure their tuxedos were just right for the wedding. Zach stood dressed in his tuxedo, surrounded by his groomsmen. They all looked sharp, dressed in black with dark crimson red vests, matching the women's dresses perfectly. Zach, who was instructed to stand out as the groom, wore a white vest to match his bride.

"You clean up nice, Zach," Grant teased, remembering how nerve-wracking it was to be standing in his shoes. "It seems like yesterday that Susie and I were getting married. I'm glad it's you this time around," he joked.

"Well, how do I look?" Zach asked, stretching his neck pretending to straighten his tie. "Do you think Ali will approve?" He turned from side to side, over exaggerating his moves.

"From the detailed instructions Susie gave me, directly from Ali's mouth, I'd say you followed her orders to a T," Grant said, giving him the thumbs up.

Will adjusted his tie, not fully understanding how Zach was feeling. He'd been a groomsman in a couple weddings for his friends, but he had yet to feel the groom-to-be jitters. The closest he had come to it was a case of the nerves from getting ready to propose to Lauren. Though he never made it to that point, he had hopes of still getting there someday — with just the right someone.

"So, Will, are you bringing a date to the wedding?"

Grant wondered aloud. "Maybe Lauren will go with you if you can't find anyone else," he said, playfully punching his arm.

"That's not even joke worthy, Grant," Will argued. "I'd rather bring my sister as my date than ask Lauren. Plus, she's probably still dating that other guy, whatever his name is," his voice trailing off.

They all knew Will didn't forget the other guy's name. That was one of those things that gets burned into your brain forever, no matter how hard you try to forget it. He hadn't heard a word about him until the day she blurted everything out. The day she decided that *he* was a better fit for her than Will was. He often wondered how many times he'd seen him around town without even knowing. Now Will felt like he was always on the lookout for him, avoiding him at all costs.

"Well, Mary doesn't have a date either," Brad suggested, getting a confirmed nod from Grant. "Maybe you two can hang out together. I don't think Alex is flying in for the wedding."

The thought of having Mary as his date for the wedding made Will's cheeks feel as though they were on fire. "Maybe," he said.

Brad gathered the men, placing Jack in front of them, and wrapped their arms around each other's shoulders. "We might just be the best-looking men around town," Brad said. "I think I may be one of the luckiest guys at the wedding, bringing two dates and all."

Brad was certain that Lily was soaking up every

second at the bridal shop. When Ali asked her to be one of her flower girls, she couldn't stop jumping up and down. He wasn't sure if it was the dress, dropping petals on the floor, or getting to walk down the aisle with Molly and Jack that made her more excited.

"I bet she's going to be beautiful in her dress," Grant said. "Molly was happy Lily was joining her so she didn't have to walk alone with her annoying little brother — her words, not mine."

The men laughed, all but Jack, who raised his brow.

Jack looked up at Grant. "She's the one who always bugs me, dad." He crossed his arms across his chest. "What about me, dad?" Jack asked.

"What about you, what?"

Jack looked at each of the guys. "Do I need a date for the wedding, too?"

Grant patted him on the top of the head. "If you play your cards right, son, maybe Lily will save a dance for you." Grant looked over to Brad.

Brad knelt down. "I suppose you can ask her to dance, but I'll have my eye on you," Brad said, pointing two fingers back and forth between the two of them.

"Well, gentlemen, I think we all look pretty sharp," Zach said, "but I think it's about time we get out of these monkey suits. One day is enough dressed like this," he said, loosening his tie.

Zach was more of a jeans and t-shirt kind of guy. Though he liked dressing up for special occasions, he was really nervous about wearing something this fancy, especially when it was for his own wedding. Maybe it was all mental, knowing that Ali always approved of his outfits before formal events. He'd just have to trust the guys this time around.

"Cora said you were thinking about stopping by the wood-workers expo yesterday," Brad said. "How did it go?"

Will slipped his shoes back on. "I decided to check it out on my way home, and I think it went pretty well. I exchanged info with a few of them, and it sounded promising. You never know what may come of it."

"What kind of products were they looking for?" Grant asked Will.

"Anything from small jewelry boxes to dining room tables and chairs," Will replied. "There wasn't much that they weren't looking for. I gave them my contact information and let them know everything I could make." He sat down on the floor next to Jack who was playing with a toy car.

"Can you make wooden cars, Will?" Jack asked.

Will smiled. "I bet I could try, but I've never made one before. Would you like me to make one for you?"

Jack's face lit up, nodding rapidly. "Yes, please." He drove his car around the floor, weaving around the chairs on his hands and knees, making loud car noises.

"I love how little boys are born with those noises already programmed in their brains," Grant said, smiling down at his son.

"I hope to have one just like him someday," Will said,

watching him drive around the room.

Chapter
Eight

The following night, Mary's family gathered at her parent's, Roger and Linda's, house, continuing on with another Christmas tradition — putting up the tree on Christmas Eve. Linda was a busy bee, buzzing around the kitchen with her daughters, preparing their holiday dinner. She had a ham cooking in the roaster, cheesy hash brown potatoes were in the oven, and fresh baked dinner rolls were cooling on the counter.

The four pies she baked earlier in the week were chilling in the refrigerator. Everything they served was homemade, right down to the gravy. The girls tried to get their mother to relax during the holidays and buy the pies, or jars of gravy, but she always insisted on making it all from scratch.

"Dad," Mary yelled from the kitchen, "do you need help putting up the tree?"

"No, I'm just about finished," Roger replied. His job every Christmas Eve was to go up to the attic and drag out the tree and ornaments. Linda has been trying to convince him to store all of it in the spare bedroom closet for years, but every year he insists that he's fine going up there.

"I'll go see if he needs any help," Grant offered.

"If you're almost ready for us, then I'll start popping the popcorn." Mary opened the pantry and pulled a large bag of popcorn kernels out. She cut the corner of the bag off and poured some into a large saucepan with a spoonful of butter, and listened as the butter began to sizzle, followed by popping kernels.

Linda wrinkled her brow at Mary as she prepared another bag of kernels. "Mary, how much popcorn are you making? We only have one tree to decorate, you know."

"I'm making two bags at least," Mary declared, "because I distinctively remember last Christmas I made only one bag, and we ended up eating more than we strung, so I'm planning ahead this year." Mary placed six small bowls on the counter and started filling them with the first pan of popcorn. She found the needles and thread in the same drawer she left them in last year and joined her father in the living room.

Molly and Jack dropped their toys and ran over to Mary, eager to help and to sneak a few kernels for themselves.

Mary lined the bowls up on the coffee table. "Who wants to help string popcorn for the tree?" she asked, both of the kids raising their hands. "Sit down on the floor and I'll get you both set up with a needle and thread."

She pulled a long strand of thread off the spool, threading a needle onto both ends. "You two can work together on this string," Mary instructed, "each of you working from one end and meeting in the middle. If you run out of popcorn, let me know. I'm going back to the kitchen to make more." She left them to stringing and went back to the kitchen to make another bag.

"Are the kids already stringing popcorn?" Susie asked, placing another cookie sheet in the oven.

"Yes, they are, I just set them up on the living room floor," Mary said. "Ali, are you helping with the cookies, too, or do you want to help with the popcorn? I could use someone to work on the other end of my string." Mary raised her eyebrows up and down at her sister.

Ali looked at Linda and Susie, then back to Mary. "I'm in," she squealed. "I think you two can handle the cookies without me."

"As long as you save a string for me and Susie when we're finished," Linda shouted as they left the kitchen. "This is the last tray of cookies, so we'll be in to join you shortly." The oven was getting a workout today; Linda was still wishing Roger would have bought her that double oven when they remodeled their kitchen a few years back.

"Ali, you go in the living room and find the Christmas

station on the radio," Mary instructed, "and I'll grab the rest of the popcorn." Mary balanced the bowls across her arms and joined Molly and Jack on the floor. "Wow, look how far you've gotten already," squealed Mary. "When you're finished, I'll cut you another string, but be sure to leave a little space at the end so we can tie them together."

Ali turned on the radio station as Silent Night began to play. It was Mary's all-time favorite Christmas song for as long as she could remember. Every time she heard it on the radio, she pictured herself sitting in an over-sized chair, curled up with her husband by the fire, covered in a cozy blanket, drinking hot cocoa while the snow fell outside. The strange part of her vision though, was that the face of her husband was never clear. It was almost as if it were blurred out and she wasn't able to make out his features. She often wondered if that meant it wasn't Alex sitting beside her.

"This is my favorite Christmas song; did you know that?" Mary said, looking over at her niece and nephew.

"I do now," Molly grinned.

"What's your favorite Christmas song?" Mary asked them.

"Mine is Jingle Bells," Molly said, "because I got to sing it in our Christmas play at school last week. I was one of only five kids in my class that got to ring the bells." She held five fingers up in the air for added effect. "Everyone wore red robes in the choir, but the bell ringers got to wear special gold robes." Her face lit up as she told Mary all about it.

"That sounds pretty special," said Mary. "I wish I could have been here to see it. Maybe next year I can come home a little earlier so I don't miss that." Mary smoothed the back of Molly's sandy blond hair, and looked over to Jack and asked, "What about you, Jack? What's your favorite Christmas song?"

Jack tapped his finger against his chin. "Mine is Rudolph the Red-Nosed Reindeer. I like it because his nose lights up and helps Santa see where he's going when it snows on Christmas Eve. Without Rudolph, Santa might never find our house." Jack got excited about the thought of Santa coming to his house. His little body began bouncing up and down on the floor. "We're done auntie Mary!" he shouted, holding his end of the string happily in the air.

"You two did a fantastic job," she said. "I think that is the best string of popcorn I've ever seen."

Molly and Jack jumped to their feet, holding their string in the air. "What do you think, grandpa? Did we do a good job?"

Roger stopped what he was doing to take a look. "That will look perfect on the tree; great job kids." He smiled at them and continued fluffing the branches.

Linda and Susie joined the rest of them on the floor and helped string the remaining bowls of popcorn until everyone had strung two strands. Susie tied them all together while Ali and Mary walked circles around the tree, placing them just right among the branches. Grant and Zach were completely content on watching it all unfold, supervising — as they called it — from the couch.

The next step was garland, followed by a large box of ornaments that had been collected since they were little girls. Linda carried the box of ornaments over to the coffee table. Molly and Jack sat close to her, mesmerized by the thought of what could be inside. Each ornament was carefully wrapped in tissue paper, partly to protect what was inside, partly to make it a surprise, not knowing which one you were choosing from the box.

Jack leaned over the box. "Who gets to choose the first one?" he asked with wide eyes.

"Well," Linda started, "the tradition when your mommy and aunties were little was the youngest went first and worked our way up to the oldest." She winked at Roger.

Jack looked around the room. "Does that mean I get to go first?"

"I suppose it does," Linda said. "And I bet you can guess who gets to go last."

He glanced around the room again, looking at each of them. "Grandpa!" he shouted, pointing to Roger who was laughing in the corner. Jack pulled his first ornament out of the box, placing it on the floor to unwrap it.

"Which one did you get?" Susie asked.

He grabbed hold of the thin gold thread and lifted it out of the tissue. Everyone watched as Jack made it as suspenseful as possible.

"Well?" Susie asked again.

"I got the pickle!" he shouted, waving it around

proudly.

"I love the pickle," Molly added, "but you can't hang it on the tree or you'll know where it is and it won't be fair."

Both Jack and Molly loved that tradition of looking for the pickle ornament, with the first one to find it getting a special prize. The girls reminisced about it from their childhood, too.

Linda stood between Jack and Molly. "I'll tell you what," she suggested, "why don't we set this one aside, and we'll have grandpa hide it later tonight after you go home. That way, when you come back tomorrow, you can both try to find it." Linda grabbed the pickle ornament and placed it safely on the mantel. "Since you can't hang it, go ahead and choose another."

Jack reached in the box and chose another, walking around the tree until he found the perfect spot to hang it, Grant lifting him up several times so he could reach. Molly went next, proceeding down the line in order of age until the last ornament was hung. When they were finished, everyone stood back and admired their work.

"I think we did a great job," Grant said, crossing his arms across his chest.

"I would have to agree," Linda said. "The cookies should be cooled enough to decorate. Who wants to come in the kitchen and help me?" Molly and Jack's hands shot straight up. Linda led the way as the kids followed closely behind. Roger decided to join them in the kitchen while the others relaxed in the living room, admiring all of their hard work.

"How's Alex doing?" Grant asked of Mary, breaking the silence. "I was kind of hoping he would've come home, too, and maybe get a little guy time out on the town." He smiled at Susie, elbowing her in the arm playfully.

"Oh yeah, you are such a party animal," Susie joked. "I'm sure you would have really shown him a good time." Ever since Grant and Susie had Molly and Jack, their night life as a couple ceased to exist. They used to take Molly out when she was a baby, but once Jack came along, they were completely content on staying home with their little family.

Mary half smiled, saying "He must be busy. I thought I would have heard from him by now." She checked her watch and shrugged it off. "He must be out with a client."

"Do you all still want to go into town for the tree lighting ceremony?" Susie asked. "Mom and dad said they'd watch the kids if Grant and I wanted to go." She looked at her sisters.

Ali and Zach nodded, but Mary sat expressionless on the couch as if she hadn't heard a word Susie said.

"Yoo-hoo, earth to Mary," Susie said, waving an arm back and forth.

Mary pushed her sleeve up, checking her watch again. "I don't think my body has adjusted to the time change quite yet. I'll probably stay home and help mom and dad with the kids."

"As soon as we leave, the kids are going to bed, so no help is needed. I guess that solves that little problem — go get ready," Susie ordered, making the decision for her.

"Well, I guess I'm going then. But you have to make me one promise first, or I'm staying home," Mary said. She looked at the four of them sitting across the room. "Don't make me feel like the fifth wheel since I'm the only solo one in the group. You can't be all cute and lovey dovey with each other and make me feel even worse than I already do about spending the holidays alone."

The four of them looked at each other.

"Deal — now go put some layers on because it's freezing outside," Susie ordered.

"Yes, *mom*," Mary replied, sticking her tongue out at her sister like she did when she was a kid.

Mary walked upstairs to her room and found several pieces of clothing that would work well for layering. She pulled on a pair of leggings and layered them with a pair of skinny jeans over the top. Not a huge fan of standing out in the cold, she layered the top with a few extras — tank top on first, followed by a tee shirt, and then her sweatshirt. For a moment, she paused, thinking of adding a long sleeve shirt in between, but didn't want to sweat if they were to go inside for a while.

Mary grabbed her cell phone off the bed and called Alex to check in before heading out for the night. After four rings, she got his voicemail. She didn't really have a specific reason for calling, nor did she think he would return her call, so she hung up without leaving a message. It was a rare occasion that his voicemail gave her the option to leave a message. Typically, when she calls, his voicemail is full with showing confirmations for his clients.

Everyone was gathered around the center island in the kitchen when she returned downstairs. In the middle of the counter, Linda lined up seven different bowls, all with a different color of food color-dyed vanilla frosting.

The cooling racks were overflowing with undecorated sugar cookies cut in every shape associated with Christmas you could imagine. There were bells, presents, Santa's, snowmen — enough cookies to last for days. A plate of finished cookies sat between them on the counter, slathered in inches of frosting and sprinkles, many of them falling onto the plate or rolling across the counter.

"Wow — it looks like you guys have been hard at work. Are they off limits, or are you going to let me taste one?" Mary inspected them, eyeing up which one she wanted to eat at the word "go."

"I suppose you can have *one*," Linda said sarcastically. "There are so many cookies over there, you could eat ten and still not make a dent in the pile," she said laughing.

"Don't temp me," Mary said, raising her eyebrows.

Jack raised his hand. "Can we go youngest to oldest again?"

"Sure, go ahead," Mary agreed.

They each grabbed a cookie, stuffing it down quickly before they left.

"The rest will be going home with each of you when we're finished," Linda said, pointing to the table. There sat a silver tin with each family's name on them. Linda made a rule years ago, that if you bring your tin back each year, she would refill it with cookies. If you threw your tin away or didn't bring it back, you got nothing. They assumed she got tired of buying cookie containers for them every year. Once the rule was in place, it was never a problem again. Just to be safe, Mary packed her tin into her carry-on to be sure it would arrive safely.

"Good night my loves," Susie said, kissing each of her kids on the forehead. "Mommy and daddy are going out for a little while, but grandma and grandpa will be here with you if you need anything. We'll be back later to pick you up before Santa comes."

"Have fun," Molly said, licking frosting off her finger.

Jack placed another finished cookie on the plate. "See you later, alligator."

"We better get going," Susie said. "The ceremony starts in an hour, and I thought it'd be fun to stop by the Pub on the way for a drink. It might help warm us up a little before we stand outside waiting for them to light the tree." She walked to the front closet and started handing out jackets, not realizing the mom in her was showing again. As long as she resisted the urge to kneel down and zip them up, she figured no one else would notice.

"Someone means business," Mary teased. "I've actually been looking forward to the tree lighting ceremony all month. It's one of my favorite Maple Falls traditions." She zipped her jacket and put on her hat and warm mittens.

"And to think, you didn't even want to go twenty minutes ago," Ali pointed out.

Mary replied with another child-like scrunched face.

"Zach and I will go warm the car up for you freeze babies," Grant said. "See you out there." He pushed his arms through the sleeves of his jacket and followed Zach outside.

"I think I have to go to the bathroom quick before we leave," Ali said, dropping her jacket on the floor. "I know once I get outside in the cold air, I'll really have to go." She ran through the living room, disappearing down the hall. A few minutes later, she was finally back and ready to go. When they were little, she was always bringing up the end of the line everywhere they went.

"I feel bad for you already if you have children someday," Susie laughed. "If you think your bladder is small now, wait until you have a giant baby sitting on top of it."

"Let me get married first, sis. One step at a time." Ali slid her jacket back on and they were out the door.

Mary pulled the collar up on her jacket, leading the way to the car where the guys were impatiently waiting in the front seat. The three girls piled into the backseat, squishing Mary in the middle.

"What took you so long?" Grant questioned. "Zach thought you had to wash your hair again or something."

"Very funny, Zach, but you can blame your fiancé this time — the woman with the tiniest bladder," Susie joked.

Ali reached across Mary and hit Susie square in the chest. "Very funny, can we go now?" She sat back and pouted the rest of the drive. Ali should be used to her sisters teasing her by now, but she was out of practice of both of them doing it at the same time.

Chapter
Nine

"I can see nothing here has changed," Mary said, pushing through the front door of the Pub. The sound of peanut shells and stale popcorn crunching under her feet as she walked to the back to find a place to sit. The only table that appeared to be available was in the back corner with beer bottles and peanut shells scattered across it. Zach waved down a waitress to wipe it down. The building was already packed as more people were piling in behind them.

"Sorry about that," the waitress said, flinging peanut shells onto the floor with her rag. "We are swamped tonight, and we're having a hard time keeping up with who is coming and who is going. Are you all headed over to the tree lighting ceremony tonight?" She wiped the rest of the table down and swished her rag along the chairs.

"Yes, I think that's the plan," Grant told her. "We were hoping to hang out here and stay warm until it starts. With a crowd this size, I don't think staying warm will be a problem." He unzipped his coat and hung it over the back of his chair.

"Whew, I was planning to order a warm drink," Mary said, "but I think a cold beer might taste better. It must be ninety degrees in here." She fanned her face with the drink menu.

Four waitresses ran around the room taking drink orders, each covering a different corner of the pub. The waitress assigned to their table flew by them twice without stopping to take any orders. Ali checked her watch as four more people crowded in next to their table, only standing room remaining.

"Why don't you tell me what you want, and I'll go up to the bar and order it," Mary said, standing from the table. "I'm the out of town visitor, so it's my treat — and don't even think of arguing with me." She took their requests and weaved her way through the crowd toward the bar. When she finally got close, she wedged her way between two large men who were waving their cash in the air hoping to get the bartender's attention.

"Excuse me, could we get a few beers over here?" Mary shouted, joining them in the money waving.

It wasn't like her to be so forward, but she was beginning to discover a new side of herself since coming home. The bartender muttered something in her direction and proceeded to the other end of the bar. Sighing, she dropped back down to flat feet. Another customer came up behind her, standing so close it was making her uncomfortable. As she was about to move away and relocate further down the bar, she heard a familiar voice.

"Well, if you can't get a drink around here, there's no hope for me," the man said, still standing close.

She darted around, and said, "What are you doing here?"

"The same thing you are I would imagine," Will replied slyly. "You probably think I'm totally lame going to the tree lighting ceremony alone, but I've gone every year. They say its bad luck to break a Christmas tradition, right?" A smile spread across his face.

Mary laughed, lightly touching his arm. "Why yes, I have heard that it's bad luck, so it's probably a good thing you came." The bartender finally made his way over to them. She ordered the drinks, adding another for Will. "We have a table in the back corner if you care to join us. I can't guarantee there'll be a chair for you to sit on, but you are welcome to come and stand by us." She was starting to like this new outgoing side of herself.

He looked at the drinks sitting in front of them. "You just need me to help you carry all of the drinks you just ordered, don't you?" Will joked.

"Well, that, too, I suppose," she giggled. "I guess I hadn't thought this through fully before coming up here alone." They each grabbed three bottles, and Will followed

Mary to the back table.

"We thought you got lost," Susie teased. "I was getting ready to send Grant up to search for you."

Mary rolled her eyes. "Oh, you're so full of jokes tonight. You have no idea what it's like up there. People are crazy around here tonight." Mary handed out the bottles she was holding. "And look who I found along the way," she said, moving to the side as Will appeared.

"Well technically, I found you," he said, handing out the bottles he was holding. "She asked me to join you all. I hope that's okay. I still think she just needed help carrying the drinks all the way back here."

Mary could feel the chill of the night's cold air still coming off Will as he stood close to her. The smell of his cologne was sneaking in under her nose, and she was suddenly very aware of how close they were actually standing to each other.

"We don't mind, I'm just glad you came with my beer," Grant teased. "I should take it right back up to the bar, and get in line now for the next round if it takes that long." He threw a stray peanut shell at Mary, causing her to blush.

"That's the last time I do something nice for you guys," Mary protested. "I expect all of you to buy the drinks for the rest of the night." She sat down in her chair and pouted.

Will moved closer to Grant and Zach and talked about work — nothing that would interest any of the women. Mary could only make out a few words of their conversation here and there with the volume in there. It was beginning to clear out as people made their way out to the tree, freeing up a chair nearby for Will. Mary held her breath, secretly hoping he would pull it up to the table next to her, but he carried on his conversation with the guys, unaware of her hopes.

"Look who the cat dragged in," Grant shouted, looking up over Mary's head. They all turned around to find Grace, Brad, and Cora standing behind them.

"Hey everyone, good job at getting a table in here," Cora said. "We've been crammed in the front corner since we walked in. I knew I should have called you."

Brad stood beside Cora rubbing her arms up and down, warming her always-frozen body. Grace, Mary's friend, was quiet, standing beside Cora, feeling very similar to how Mary was feeling being the fifth wheel to their group.

"I'm afraid I didn't get the date memo," Grace said, looking around the table.

Mary's eyes instantly met Will's, although he tried to play it off. She wasn't sure if this had turned into a date or not, but being that she wasn't single, she didn't want to make too much of the situation.

"Don't worry, I didn't either. I'll be your date if you want," Mary suggested.

Grace laughed. "Well, it wouldn't be the first time you filled in for my date. Are you guys headed out to the tree soon?" She looked around the room and noticed it was half empty already.

"Shall we?" Zach asked, helping Ali with her jacket.

Grace zipped her jacket all the way to the top, tucking her chin into the collar. "Is it bad that I'm already cold just thinking about going outside?"

Everyone stared at her like she had three eyes.

"I think you've been living in California too long," Mary teased.

The number of people surrounding the tree was unbelievable. The tradition has been drawing more and more people in from smaller surrounding towns each year for the event. The evening temperature outside had drastically dropped compared to how warm it felt inside the pub. The wind had picked up sending snowflakes sailing across the area. Although Grace didn't seem to care for it, the rest of crowd welcomed it, adding to the Christmas mood. The small string orchestra in the gazebo began playing *Canon in D* as the crowds gathered in tighter, huddling together to keep warm and listening to the delightful music.

Mary pulled her mittens out of her pockets and slid them on. She tightened her scarf a little closer to her face to keep the snow from blowing down her jacket. While she was pretty much frozen to her core, she didn't want to sound like a baby whining about the cold.

Will, being the attentive man that he was, could tell she was freezing without her uttering a single word. He stood behind her and rubbed her arms up and down to help warm her. Though he wished he could wrap his arms around her like Zach and Grant were doing with their ladies, he didn't want to cross that boundary with Mary. Her face was the first thing to warm, her cheeks flushed from his attention. Out of the corner of her eye, she could see her sisters watching her. Trying to avoid their eye contact, she glanced down at the ground, not wanting them to notice how red her cheeks had gotten. She could have, however, blamed it on the cold wind blowing against them.

Her stomach began to flutter as he tried to warm her up, his soft breath falling against the side of her face as he looked around from behind her.

"Good evening, everyone," the mayor greeted over the microphone. The crowd silenced as he continued. "Thank you all for coming out on this chilly evening. I see a lot of you brought your families out. I love to see so many of you carrying on this Maple Falls tradition with the next generation. I'm so honored to be your mayor and to be able to share this night with all of you."

Mary listened to the mayor as he spoke as if he was speaking directly to her. She didn't have a family of her own, nor did she have a significant other to spend this night with. For some reason, however, since coming home, she really began to picture herself living back there. She felt this is a place where she could carry on her family traditions with her own children someday. She hadn't realized all she had given up to move away with Alex. It became very apparent to her while being with everyone tonight as to what she was missing the past couple years.

Shutting off her mind and letting her heart do the talking for once, she allowed herself to lean back into Will, the warmth of his chest radiating against her back. Was this where she was supposed to be? Maybe she was supposed to raise her family in Maple Falls and make this ceremony one of their traditions. Her mind began to race again, filling with so many questions she couldn't find the answers to.

"I don't want to keep you all out here any longer than necessary," the mayor continued, "and I can see several yawns coming from the little faces among the crowd. So, without further ado, I give you the 2017 Maple Falls Christmas tree." The mayor set down the microphone and walked to the podium that contained the switch.

The crowd began the official countdown. "Five, four, three, two, one!"

Using both hands, he flipped the large switch, illuminating the giant blue spruce. The bulbs were the size of golf balls, glowing red, green, yellow, and blue. The cheers from the crowd were sure to be heard for blocks around. The joyous sound of *We Wish You A Merry Christmas* began blaring through the speakers as the crowd joined in the lyrics.

Mary glanced around at all the couples embracing around her, celebrating this time-honored tradition together. Her mind briefly wandered, wondering what it would be like to kiss Will. But knowing she had committed herself to Alex, she pushed the thought away, offering him a warm hug instead. Feeling his arms wrapped around her felt foreign to her, something she hadn't felt with Alex in forever. She tried to remember the last time Alex embraced her, but her mind came up blank.

Was she only feeling this because it was something she was missing in her life, or was she actually developing feelings for Will? More and more questions came flooding to her thoughts, bogging down her mind. Her sisters turned towards Mary and Will.

"You two are so cute together," Susie said, making Mary's cheeks turn red again. "Should we head home, or do you all want to grab another drink? I'm sure the kids are passed out by now, so another hour won't really matter."

Not wanting to let go of the feeling she was having quite yet, Mary spoke up. "I vote for more drinks!" she blurted out, hoping it didn't come off as too desperate.

Will shrugged. "I'd be up for another drink if you guys don't mind me tagging along a little while longer."

"As long as the pub is cleared out, we're up for it," Zach said, nodding at Ali. "I could go for some darts or a game of pool. Are you guys in?" he asked, surveying the rest of the group.

"I promised Nancy that we would be back to pick Lily up right after the tree was lit, so we have to get going," Cora said, holding onto Brad's hand.

Mary looked over to Grace, raising her eyebrows up and down.

"I came with them," Grace said, "plus, I have to get some last minute wrapping done tonight so I'm ready for tomorrow. Have a great night you guys." Grace hugged Mary good-bye and told her to call her in the morning.

The family crowds didn't return to the pub following the ceremony, so there was plenty of tables for them to choose from. Grant led the way to the table closest to the dart boards. Still warm inside from earlier, they all removed their jackets again and draped them over the chairs, reserving them from anyone else moving in.

"I'll grab the first round of drinks if you guys don't mind getting the game set up," Will told them. "Mary, would you mind helping me carry them since I helped you last time?" He reached his hand out to her.

"Well, it's only fair." She grabbed his hand as he helped her up from her chair. "I'm still pretty cold from being outside, so I think I'll switch to coffee and Bailey's."

Will grabbed the attention of the bartender much quicker this time around. He ordered the beers and then handed the coffee over to Mary. She breathed it in, letting the steam warm her face.

She took a small sip. "Wow, one of these should warm me up quickly."

"That strong, huh?" he teased. He handed her another drink to carry as he grabbed the rest, leaving a tip at the edge of the bar. "Shall we?" He motioned her back to the table.

Grant had the game all set up by the time they returned. "We thought we could play three teams of two, so you two will be on a team together," he said, looking over at Mary with a wink.

Will didn't seem to have a problem with that arrangement. He raised his beer in the air. "May the best team win," he said. He leaned over toward Mary and whispered, "We've got this."

Will walked over to the dart board first to get the game started. Tossing his first dart, he hit the edge of the board hard, sending the dart crashing to the floor. Everyone laughed.

"Hey now, I guess I'm a little rusty," Will told them. "I just need to warm up a bit. I haven't played in a few years." Mary stared at him, wondering if he was really that bad, or if he was just trying to get everyone to think that he was. His next dart hit a triple twenty.

"Yeah," Mary cheered. "Now that is how you play darts!"

After they went through the teams once, Grant went over to the bar and bought the next round of drinks. He was the group's designated driver for the evening, so he switched over to water and allowed the others to enjoy themselves. Mary couldn't remember the last time she had more than two drinks, which for her, was already pushing her limits. Each drink that was brought to her seemed to go down better and faster than the one before.

Susie threw her last dart and looked at her watch,

noticing it was almost eleven o'clock. "I think we better start wrapping it up so we can get the kids home before Santa comes." She motioned to Grant as she took the last sip of her drink.

Will set his empty beer bottle down on the table. "I had a lot of fun with you all tonight. Thanks again for letting me tag along with you." He walked over to the chair and grabbed Mary's jacket, holding it out for her to put on.

"Thank you, Will. You're quite the gentleman." Mary zipped back up and waited for the rest of them.

Grant and Susie went outside first to warm the car while Ali, of course, had to run to the bathroom again. Zach stood guard outside the bathroom door like the good fiancé that he was.

"I had a really nice time tonight," Mary said. "I can't remember the last time I laughed so much." Mary stared into Will's eyes, very aware of how close they were standing to each other.

"I did, too," Will admitted. "You mean to tell me that you don't do this every weekend back home with your friends? I have a hard time believing you aren't always this fun."

Back home, she thought. To her, she was back home right now, and felt it now more than ever. "No, I don't go out very much," Mary said. "Alex works all the time, and I still haven't found a job. The opportunity to make new friends is pretty slim." She looked down at her feet, wishing she hadn't just said Alex's name out loud.

Will placed his finger under her chin, gently lifting her

head back up to look at him. "If I were Alex, I would take you out every night to show the whole world what an amazing woman I was lucky enough to be with."

She looked into his eyes, holding his gaze. She could feel him getting closer, their lips mere inches from touching. She leaned her head, ready to give in. As her eyes began to close, her phone started ringing on the table, snapping her out of the trance she was in. She shot a quick look down at the table — it was Alex.

Chapter *Ten*

Mary woke the next morning to the bright sunlight blaring through her bedroom window, causing her head to pound a little harder than it should have. She thought she may have a little hangover as a result of those few drinks last night, but this is more than she bargained for. She lifted her head off the pillow, but the quick motion made her borderline nauseous.

Reaching for the nightstand, she grabbed her cell phone, curious to see if Alex tried to call again last night. A guilty feeling fell into the pit of her stomach thinking back to last night. Not that she had done anything wrong, but if Alex hadn't interrupted with his call at that exact moment, she knew she would have kissed Will.

She sat there in bed wondering if she should just pick up the phone and call him, ending it all right now. But she wasn't sure that big of a decision should be made so quickly. Ending a relationship on normal circumstances — face to face — was difficult enough, but ending a relationship where one person lives across the country from the other, now that, for Mary, would be one of the most difficult things she could ever dream of doing. Not to mention that once she broke off the relationship, she wouldn't have anywhere to live, and there would be a domino of decisions thrown in her face. She wasn't quite ready to deal with the chain of events that would come along with that decision. Mary glanced at her phone.

No missed calls.

She thought that maybe, just maybe Alex would send a Merry Christmas text, but there was nothing. She decided to call him at home.

No answer.

Since his cell phone was never more than a foot away from his ear, she tried that next. It rang three times before he answered.

"Hello?" he answered, sounding caught off guard.

"Merry Christmas, Alex," she replied. There was a pause on the other end.

"Oh — hi Mary," he answered — sounding somewhat abrupt. "I didn't look to see who was calling before I answered. Is something wrong? Why are you calling?" He sounded distracted. She could hear the faint sound of another voice in the background, but it was too soft to make out.

"No, nothing is wrong," Mary said apologetically. "I missed your call last night, and I wanted to call you back and wish you a Merry Christmas." She paused to listen again, unsure if she should have brought up his call last night, all the while her experience with Will was racing through her mind. "Where are you?" she said. "I tried you at home first, but you weren't there. Certainly, you can't be at the office on a holiday."

She sat back down on the bed slowly after making one lap around the room, trying to concentrate on the voice she heard in the background. She rubbed her temples, attempting to lessen the throbbing.

"Actually, I *am* at the office," Alex admitted. "I figured since you were out of town, I might as well come to the office and get a jump start on setting up the showings I have to schedule for next week. If I call today, they will set them up first thing in the morning when the office is back open."

Mary could hear him shuffling papers around, sounding almost staged at the pace in which he was doing it, but yet almost sounding like crumpling, rather than shuffling.

"Couldn't you have just done that from home on the couch?" Mary asked. "I would think the traffic around town would have been too much for you to handle what with all of the people out and about today." She squinted her eyes to help her concentrate, waiting for Alex to speak again, but hoping to hear the voice of the other person who was with him. "Is somebody else in the office with you?" she said quizzically. "Don't you agents ever take a day off?" She forced a laugh, trying to make a joke.

"Oh, yeah that —," he stuttered, shuffling around some more papers. "That's just Trish, my new assistant. She came in to help me organize the showings I have to set up for two of my clients. One is looking in the north and the other in the south. I'd be sure to mess them up if I tried to do it myself."

Alex was one of the most organized agents she'd ever met, insisting on doing everything himself to ensure it got done correctly, and more importantly, on time.

Mary huffed. "You made your assistant come in today? For goodness sakes, Alex, it's Christmas!" Her voice got a little louder than she intended.

Alex rolled his eyes. "I did give her the day off," he shouted, "but she just moved here a few months ago, and she doesn't know anybody else yet. She offered to come in and help me this morning, so I took her up on it. Plus, I didn't want her to spend the holiday alone in a new city. It's hard meeting new people, you know. Besides, I didn't think you'd want me to be alone today either." He stopped talking, feeling like he already dug a big enough hole.

Mary knew how hard it was to meet new people. If there was anyone who would understand exactly what that felt like, it was her. She shook her head. "Of course, I wouldn't want you to be alone today, but you spending the day with your assistant wasn't exactly what I had in mind. I was thinking more along the lines of spending the day with Brian's family. Doesn't Trish have a boyfriend to spend the day with?" She threw that out there, trying to indirectly find out if she was single or not. Not as subtle as it should have been, but she was annoyed, and at this point, she didn't care. "And when did you hire an assistant? I don't recall you telling me this before."

"No, Trish doesn't have a boyfriend," Alex came back somewhat sarcastically. "Like I said, she just moved here a couple months ago and doesn't have any friends yet. Kind of like you in a way, except she has a job where she can meet people."

His words stung, her breath catching in her throat. "That's not my fault. I've been applying everywhere, but nobody is hiring," she argued. "I've been trying ever since you made me move there." She tried to throw it back in his face, but she felt her comebacks were never very good. He never did answer her question. "When did you hire her? She must have a lot more experience than I do since you turned me down for the job."

"I didn't mean it like that," he said, trying to back pedal. "I'm really busy here, and I don't want to fight with you right now. I have to set up about twenty showings before I can leave. Not to mention that Brian is having an office get together at his house later, so I want to finish up here so I can stop by Brian's. Tell your family I wish I could have been there."

"You could have if you really wanted to." She paused, knowing if she kept talking, it would only make it worse. She took a deep breath. "Is Trish going to be at Brian's house, too?"

"Mary, I have another call coming in. I'll try calling you later tonight before I go to Brian's. Good-bye." And with that, the line cut off.

Mary slammed her cell phone down on the nightstand, her hands shaking. She stomped to the bathroom to brush her teeth. Opening the bathroom door, the sound of pots and pans banging around down in the kitchen made her head pulse again. She tied her robe, took a couple deep breaths, and shook off her horrible conversation.

She grumbled as she walked down the stairs, her body still tense from her conversation with Alex. She stopped on the landing, just in time to see her parents' paths cross each other in the kitchen doorway as they paused under the mistletoe. Her father leaned in and kissed her mother gently, taking in the moment. After all these years together, it still touched Mary's heart seeing the love they still have for each other. It was witnessing those little moments such as that, that made Mary long to have the same in her life. The step creaked as she continued down, alerting them to her presence.

"We were wondering when you were going to get out of bed," her mother teased. "Can I get you something for breakfast? I have eggs, sausage, bacon, and pancakes cooking in the kitchen. Come on down, I'll make you a plate." She walked away before Mary had a chance to answer.

Mary wasn't sure if it was her mother's generation, or if it was just the mother in her, but she always insisted on making food for her family whether they were hungry or not. She went to the kitchen, following her nose, and pulled up a stool at the counter.

"Do you have any coffee made? I could use a pot — or two," Mary kidded.

Linda turned around, giving her a sly smile.

"I know, mom, that's a dumb question. You own a coffee shop. Of course, you have fresh coffee brewed."

Linda poured a cup, and placed it in front of her without a word. Mary grabbed it and wrapped her hands around it, closing her eyes, still trying to shake off her rough start to the morning.

"Thanks, mom, this is just what I needed." Mary breathed it in, her headache slowly fading away. "Can I have a little sugar and cream?" Her mother gave her a puzzled look over her shoulder. "I don't drink mine black like you do, mom. I need to sweeten it up a bit."

Linda slid the cream and sugar bowls across the counter to her. Mary scooped a little sugar in from the small silver dish and poured in some creamer.

"Could I trouble you for a spoon to stir it with, please?"

"Anything else, your majesty?" her mother teased. She tossed Mary a spoon and returned to the stove in time to flip the next batch of pancakes. Mary took in another breath as she sensed the smell of fresh blueberries filling the kitchen. As Mary sat sipping her coffee, she enjoyed the stillness and quiet of the house. The serenity was wonderful; the only sound to be heard was that of bacon sizzling in the pan.

"Sorry, I could have gotten it myself," Mary said to her mother, "but I know how you are in the kitchen and didn't want to get in your way." Stirring her coffee, she watched it twirl in the mug.

Linda gave her a look, even though she knew Mary was right. "Did you guys have a good time last night? I didn't hear you come in, but I'm guessing it was pretty late." Linda piled another batch of pancakes onto a plate and carried them over to Mary.

"We did have fun. We went to the tree lighting and then to the pub afterward for a few drinks and darts." Mary buttered two pancakes and scooped some eggs onto her plate.

"I mean this in the nicest way," Linda smiled, "but you look like you may have had more than a few. Did you see anyone else you knew there? It's such a big event that everyone comes out for it."

Mary brushed off her mother's comment and took a bite of her pancake. She debated on whether or not to tell her mom that she ran into Will, but she knew her sisters would blab the second they walked in the door. She figured it would be better to get her version out there first.

"I did, actually." She could feel her cheeks begin to get hot again. "We ran into Grace, Cora, and Brad at the pub and they joined us. Oh, and Will." She added him in at the end very matter-of-fact, hoping she wouldn't hear it.

"That sounds like fun, dear. I bet it was nice to have some other friends to hang out with to lessen the fifth wheel feeling with your sisters. It's really too bad Alex wasn't able to come home with you — we sure would have liked to have seen him. Remind me to send his Christmas gift home with you."

"That's nice, but you didn't have to get him a gift." She wanted to tell her mother about her phone call this morning with Alex, but thought she would assume she was being paranoid. It was still eating at her, unable to push it from her mind. He seemed to be dodging her questions, and he never answered her about whether Trish was going to be at Brian's house or not. On the other hand, she *was* hanging out with Will, so how could she get mad at Alex for doing the same thing?

"Was Will happy to see you last night?" her mother asked. "It was sure nice of you to invite him to join you." Even though her mother's back was to her, Mary knew she was smiling.

Mary cleared her throat. "Yeah, I think so. He was the only reason our team won in darts. He hit the bulls-eye three times. I think my dart bounced off the floor more than that." Linda warmed up her coffee and brought over more pancakes. Mary set her fork down. "If you keep feeding me like this, I'm not going to fit into my bridesmaid's dress."

"You could stand to put on a pound or two," Linda said, looking her up and down. "You've gotten so thin since you moved away."

She didn't have the heart to tell her it was probably from stress and being unhappy. "I haven't lost *that* much.

Maybe it's from the stress of trying to find a job. Picking up and starting over wasn't as easy as I thought it was going to be. If Alex was around more, maybe it wouldn't be so bad." Mary stirred more sugar into her coffee.

Linda stopped what she was doing. "Well if he's so busy out there, then why don't you stay here a little longer? You don't have a job to rush home to, so why hurry back?"

Her mother did have a point, but she wasn't sure she should stay. Running home to be alone all of the time was not on her list of high priorities, but she couldn't hide forever. Eventually, she would have to make a decision about all of it.

"I have to get a job sooner or later, mom," she said. "The longer I wait to apply, the harder it will be to get one. A few months from now, the college kids will be returning for the summer and will take all of the available jobs. Before I know it, it'll be fall again before anything opens up."

Linda nodded. "But if you stay here, your sisters and I would really enjoy it. I know your father would love to have your help around the shop again. I bet Will would enjoy it, too."

Mary froze. "Why would you say that? Isn't he still involved with Lauren? Besides, I'm with Alex if you have forgotten." She stared at her mother, trying to see if she knew anything, but she was impossible to read. Mary knew what she was feeling about her relationship with Alex, but she just hasn't had the right opportunity to talk to him about how he felt.

Linda simply smiled and walked back to the kitchen sink without another word.

Chapter
Eleven

Later that morning, Mary could hear voices begin to fill the house as she came downstairs after her much-needed shower. Susie and her family arrived first as the kids darted through the door; their boots and jackets barely off before they raced each other to the tree to check out the gifts that were spread across the tree skirt underneath. As they cleared the foyer, Ali and Zach came in right behind them. Mary stood in the doorway of the kitchen, watching all of them pile into the living room, something almost magical about it.

Molly and Jack went right to playing on the floor with a few of their new presents they brought with from home. Zach and Grant settled in immediately on the couch, turning on the football game, kicking their feet up on the coffee table. Mary glanced at them, trying for a moment to picture Alex sitting there with them, talking about sports and having a great time — but she couldn't see it. Instead, she pictured him pacing the room on an important phone call and ignoring the rest of the family.

"Merry Christmas, Mary," Susie said, as both of her sisters ran over to her, bringing her back to the present. They both attacked her with kisses on either cheek, smashing her face together with theirs.

"That's what you get for standing under the mistletoe," Ali said. "You look better than I thought you would today. How are you feeling?" All three of them burst into laughter.

"It was a bit of a rough start," Mary admitted, "but nothing a little coffee and homemade breakfast couldn't fix."

Her mother's meals were always the go-to fix for any problem. Whether it be boy trouble, a bad day at school, or just not feeling well, her mom's meals always made it better. The girls were convinced she had a magic potion she put into it, but her answer was always *a mother's love.* She supposed that was magical.

Linda and the girls went straight to the kitchen as Roger joined the men in the living room. The ham was already cooking in the roaster and the potatoes had all been sliced, ready to be made into their mother's famous homemade au gratin potatoes. Fresh dough was rising in a large mixing bowl to be made into dinner rolls. Ali took charge of the place settings, bringing out the fancy dishes for the second time this week, placing cloth napkins near the edge of each plate paired with freshly polished silverware. The extra leaves were placed in the table to accommodate them all, requiring two poinsettias for centerpieces, spacing them evenly apart.

When the dining table had been set and all of the food preparations had been made, the women joined the rest of the family in the living room.

"Who is ready to open some presents?" Linda asked, immediately getting the kid's attention.

Molly and Jack both dropped what they were playing with and hurried over to the tree, sitting as close as they could to the presents. Roger put the kids in charge of reading the tags and handing out the presents to keep them occupied. Mary sat close by to help them with the tough names.

"Who is this one for, auntie Mary?" Molly asked, holding up a gift.

"That one is for your mommy," Mary said, tapping Molly's nose with her finger. She darted over and placed the package on Susie's lap.

"What about this one?" Jack asked. Mary whispered the name into his ear as his face lit up. "Dad! This one is for you!" He ran over to Grant and tossed it to him, and raced back for another.

When the kids finished handing them out, they all opened their presents — gift wrap and bows sailing through the air. Ali stood to take pictures, wanting to capture the moments of pure joy and chaos.

"Ali, aren't you going to open your gifts?" Mary wondered. "You're the only one left."

Ali looked around the room, still sneaking photos of everyone. "Okay, okay. I wanted to watch everyone and see what they got. If you look away for even a second, you would miss something among all the craziness."

Ali picked one of her gifts up, wrapped in a shiny silver snowflake paper. Sliding her finger carefully under the taped edge, a white gift box was revealed. She opened the box to find a beautiful guest book for her wedding. It was covered in white satin and dark crimson red lace trim, finished off with a crimson red ribbon tying it closed. She ran her hand along the smooth satin, untying the bow. Inside the front cover, there was a handwritten note.

Ali and Zach,
Today is a day you will remember for the rest of your lives.
May you take in each moment and enjoy it. I know
it'll go by fast, so here is a book for you to remember who was
there to celebrate your special day with you.
I love you both so much, and I'm so thankful you chose me to
be a part of this wonderful day.
Love, Mary

"I asked mom if you had a guest book, and she didn't think you did. Hopefully she was right." Mary looked over to Linda.

Ali shook her head. "No, she was right. That was the

last thing on my list to get this week. Thank you, I love it. The colors are a perfect match and it'll look great on the table at the reception." She stood and embraced Mary. "I'm so glad you came home early. I couldn't imagine Christmas or my wedding without you here. It would be like a part of me would have been missing." She wrapped her arms tightly around her again.

Mary kissed the top of her sister's head. "I wouldn't have missed it for the world. It's not every day your little sister gets married before you do," Mary laughed, trying to lighten the mood. She wiped a small tear from the corner of her eye. "Someday I'll get married. You may have to push me down the aisle in my wheelchair and make sure I remember to put my teeth in that morning, but it'll come."

"I'm sure Alex will ask you," Linda assured her, "but he's just really preoccupied with work right now. That's a good thing though, right?"

Mary looked at her mother. Perhaps she was right, but she was starting to wonder if that's what she even wanted anymore. Maybe there was a reason Alex hadn't asked her yet. Lord knows he's had plenty of time and opportunities to do so. Maybe it wasn't in the cards for them. She tried to shake it off, hoping that she would realize eventually what she truly wanted. Until then, she wasn't going to obsess over it anymore and just enjoy the real reason she came home. It was Ali's time now, and that was what she was going to focus all of her attention on.

"Are there any other last-minute things you still need help with?" Mary asked. "I have no plans this week, other than helping out around the shop, so if you need me just say the word. I feel like I missed everything, and I'm dying to earn my keep in your wedding. Then I can at least say I helped plan my sister's wedding, even if only a little."

Ali thought about it. "Nothing major left, but plenty of small things you can help with. It seems like every time I cross one thing off, three more get added." She waved her hands through the air for extra drama. She froze and pointed at Mary. "The dresses need to be picked up, and I need to check with the florist to be sure the bouquets and centerpieces are scheduled for delivery. I'm sure I can find plenty of things for you to do."

Zach grabbed Ali's hand and pulled her back down to sit by him. "I can't believe the wedding is right around the corner. It seems like so long ago that we got engaged." Considering how long it took him to plan the day he proposed, it really was a long time ago.

"Thank you all so much for everything you've done to help us get ready for the wedding," Zach chimed in. "You've all been so welcoming to me, and I couldn't be happier to become a part of your family." Ali leaned over and kissed Zach. Everyone in the room could see the love they had for each other.

The demand for coffee at the shop on the day after Christmas was out of control. It seemed as though the entire population of town was out and about looking for any after Christmas sales they could get their hands on, not to mention exchanging the gifts they pretended to love, but secretly prayed there was a gift receipt for.

The line was out the door of the shop mere minutes after they opened. Mary grabbed a cup from the first pot she brewed to keep up with the continuous lines of customers. Many of their regulars popped in and out, happy to see her back behind the counter, asking if she was back for good.

"Good morning, Mary," Ellen said, walking up to the counter. Ellen was an elderly woman that lived in an apartment a couple blocks away. She came in the same time almost every day and ordered the same house blend coffee every time. She was definitely a creature of habit.

"Good morning, Ellen. Merry Christmas. Are you still ordering the usual these days?" Mary asked, reaching across the counter for a to-go cup.

"That's right, dear. One cream and one sugar, please." Ellen pulled her coin purse out of her jacket pocket and twisted the gold clasp open. Pulling out the exact change, she placed it on the counter and slid a dollar bill into the tip jar.

"Here you go, Ellen," she said, handing her the steaming cup. "Are you off to do some after Christmas shopping? I've heard there are some pretty good deals out there today."

Ellen shook her head. "Not me. I don't like all the busy crowds of people. The crowd in here is about as much as I can handle. The streets are filled with cars today. I'm thankful I live close enough to walk down here and not have to find a parking spot." She slipped her gloves on and grabbed her coffee.

"That is a nice perk of living close," Mary agreed. "Be careful walking home; it looked a little icy out there when I came in this morning." She waved to her and watched as she walked by the front window and out of sight.

Once the town was caffeinated and the lines calmed down, Roger and Linda spent the rest of the morning taking inventory on what they needed to order before the end of the year. Mary stayed up front and managed the rest, seeing more regulars and crushing any rumors about her moving back home. She walked to the front tables to wipe them down as she saw Will's delivery truck pull up out front. Her heart did a flutter of part excitement, part fear. With a quick hair check of her reflection in the window, she ran to the door to open it as he wheeled up a cart full of boxes. The rush of cold air felt nice against her flushed cheeks.

"Thanks, Mary. How was your Christmas?"

Her first thought was her call to Alex that could have ruined her entire day — but it didn't. "It was great, thanks. It's so nice to be home again and spend time with my family. How was yours?" She couldn't take her eyes off him, hoping he didn't notice.

"It was relaxing, definitely needed that after the busy delivery season I've had," Will said, dropping his shoulders. "I spent the morning at home and then joined the rest of my family later in the afternoon. My parents hosted this year, and I got to play with my niece and nephew. I made sure I bought each of them the loudest, most obnoxious toy I could find in the store." He threw his head back with an evil laugh.

Mary laughed. "That was nice of you. I'm sure your siblings appreciated that."

"No — not so much. I'm pretty sure that if I ever have kids, they will buy them drums, recorders, and harmonicas to pay me back. I can't say as I'd blame them though, since I've purchased a fair amount of those noisy things for *their* kids," he smirked.

His smile was crooked and had a playfulness about it. She could picture him playing on the floor with the kids, imagining him being as excited about a new toy as they were. The father gene was definitely there inside of him, that she could tell for sure.

"Merry Christmas, Will." Roger said, coming out of the office. "Linda and I were just taking inventory in the back. After seeing what little is left back there, I'm very glad to see you today. How was your Christmas?"

"I had a nice time with my family, thank you for asking. From what Mary said, it sounds like you all had a nice day as well." Will handed the packing slip to Roger. "Sign there on the bottom, and I'll be on my merry way. I have double the deliveries today since we were closed yesterday. Holidays make work busy no matter what kind of job you have."

Linda came to the front to help Roger with the boxes. Will walked over to the counter where Mary was wiping coffee pots down. He stood there and watched her for a moment, unaware if she knew he was there. He cleared his throat, trying to get her to turn around.

"Can I get you some coffee? It's awfully cold out there," she offered.

He cleared his throat again, suddenly feeling very dry. "Actually," he started, clearing his throat again, "I was wondering if you had plans tonight. I'm just going to be hanging out at home, and I thought if you didn't have any plans, I'd invite you out for dinner. Eating alone gets pretty boring after a while." He smiled, hoping it didn't come off as too pathetic.

"I can relate. I'm sure my parents won't miss me for one meal. In fact, they'd probably enjoy the break," she laughed.

"She's such an awful house guest — please take her off our hands for a few hours," Linda shouted as she carried a box to the back, obviously eavesdropping on their conversation.

"Thanks a lot, mom," Mary shouted back. "I'd love to join you for dinner. I don't have a rental car, but I'm sure I can borrow my parents' car for a while."

"If it's alright, I'd be happy to pick you up," Will volunteered. "I'd hate to leave them stranded at home if they needed to go somewhere."

Mary nodded. "That sounds perfect. I'll be ready at six."

Will let out the breath he was holding in. "I'll see you then," he said, relaxing his muscles a little more. "I'd better get running so I can finish my deliveries on time."

With a quick wave, he pulled his cart behind him as she watched him go. When his truck was out of sight, she fell back against the counter, not realizing how tense she was standing there. Linda peeked back out of the office, waiting for Will to go before she interrogated Mary.

"Was that a date you just set up?" she asked, sneaking up behind Mary.

She turned around, startled. "It's just dinner, mom. I'm sure he's just trying to be nice to me, a poor pathetic girl who is home for the holidays, alone, without a car. Wow, I just made myself sound like a real catch there, didn't I?" She tended to make jokes when she was trying not to sound so pathetic. She was fairly certain she was at a record high for joke telling on this trip.

Linda hit her playfully with the towel that was draped over her shoulder. "I think it's a date, but you can call it whatever you like." Without another word, she walked back to the office to help Roger unload the new inventory.

Chapter
Twelve

Will strolled through the front door and plopped down on the bench to remove his boots. With each lace he loosened, his feet breathed a sigh of relief. He went to the kitchen to add another stack of mail to what was already piled high after gathering for the past week. Going through the mail regularly was never something he cared to do. It was one of the little things Lauren used to take care of when she was still living there. He wasn't sure why he didn't take an interest in it — maybe he halfheartedly thought if it sat there long enough, she'd be back to take care of it.

He finally decided to take the time to separate the bills into one pile and the junk into another, pausing at a hand-addressed envelope. He slid his finger under the flap and opened it. The formality of the letter caught his eye immediately, using his full name to address him. The only time he ever heard the name William, was from his mother, and he was likely running the other way. Taking a seat at the kitchen table, he read through the letter twice, not believing what he read the first time through.

He wasn't expecting a reply to his correspondence at all, but that it would come this soon was a little alarming. He checked the date on the envelope. Post-marked four days ago. If anything, this may have just taught him a lesson to check his mail daily in fear of missing something important. Important like the letter he was holding.

His thoughts were interrupted by his phone alarm reminding him of his date with Mary — as if he'd forget. He had a half an hour to shower and change out of his uniform into normal clothes. He tucked the letter back into the envelope and tossed it back on the counter with the rest of the mail. Pulling one sock off at a time as he hobbled down the hall, then jumped in the shower, not wanting to be late for his date.

Mary pulled her sweater on, finally deciding what to wear after three changes, as the doorbell chimed in the living room. Six o'clock on the dot. Clearly, Will was not a fashionably late kind of guy. She appreciated a man that could be on time, since all she'd been used to over the past few years was waiting. She grabbed her purse off the bed and got downstairs just as Linda was opening the front door.

She grabbed her jacket from the closet and slid it on quickly. "Right on time — very nice," she said with a grin from ear to ear.

"I wouldn't want to keep a beautiful lady waiting," he said, causing her to blush for the millionth time since she had come home. "Shall we?" He held out his arm. "Have a nice night, Mrs. Bradford."

Mary felt like she was a teenager again getting picked up from her parents' house for a date. Only this time, her father wasn't answering the door, drilling the poor guy with questions that didn't even pertain to the situation.

"Is there anything in particular you're in the mood for tonight?" He walked her to the passenger side of the door, opening it for her. The last time she was in the car with Alex, he wouldn't even set his phone down to give her a proper good-bye, let alone open the door for her — or the trunk for that matter.

"I'm up for anything," Mary chimed. "I had an early lunch at work today, so I'm starving."

He started the car. "You aren't one of those girls that say they're starving and all you order is a side salad, are you?" he asked, backing out of the driveway.

"No way," she said. "Give me a burger and fries over a salad any day. I need real food, especially for dinner. Take me out for lunch, then maybe a salad."

Will chuckled. "I love that. There's nothing worse than taking a girl out for a meal and watch her push her food around on the plate, only taking a few bites. Needless to say, that would make me think twice about a second date."

"I should warn you though," she said. "I'm kind of a dessert girl. I like to have something sweet after dinner." She slipped her gloves off and placed them in her lap. Part of her wondered what kind of girl Lauren was. Since they were together so long, she must have been a burger and fry kind of girl, too. She wanted so much to ask him about what happened between them, but now wasn't the right time.

Twenty minutes later, they pulled up in front of Kline's Steakhouse in one of the neighboring towns. Mary was relieved to go somewhere that Lauren wasn't the hostess. Maybe that was Will's plan all along. She couldn't imagine he'd want to run into her either, especially being out with another woman — more specifically, her.

"I hope this place is okay," he said. "I figured if you weren't a salad person, perhaps you would be a steak person." Will parked the car and hurried around to open the door for her. He offered his arm again, walking together to the entrance.

She walked inside ahead of him. "This place is perfect," she smiled. "I never got a chance to eat here before I moved away, and I was so bummed. My mom was telling me all about their soup and that I needed to try it while I was home."

"How many?" the hostess asked, looking no older than sixteen and not in a very friendly mood.

Will glanced around the crowded restaurant. "Two, please, and if you have a booth available that would be great." He scanned for an empty spot, but couldn't spot any.

The hostess referred to her map on the podium and looked around the room for the available spot. "I have one left near the window. Follow me." She grabbed two menus and walked to the back of the restaurant.

Mary checked out the other diners on the way, curious to see what they ordered. Having seen steak on many of their plates, it was an easy decision of what she would order. She tried to remember the last time she and Alex went out for a nice dinner other than one associated with clients — she couldn't think of one.

"There's a hook on the outside of the booth for your jackets if you wish to hang them," the hostess said as they arrived at the booth. "Your server will be right with you."

Will helped Mary take off her jacket and placed both her jacket and his on the brass hook. The tree-lined sidewalk glowed ever so brightly from the hundreds of strands of white twinkle lights. The snow coated them lightly, allowing them to glow and sparkle through the soft white powder. The table was perfectly located for watching people passing by, many strolling through the park hand in hand.

Will opened his menu. "Are you interested in an appetizer, or would you rather wait for the entree?"

The waitress arrived with a loaf of fresh baked pumpernickel bread before Mary had a chance to open her menu. A thin trail of steam rose from the top of the bread, fresh out of the oven.

"I think the bread is enough for me," said Mary. "Feel free to order something for yourself, though, if you'd like, but I'd rather wait for my dinner."

When the waitress returned, Mary ordered the sirloin, a loaded baked potato, and a side salad to come before the meal. When Will ordered the exact same meal, she couldn't help but wonder if she ordered way more than she could possibly eat. If she were out with Alex, she would never have ordered the meal she just did. She most likely would have ordered a salad, maybe with a cup of soup on the side. Something she just finished telling Will she would never do. It wasn't the person she was — this was. The steak and potato kind of girl. The one who was looking for another person that she could be herself around.

They talked a lot while waiting for their dinners to arrive. He told her about his job, and a little more about the holiday. The conversation was wonderful and refreshing as they both spent time catching up with each other after the past two years of Mary being gone. There was so much that Will had to tell her about what had changed in his life, but he didn't want to info dump on her too quickly.

He was intrigued by hearing about her life now, since it seemed as though her entire world changed. Other than Lauren leaving him unexpectedly, his life was relatively the same as it was before she left. Some may find that boring, not changing in nearly two years, but his life was comfortable. He wasn't one for change, and he liked the routine he had.

After listening to Will talk about how his life has been going, Mary became even more curious about what happened with Lauren, especially since that was the one topic he clearly steered away from. They'd talked about everything but relationships. In her heart, she didn't really want to hear about Lauren or anything having to do with them being together, and for Mary to bring up Alex's name was the furthest thing from her mind. She had resisted the urge to call him and find out how the party at his boss's house went last night, not wanting to hear about lonely Trish again.

Like any other topic, at some point you had to break the ice, rip the band-aid off, or in this case, simply blurt it out. "So, I feel like I am caught up on every aspect of your life except for one little detail," Mary said sheepishly. "Is there a special lady in your life that I need to watch out for after she finds out we are having dinner together?" Mary assumed there wasn't since he was alone at the pub the other night, but it was her way of indirectly asking if she should fear for her life if she ran into Lauren again.

"No girlfriend for me," he said, pressing his lips together. "I was seeing someone a while back, but it didn't work out. Probably for the best, now looking back. I thought she may have been the one, but now being apart for a while, I realized that we weren't meant for each other." He ate the last bites of his salad and pushed his plate to the edge of the table.

"Do you mean Lauren?" She paused, hoping she

wasn't being too forward.

He nodded slowly. "Yes, it was, actually. I forgot I was with her when you were still living here. I thought she would be the woman I was going to marry. I had a ring picked out and everything." He took a long drink of water, and continued, "The day before I planned to ask her, she came to me and told me there was somebody else and wanted some time apart to figure out what she had with the other guy before moving forward with me."

Mary could tell how much pain he was still in when he said that. He barely made eye contact with her, spinning the ice cubes around in his glass with his straw.

"Had she been with him the whole time you were together?" Mary inched to the edge of her seat, eager to hear the rest of his story.

He shrugged. "She claimed she only met him a few weeks before she told me. I'm not sure if I believe her or not, but it doesn't really matter now. I gave her the space she asked for and made the decision for her. A few weeks later, this guy told Lauren that he really didn't want a commitment and left her. After their breakup, she heard from one of her friends that I had intended to propose to her, so she tried to get back together with me."

Just as he was finally starting to open up, the waitress arrived with their dinner. Mary quickly asked for a refill on her water and returned her attention back to Will.

"That's awful — what did you tell her?" She cut a few pieces of her steak quickly so she could concentrate on his story, not on her plate.

He cut a few pieces, pouring steak sauce onto his plate. "It was pathetic, really. I think in the end, all she wanted was to be married. I don't even think she cared who she was married to. It was one of those blessings in disguise, I suppose."

Mary always suspected that Lauren was a little crazy and self-centered, but didn't realize to what extent. Part of her never really cared for Lauren, especially as they got older, but she could never really put a finger on why. After hearing him explain what happened, she now had a valid reason for her feeling the way she did.

"She finally backed off a few months ago," Will said breathing in deeply, "so I'm hoping that's the end of it. I saw her a couple weeks ago with a guy, so who knows. Honestly, I wasn't sure if I felt relieved seeing her with another guy, hoping she was moving on, or if I should run up to the poor guy and warn him about who he was with." Apparently, Mary thought to herself, he used jokes to lighten up the mood like she did, trying to laugh at the crazy situation that he had endured.

Mary burst out laughing, causing a few of the tables near them to stare.

"I'm sorry," she said apologetically, "I didn't mean to laugh, but the way you said that was so funny. It's probably best that you left it alone. Some surprises are better left to be found out later."

"Don't be sorry," he said. "It is kind of funny — now. Back then it was a nightmare. I felt like I needed to wear disguises when I left the house so she couldn't follow me. I finally feel like I'm starting to get my life back, and I'm able to breathe again." He took another sip of water. "What about you? Would Alex be upset about you having dinner with another man?"

Mary looked away, taking a long drink. She knew the other shoe was likely to fall, but she still didn't want to answer him. "Um, I'm sure he'd be fine with it. He has dinner with female clients all the time, and I never get upset."

He slowly nodded. "Clients are one thing; people you don't work with are another."

Mary wrinkled her nose. "Well, technically we do work together, sort of. My family runs a business, and you are our client that happens to deliver all of the supplies to our building." She knew it was a far stretch, but she was proud of herself for coming up with it. Whether it needed to be justified or not, she didn't really care. Like him, she was also starting to feel like her old self again, and she had him to thank for a lot of it.

"I stand corrected. Well done," he said, clapping his hands together. "But in all seriousness, do you think he would have a problem with us having dinner together? I'd hate to cause a rift between the two of you."

She wasn't ready quite yet to tell him that the rift was already there, though he had nothing to do with it. She wasn't feeling a connection with Alex anymore, and frankly, she really has never felt a connection with their new city. She was tired — tired of trying to make something work that maybe wasn't supposed to work. She felt as though she wasted so much time on them as a couple that she wasn't sure she wanted to try anymore. It wasn't working, plain and simple.

"Honestly," she said, "he probably wouldn't think twice about it." That, she knew, was the truth. He was far too busy hanging out with his new assistant and taking her to office holiday parties to be worried about what Mary was doing.

She debated telling Will about the phone call she and Alex had yesterday morning, but it wouldn't really change anything. Making Alex more of a topic of their conversations wouldn't do any good, and if anything, it would make her sound even more pathetic than she felt she already was just being with Alex. To Mary, admitting and saying out loud that she was unhappy and hated every aspect of her life sounded good in theory, but in reality, it would probably only scare Will away. She didn't know what she wanted at this moment, but she did know that scaring him away was not a good idea.

"He wouldn't mind," Mary admitted, "in fact, he'd probably be happy that I finally had someone to hang out with so he wouldn't have to listen to me complain any more about having no friends. He'd probably be happy that I got out of the house. I'm sure he wouldn't mind." She wondered if he realized how many times she said *he wouldn't mind*, like she was trying to convince herself as much as him.

"I hope that's the case," Will said, holding his glass in the air. "To us — friends, or clients, having a nice dinner out together. And to getting to know each other better while keeping each other's lonely old souls company."

They touched their glasses together, holding their gaze. "Cheers to that," Mary chimed in.

Chapter
Thirteen

Linda had the volume on the television turned up as high as it would go in order to hear the weatherman all the way in kitchen, making the doorbell nearly impossible to hear. They were predicting a snowstorm to come later that afternoon, but Maple Falls was right on the edge.

"What are the chances of the storm coming here?" Linda shouted from the kitchen.

"Maybe you should stop what you're doing in there and come watch for yourself instead of trying to listen to the weather over the running water," Mary yelled back. "The storm looks enormous, but it looks to be moving northeast. It may not even come here." Mary knew the sounding of the doorbell would mean that Will arrived, so she grabbed her jacket and scarf from the closet and opened the door. "Hey, come on in," she said in her most welcoming tone. "I was just shouting weather updates to my mom in the kitchen. Looks like over two feet of snow is coming, mom." Mary waited for a reaction.

Linda appeared from the kitchen, wiping her hands dry on a dish towel. "Good morning, Will." She walked into the room to get a better view of the TV. "Two feet? Really?" She stared at the screen, waiting for another update. "Where are you two off to today? What if the storm pattern changes and starts moving this way? You could go off the road and get stuck in a ditch. Do you have a full tank of gas? You know you should never go below a half tank of gas in the winter in case you get stranded."

Mary placed her arm around her mother's shoulder, hoping she got the hint to calm down with the twenty questions and winter interrogation she was throwing in Will's direction.

"I've got it covered and filled up on the way over here," Will reassured, "but I wouldn't worry too much. The weatherman said the storm was going to miss Maple Falls, maybe a dusting at best." He looked at Mary and smiled, sensing her annoyance.

"Well if you insist on going, you better hurry," Linda responded in her worrisome voice. "The quicker you go, the quicker you can get back just in case it shifts."

The map appeared on the television screen again, showing the predicted totals for the surrounding areas. Linda's eyes widened.

"What are you waiting for?" Linda, the mother hen,

blurted again. "Do you see the totals on the screen? There is no way you two should be chancing this storm." She began pacing the room.

Mary zipped her jacket. "Mom, I'll send you updates along the way if that'll help ease your worries. And besides, we're just picking up his tuxedo and the dresses for the wedding. What are they, five miles away?"

She did everything she could to assure her mother that there was no need to panic and start stocking up on bottled water and canned goods. Before Mary could say another word, Linda pushed them both toward the door to get them going faster. She stood by the TV a few minutes longer before heading back to the kitchen.

The roads were clear, and the traffic was light. Everyone else in Maple Falls must have gotten spooked by the weatherman, too, and chose to stay home today. The dress and tuxedo shops were only a few miles apart from each other, so they didn't anticipate being gone very long. Snowflakes began flying around, swirling on the roads in tiny tornadoes as the wind whipped by the passing cars.

"Where should we go first?" Will asked, stopping for the red light. He held onto the wheel with both hands, tapping his fingers along to the beat of the music.

"I suppose we should pick up your tuxedo first," Mary answered. "Ali left me in charge of picking up her dress, and she'd probably kill me if she knew I left her dress unattended in the car for even a second."

Will nodded, unsure of what the big deal was, but went along with it anyway. "Tuxedo it is," he said in agreement. "Do you want me to drop you at the door? The wind is really whipping out there, and I wouldn't want it to mess your hair up."

Mary hit him in the arm. "I'm sorry," she quipped back at him, "do I look that high maintenance to you?"

"I'm just teasing you," he laughed. "I'm allowed to do that, aren't I?" Will parked the car as close to the door as he could.

Bang, bang, bang. The sudden noise startled Mary and Will as they looked around, only to find two men running around their car, pounding on the windows. Will pushed his door open and jumped out of the car to find Grant and Zach, laughing and running in circles. Mary pushed her door open when she knew it was safe, pressing up against the wind. Pulling her scarf up over her chin, she joined them near the back of the car.

"Did you already pick up your tuxedos, or are you just here to harass the other customers in the parking lot?" Mary asked, rolling her eyes at their immaturity.

"No, we like to carry giant garment bags around for fun," Grant joked. "Do you think this bag goes with my shoes?"

"Yours is the last one hanging on the rack, Will," Zach said. "You may want to hurry because it looks like the storm is coming this way."

Mary rolled her eyes. "You sound like my mother. She

was trying to convince us to stay home so we wouldn't get caught in it." She pulled her scarf further up on her face. "I'm freezing, so I'll meet you inside." She pulled her hood down to her nose to protect the top of her face from the wind, watching the snow swirl on the ground as she walked.

The tux shop was warm with a small fireplace crackling in the corner. The saleswoman was helping a young man near the fitting room when Mary walked in.

"Someone will be right with you," she said to Mary as she measured the cuff of the man's pants.

Mary smiled and grabbed a seat next to the fireplace to warm up. The bell rang as Will walked in, his ears as red as a pair of tomatoes and his cheeks bright and rosy.

"It feels good in here," he said, pulling up a chair next to her, rubbing his hands together.

"Maybe if you didn't stand out in the parking lot goofing off with your friends in the freezing cold, you wouldn't be an icicle," Mary kidded. "Or perhaps you should invest in a pair of mittens and a hat. Have you forgotten where you live?" Mary figured if he can tease her all the time, she was going to dish it right back.

"Have you been helped yet?" an older woman asked, carrying a handful of garment bags over her arm.

"Not yet," Will answered. "I'm here to pick up my tuxedo for the Reiter wedding this weekend."

"Yes, you must be Will." She hung the bags on an empty rolling rack. "I think I have yours right here." She checked the names, finding his near the back of the rack.

"Have you had your final fitting, or do you need to try it on?"

Will looked to Mary. "I better try it on just in case. I wouldn't want to upset the bride on her wedding day by showing up in a tuxedo that's the wrong size." He grabbed the bag off the rack and carried it to the closest dressing room.

Mary's phone started ringing as Will closed the door, and she answered, "Hello?"

"Mary — it's mom. I was just watching the weather again, and it looks like the snow storm shifted and is headed right for us. They are advising everyone to stay off the roads unless absolutely necessary. Are your errands really necessary?" She was rambling again with questions.

Mary sighed, suddenly realizing this was the one thing she didn't miss since moving away. "Mom, I'm sure we'll be fine. We're at the tux shop now and as soon as he's done trying his on, we'll hurry over to the dress shop. The weather people just say those things to scare people so they'll run out and fill up on gas and groceries. It's all a ploy to get people to spend more money."

"I know you'll be fine," Linda answered, "I just wanted to give you an update on the weather so you'd move faster. It isn't snowing here yet. Is it snowing where you are?" Linda paused from pacing the room again.

"No it isn't," Mary answered. "We are only a few miles away from you. I appreciate the update, mom. We should be home in the next hour or so." She hung up the phone as the dressing room door opened. Will stepped out, doing a twirl to show off.

"So, how do I look?" he said with a big smile on his face. "Do you think Ali will approve?" He did another twirl for effect.

"Very handsome — are all the pieces there?" Mary said as she stood up to inspect him. Ali gave her very specific instructions on what to look for. "Handkerchief, cuff links, tie — looks like everything is here. How does it fit?" She walked around him, checking his suit coat to be sure it wasn't too tight in the shoulders.

"It feels great," Will answered, "nothing is too small. Do you want to do the mommy jiggle on my pants to be sure they fit, too?"

Mary stopped inspecting him, whacking him in the arm again. "Hey, I'm just trying to save you the headache of my sister attacking you at the wedding for your tuxedo not fitting right or missing an accessory. Typically, Ali is pretty easy going, but when it comes to the wedding, you better look out."

He shook his head as he walked back to the dressing room.

"Don't forget any of your accessories and make sure to pack it up neatly so it doesn't wrinkle," she shouted through the door.

"Yes, mo—, um, Mary," he corrected himself quickly.

"If you were going to say mom again, you're lucky you stopped." She sat up straight in her chair, trying to not get too stressed out. If he forgot something, it would be on him, not her.

Will paid for the balance of his rental while Mary inspected the garment bag, unzipping it just enough to check for folds.

"Are you checking my work?" he asked, busting her in the act. "I do wear a uniform to work every day, in case you forgot. Who do you think irons them and hangs them neatly in my closet?" He tucked his wallet into his back pocket and grabbed the garment bag back from her. "I'm not the messy bachelor you are implying that I am."

Mary took a deep breath. "I was just double checking to make sure all of the pieces were inside. It never hurts to have a second look."

His mouth opened wide, and added, "Are you sure you trust me to carry it out to the car all by myself? What if the wind gusts blow it out of my hands and it falls to the ground and wrinkles?" he asked, flaring his hands about.

She shot him a pathetic look as she stood quietly by the car door, waiting for him to unlock it.

The bridal shop wasn't nearly as quiet. Women were running through the parking lot to the front door as tiny snow tornadoes began whipping around, the flurries turning into larger snowflakes. Four brides in big white fluffy dresses stood in the front window as Mary and Will passed by, each of the brides admiring themselves in the long wall of mirrors. Mary pulled on the door hard, fighting against the gusting wind.

A young woman working behind the front desk was on the phone, frazzled as she frantically jotted down messages on post-it notes, attempting to balance the phone between her chin and shoulder. She looked up briefly and acknowledged them, but quickly returned to her notes.

Mary gazed around the sequined-filled room, each gown catching the reflection of the bright lights overhead. A large group of women came charging through the door, laughing and horse playing, the cold breeze following in behind them.

"I'm sorry about the wait. Are you here to pick up or try on?" the receptionist asked Mary as the phone began ringing again.

"Both, actually," Mary said. "I'm here to pick up my sister's wedding dress and to try on my bridesmaid dress one more time to check the alterations."

The receptionist tossed a pen and notepad at Mary. "Write your names down on here, and I'll let someone know shortly that you are here." She cut Mary off before she had a chance to say another word and answered the phone again, placing a second caller on hold.

Twenty minutes later, a woman came out of the back room carrying their dresses. "Are you Mary or Ali?"

"I'm Mary," she answered. "I'm just picking up my sister's dress while I'm here as part of my bridesmaid duty."

The saleswoman raised her brow, clearly uninterested in what she had to say. Will held on to Ali's dress while Mary followed the woman into a fitting room. The other women in the shop weren't holding back their looks towards Will, like the place was forbidden to all men.

Mary unzipped the bag, revealing the dark crimson red dress. She only required one small alteration, but Ali insisted she try it on one more time to make sure it was perfect. Mary got the feeling as though she may have missed out on a little craziness with her sister while being away. Normally a happy and calm person, Ali the bride seemed to lack either of those qualities when it came down to the wedding details.

"Let me know if you need help zipping it up," the woman said, closing the fitting room door. "I'll be waiting right outside."

Mary pulled the bottom of the dress out of the garment bag slowly, careful not to catch the sheer overlay on the zipper. She stepped into it and called the woman back inside the fitting room to zip her. Holding her breath, she waited as the zipper rose, praying it would fit.

She exhaled loudly, scaring the saleswoman. "It fits!" she exclaimed. "I was so worried after they wanted to take it in a little more," Mary explained. "I was already mentally preparing myself for a crazy diet over the next few days just in case." She spun around from side to side, checking every angle in the mirror.

"So, do I get to see you, since I let you see me?" Will shouted from the other side of the door.

Mary laughed, opening the door slowly, just popping her head out. "Here I am, and now you've seen me."

"Come on," he whined. "I've already seen your head

before. Let me see what the dress looks like." He stood up and walked closer to the fitting room before she had a chance to close the door again. He pulled it open the rest of the way, looking her up and down.

"So — what do you think?" she asked. "If you hate it, I wasn't involved in the selection process. You can blame Cora, Susie, and Katie." She waved her hand in front of him, snapping him out of wherever he'd gone.

He shook his head slightly. "You look beautiful. The color looks great on you."

Mary felt her cheeks get warm, sure to match the color of her dress. "Thank you, Will. I think the girls picked a pretty one. Typically, when you agree to be in a wedding, the dress is dreadful, but I think I'd actually wear this one again. I don't know where to, considering I never leave my house and have no friends, but maybe I'll throw it on to wash the dishes one night and spice things up a bit." She did a few more twirls before she asked the woman to unzip her. The line for the fitting room was starting to pile up.

"Don't forget to hang it neatly on the hanger so it doesn't wrinkle," Will teased. "I'm going to check your work when you are finished."

"Ha-ha, very funny," Mary yelled back. "You'll thank me later when you have a wrinkle-free tuxedo with all of its accessories in place on the day of the wedding. Not to mention the fact that I saved you from the wrath of Ali."

Mary opened her fitting room door at the same time as the woman next to her, almost knocking her over with the swing of the door. Pushing it back, she startled the woman on the other side, apparently unaware that Mary was standing there. The woman swung around to give her a piece of her mind, but annoyance quickly turned to shock when their eyes met. The woman stood frozen like a deer caught in the headlights.

It was Lauren.

Chapter
Fourteen

"Mary!" Lauren shouted. She turned her head toward the chairs and saw Will sitting there, holding a wedding gown across his lap. Making eye contact with him made all of the color drain from Lauren's face, matching the white color of the wedding dress she was wearing.

"What are you guys doing here?" Lauren said in a shocked tone. The look on her face made them think she had more questions spinning in her head, but she was unable to get them out.

Will had a look of shock himself, looking quick to Mary, then back to Lauren. "I guess I could ask you the same question. Apparently, you finally got that new boyfriend of yours to marry you. Looks like you got what you wanted." He stood from the chair, adjusting the wedding gown in his arms. "Mary, we better get home before the storm gets worse," he said, holding out his hand to join hers, looking to rub it in Lauren's face even more.

His statement was harsh, but he'd been hurt by Lauren, and he was not willing to give her the satisfaction that she'd won. He left her standing there in shock, unable to form a comeback before they were gone. The sight of the two of them made Lauren's stomach turn. She hadn't thought about how it would feel to see him with another woman. Knowing how she felt at that moment made her realize how he must have felt running into her with her boyfriend all those times. She didn't like it — not one bit.

The women she was with came over to her immediately, witnessing what just happened from afar.

"What just happened?" one of them asked, all of them glaring in Will's direction.

Lauren didn't answer. She simply stood frozen in the doorway of the fitting room, wearing this beautiful wedding gown. This was supposed to be a fun experience with her friends, and all she wanted to do was rip the gown off her body. When her friends convinced her to go try on wedding dresses for fun, she knew in the pit of her stomach, that it was a bad idea. She never in a million years could have guessed that this would be the outcome. Will was the last person she imagined running into there, especially accompanied by Mary.

Lauren stood frozen until they walked out the door, watching them through the front windows, hand in hand, as they rushed to their car. The blowing snow was making it harder to see them as they ran further away, and Lauren's feet felt like they were stuck in mud. All she could do was stand there in disbelief.

Will opened the door for Mary, placing the dresses across the back seat. He jumped in quickly and sat in silence, starting the car as he stared out the windshield, his focus far beyond anything right in front of them. Mary wasn't sure what to say to him, trying to imagine how he felt seeing her.

She pulled out her phone and checked for more weather updates from her mother. "I guess my mom was right. The storm definitely shifted." She looked over to him, waiting for him to snap out of his thoughts. She wasn't sure she wanted to say Lauren's name out loud. The weather was a safe enough statement for now.

"Oh, yeah, you're right," he said, shaking his head and turned on the windshield wipers. The snow moved back and forth with each swipe of the blades, almost mesmerizing them both as they sat staring at the blades waiting for the car to warm up a bit.

"Do you want me to hop out and scrape the windows?" Mary volunteered. "I'm happy to do it if you have a scraper in the trunk." She waited for him to answer.

He took in a deep breath, letting it out slowly, finally saying, "No, no. You don't have to do that, you'll blow away out there. Just wait here — I'll take care of it." He popped the trunk and climbed back outside, brushing the piles of snow that drifted onto the car while they were inside.

Mary turned up the heat in the car, hoping to melt the fresh snow that was continuing to fall back on windshield. He climbed back inside, shaking the snow off his head, and placed the car in drive.

"If the parking lot is any indication of the road conditions," he said with a worried tone, "the drive back to your house should be interesting." He turned the defrosters up a notch since their breath was fogging up the side windows quickly.

"I don't need to be home for anything," Mary added, "so if you want to go to your house instead until it passes, that's fine with me." Mary knew his house was a lot closer to where they were, but wasn't sure if he was interested in her company right now.

He pulled up to the stop sign and waited for the cross traffic to stop. Agreeing with her idea, he turned on his left signal and started for his house.

The drive to Will's house was silent and tense; partly from the weather, partly from the experience of running into Lauren at the bridal shop and having that awkward conversation. Mary's body began to ache from sitting so stiff, and her hand hurt from gripping the door handle so tightly.

For most of the drive, she helped him navigate the road, and in some places, help him determine where the road actually was. Linda called Mary several times on their drive, but Mary chose not to answer, not wanting to take her focus off the road.

When Will turned off the main road, the visibility seemed to get better as the tall pines that lined the road blocked most of the wind. Near the end of the road, a beautiful log home appeared, a long porch stretching across the entire front. A large stone chimney climbed up the side, a steady trail of smoke coming out of the top.

Leaving the dresses in the car, Mary reached to the back to grab his tuxedo as he helped her open her door. They ran up the front steps to his home, and he quickly unlocked the door, allowing her inside first. The warm air was inviting as she pulled her hood down, brushing the snow off her shoulders.

"Your place is beautiful, Will. How long have you lived here?" She slipped her boots off and placed them to the side.

"I bought it a few years ago," he said, "and I work on it in my spare time. It needed a lot of TLC when I purchased it, but I have it just about the way I want it." He took her jacket and hung it in the front closet, the bi-fold doors squeaking as he closed it.

"I don't know what it looked like before," she said, impressed with how beautiful it was, "but it looks amazing now." She walked into the living room, looking each wall up and down. The log shape carried to the inside, giving it so much character. A loft up above overlooked the living room.

Will lit the logs in the fireplace. "Have a seat while I

get the fire going," he offered, motioning to the couch. "I'll give you the grand tour when I have this thing roaring." He pulled a few extra logs from the brass basket next to the mantel.

"Are you sure you want to light a fire?" she asked. "I'm not sure we should stay very long, since the roads are just going to get worse." She sat in an over-sized chair next to him.

He looked out the window. "I think we may be here for a while." He pulled the curtain back further, showing Mary how much snow had already fallen on the car since they came inside. She glanced outside to see that their footprints were almost completely covered.

"The car is practically buried," Mary said with concern. "I think the weatherman needs to find a new job because he was terribly wrong. This looks to be a little more than a dusting." She stood there for a moment, watching the flakes accumulate.

"Technically, he was right about the fact that a huge storm was coming," Will explained, "but maybe he needs a little more training in map reading." He smiled for the first time since leaving the bridal shop as he walked into the kitchen. He opened the refrigerator, only able to offer her milk, water, or orange juice. He closed the door and walked around the room. "Are you up for a glass of wine? I think it should be safe since we obviously aren't driving anywhere any time soon."

"I'd love a glass," she replied. "Do you mind if I use this blanket to cover up with? My legs are still a little cold." Leggings were cute, paired with furry boots, but once you take the boots off, they weren't a very wise choice for winter.

"Of course. Make yourself at home." He poured two glasses and joined her in the living room.

She reached for the glass and took a sip, resting it on her knee. "If I had a house like this, I would do this every night," Mary said, feeling the coziness and warmth. "I'd definitely curl up with a blanket by the fire and watch the snow fall, but I'd probably replace the wine with hot chocolate every few nights."

Will laughed. "I love it here. My family thought I was crazy for buying a house out in the middle of nowhere, but I love the quiet. Other than the frogs and crickets on hot summer nights, it's pretty serene for the most part."

"I miss the slower pace of living here sometimes," Mary admitted. "I thought it would be torture coming back here, but the longer I'm here, the more I really miss living here." She took another sip of wine. "Being home reminds me of how impersonal the city can be. Everyone is in such a hurry, that no one ever stops to say hello."

"I can see that," he agreed. "On the other hand, the part about everyone knowing you around here can be tough, too. When something happens to you, good or bad, everyone knows almost immediately. Gossip flies around this town like wild fire."

She was sure there was more to that statement, assuming it had something to do with Lauren.

The snow continued to fall for hours, and it seemed to be accumulating faster than before. Linda had called Mary again with more weather updates, checking in to be sure she and Will weren't out on the road. Mary assured her mother with every call that they would stay put until the storm passed. Trying to get her mother to relax a little with the updates, Mary told her that her phone battery was getting low and that she needed to save it in case she needed to call for help. It probably wasn't the best scenario she could have used, but it worked.

"Is that large building near the back of the property yours, too?" Mary asked. "I thought I saw it when we pulled in." She shifted in her chair, removing the blanket from her lap. Between the warmth of the fire and a couple glasses of wine, she was plenty warm.

"Yes, it is mine. That's the workshop I built last year. I can show you if you'd like." His eyes lit up.

She turned to look out the window. "I'd love to, but if you haven't noticed, it's kind of a blizzard out there. I'm afraid I left my sled dogs at home." She laughed as he jumped off the couch and disappeared down the hall. "What are you doing?" Mary asked, wondering what he was up to.

Moments later, he returned. "Care to give these a try?" he asked, holding out two pair of snowshoes. "I bought these last winter, but never got a chance to try them out. No time like the present." He stared at her, raising his eyebrows up and down.

She set her empty wine glass on the coffee table. "Why not?" She grabbed a pair from him and carried them to the front door. Since she wasn't really dressed for the adventure, Will offered her a pair of extra snow pants and boots from his closet. She pulled the pants on, tripping over them as she stood up. They were about a foot too long for her, but the boots helped keep them up. He gave her two extra pair of socks to help fill the gaps of the oversized boots.

He grabbed her jacket from the closet and pulled a hat down over her eyes. With a hearty laugh, he said, "You look like you can survive out in the cold for a week in all of those layers. Do you need mittens, too?" He dug in a basket on the top shelf of the closet.

"That's actually something I *do* have," she chuckled. She pulled them out of her jacket pockets and waddled to the front door to wait for Will. "I probably should have put the snowshoes on before bundling up so much."

Will got a good chuckle out of watching her walk out onto the front porch. Helping her out, he bent down and strapped the snowshoes on for her. The snow was still coming down steadily, but the wind seemed to dissipate. Both of them were completely covered in white by the time they were ten feet from the house. Nearly tripping several times, catching the toe of her snowshoes in the piles of snow, she used the trees along the way to help stabilize herself. If nothing else, it kept the mood light between the two of them.

After what seemed like a ten-mile hike, they arrived at the side door of his shop. "I sure hope that door isn't locked," quipped Mary, "because I'm not trekking all the way back to get the key." She watched him as he grabbed the handle, pretending it was locked, and she slugged him, yet again.

"You know, you could at least trade arms every few times if you're going to keep hitting me," he said. "At this rate, I'm sure to have a big old bruise by the end of the night." He rubbed his arm, hoping for a little sympathy, but received none. He unclipped his snowshoes and used his boot to clear the snow away from the door. The air wasn't much warmer in the shop, but it was shelter from the wind, nonetheless.

He flipped on the lights as the fluorescent bulbs came to life, a dim glow filling the room. He walked to the other corner of the shop and plugged in a large space heater, cranking it up to high in hopes of at least taking the chill out of the air while they were back there.

"This place is amazing, Will," Mary said in amazement. "Did you make all of this stuff?" Mary walked around the shop, admiring the beautiful wooden furniture spread throughout the room.

"Yes, ma'am," he answered proudly. "It's been a hobby of mine since I was a little boy. My parents bought me a toolbox for my fifth birthday, and I've been building things ever since." He stood by her, watching her inspect each piece, nervous of her reaction having only shown his work to a few people.

"I'd say this is a little more than a hobby." Mary was very impressed with what she saw. "The details on this chair are fantastic — so intricate." She ran her hand along the peaked edge of the rocking chair, the bottom of the legs curved at a perfect angle. "May I?" she said, motioning to the chair.

"Be my guest — it should hold you," he snickered.

She sat down gently and rocked back and forth, closing her eyes, imagining herself rocking in it next to the fireplace in his living room. She could picture it perfectly, very similar to the vision she'd had many times over. The vision of her curled up by the fire with the one she loves. But now, that person finally had a face. What had always appeared to be a blur, was now clear as day. It was Will. A chill ran over her body as she looked over at him, as he was unaware what thoughts were rolling through her mind at this very moment. She smiled.

"You're lucky there's two feet of snow outside," Mary laughed, "or I would pick this chair up and start running for the hills." She ran her fingertips along the armrests, admiring the smooth finish.

"Good thing," he laughed. "I'm glad you like it. It took me many years to get good at building furniture. The first thing I ever built was a house." He smiled at the surprised look on her face.

"You built a house?" she said, surprised. "How old were you?"

He closed his eyes, trying to think, adding to the suspense. "I think I was five." He opened his eyes to see her reaction. "Okay, so it was a doll house, but still technically a house. I made it for my sister." He stood back, hoping to avoid another arm hit. "It was an uneven two-story that was far from passing any city codes. It was full of windows and fully open on one side. My sister's dolls thought it was great, though." He leaned back against his workbench, still proud of that project.

"That's amazing!" Mary said as her smile brightened even more. "I bet she loved it." She stood from the chair and continued walking around to see the rest of his pieces.

"She still has it," Will said proudly. "I was over at her house a few weeks ago, and she showed it to me. She told me she was saving it for her kids to play with."

Mary could see how much it meant to him that she kept it. "That's so sweet, Will," Mary said, thinking what a sweet man he was. "It could become the next Roberts family heirloom." Walking around, she found a dresser, a small desk with drawers, and a few small tables. "Have you ever thought about selling your work? You could make a lot of money on these pieces. I'm considering making you an offer on that rocking chair."

"I have, actually," Will admitted. "I went to a trade show at the hotel last week and got some information from some of the buyers. One of the companies already sent me a letter a few days ago showing possible interest in my stuff."

"Will, that's fantastic!" Mary cheered. "Are you going to look into it?" She retreated back to the rocking chair.

"I'm not sure, yet," he said with some doubt. "I have to

find out how much equity they want, what the percentages will be. There are so many moving parts which makes it a little overwhelming. Before all of that, I have to show them my best work. I'm not sure if they'll want to buy inventory or not."

She nodded. "You know, you could always open your own shop, too. There are a few vacant buildings in town near my parents' shop. One just went up for rent a few days ago with great front windows that would showcase your furniture perfectly. It's just a few doors down from Cora's bakery." She sat on the edge of the chair, getting excited, her voice climbing a few levels.

Will tried to picture which building it was. "What was in there before?" he asked, mentally picturing his delivery route.

"I think it was Steven's Shoe Repair, about three stores down from the bakery." She pointed her finger in the air, trying to count the doors from her memory. "I heard he wants to move his business into his basement to save on the rent fees. You should at least check into it. You already have some great pieces here to stock your shop and get you started." She could see his wheels start to turn.

"I suppose that could be an option if the other company doesn't work out." He shrugged. "I wasn't sure my furniture was good enough to sell to the public." He walked over to the desk and opened the top drawer, pulling out a stack of papers and handed them over to her. "I made these plans a few years ago, dreaming that one day I could sell my stuff. I hadn't really thought about actually making it happen."

She read through the papers, checking out his business plan, his sketches of future designs, and a list of names for his shop. His plans were very detailed, down to the placement of the furniture arranged on the showroom floor.

"These are wonderful ideas, Will," Mary said proudly. "Between these plans and the other company interested in you, you should be set. You'll have to look into which route is best for you, but you need to make this happen. These pieces are too beautiful to hide inside the shop behind your house."

He hesitated for a bit. "You've definitely opened my eyes to rethinking the possibility. I pushed the idea of pursuing it as a career or business about a year ago and haven't given it much thought since." All of a sudden, he started pacing the room, feeling overwhelmed about the subject. "We should probably get back to the house before the snow blocks the door again."

He unplugged the heater and strapped their snowshoes back on. The snow was still falling on their walk back, the light of the moon lighting their way. Just as they closed the front door, headlights filled the driveway as a car pulled in behind Will's.

Chapter Fifteen

Will thought to himself, *Who would be out driving in this weather?* The driveway was dark, and it was hard to make out the vehicle outside. It wasn't one that looked familiar to him, perhaps they were lost or at the wrong house.

"Did someone just pull into the driveway?" Mary asked, slipping off her boots and snow pants.

"Yes," Will answered, "but I have no idea who would be crazy enough to drive in this storm." Just as the words finished coming out of his mouth, he recognized the person climbing out of the driver's side door. There was indeed a person crazy enough to drive in a blizzard. It was Lauren.

She climbed the front steps, her boots completely beneath the deep piles of snow. She stomped her feet on the front rug, standing there trying to get the nerve to knock on the door. As her hand went up, the door flung open.

"What are you doing here?" Will demanded, not at all happy to see her. If anything, seeing her again after just having run into her at the bridal shop, it angered him even more.

She was caught off guard by the way he answered. "I think we need to talk," she said, her voice cracking. "I think you might have gotten the wrong idea from earlier."

He stood there glaring at her, really letting her know that he was not in the mood. "I don't think there is anything to talk about," he answered abruptly. "And besides, I have company right now, and I don't want to be rude keeping her waiting."

Her? Lauren thought. "Oh. I just want to come in for a minute and explain what you saw earlier. It's not what it looked like."

His expression didn't change. He held his glare, his eyes narrowing as he blurted out his answer, "No."

Lauren flinched at his aggression, something she'd never seen before. "What were *you* doing there, anyway? Are you getting married?" She held her breath, expecting his answer to knock her flat.

The thought of her thinking that brought him a little more pleasure than it should have, but he wanted her to feel what he's been feeling over the past year. "I don't think that is any of your business, really. You lost the privilege of knowing my personal life when you walked out on me a year ago." His words were harsh, but he wasn't going to back down. "You wasted your time coming out here. Have you seen the weather?"

She stood there still trying to process what he was telling her. "I just thought —," her voice trailed off, catching in her throat the moment she saw who his company was.

Mary tiptoed over to the chair she'd been sitting in earlier, hoping Lauren didn't see her, but she failed.

"Are you with *her* now?" Lauren's face turned from desperation to anger at the drop of a hat. "I knew you always had a thing for her, even when we were together. Maybe I shouldn't have come out here. Clearly it was a waste of time."

Will nodded in agreement.

"I didn't think she even lived in Maple Falls anymore?" she shouted, increasing the volume of her voice so Mary could hear.

"Again, that's none of your business," he said angrily. He grabbed the edge of the door. "I think we're done here." And with that, he slammed the door.

Lauren stood there in shock, never seeing this side of him before. He'd never been so cold to her when they were together. "Fine!" she shouted at the closed door.

He watched from behind the curtain as she stumbled back to her car, his blood still boiling at the sight of her.

"Are you sure you don't want to ask her in?" Mary said with concern. "She probably shouldn't be driving out there in this storm." Mary joined his glare out the window.

"She got herself into this mess, she can find her way out." He pulled the curtains closed and stepped away from the window. "I'm sorry you had to see that, but she makes me so angry. She thinks she can just barge back into my life whenever she wants and start demanding I talk to her. I'm sorry, but I'm not letting her control me anymore."

Will turned on the TV to see if they could catch the next segment of weather on the local news. The weatherman showed the map, and the storm appeared to be moving slower, anticipating it wouldn't move out until early tomorrow morning. After one more phone call from her mother, Mary made the decision to stay the night. At this point, she didn't really have a choice, unless she wanted to flag down Lauren and risk riding with her. Obviously, that would not have been an option.

The question loomed heavy in the air. She wasn't sure it was best to ask, but if there was any chance of recovering the rest of their night, she needed to get the subject out of the way.

Mary cleared her throat and asked, "Why did she come here?"

Will threw his arms up in the air. "I have no idea. She said she wanted to explain what I saw earlier, but hearing about her and her boyfriend is about as low on my list as it gets." He began pacing the room. "All she ever wanted was a husband, so I guess she is getting what she wanted."

"I don't think it was about that, Will," Mary said, trying to calm him down. "Maybe she just panicked after seeing us there together." Mary tucked her feet up in the chair.

"Good," he said, not missing a beat. Will knew he was cold toward her and that wasn't how he normally was. "I'm just so tired of her controlling my emotions for so long. I'm done with it. If there was anything good that came from today, it made me realize that I'm finally ready to move on. I'm done thinking of her and wondering *what if*."

Mary watched him as he slowed his pace. "I suppose after all that, moving on is a good thing, don't you think?"

He stopped in his tracks and looked at her. "I think it can be, especially when it's moving on with the right person."

She knew what he was getting at and was suddenly very aware of them being alone. No matter how hard she tried to block it out though, Alex kept coming into her mind. Though she no longer cared about what he was doing or who he was with, she couldn't help but feel a pang of guilt deep in her stomach.

Will looked at her, wondering what she was thinking. It took all he had not to blurt out every feeling he'd been keeping inside. He resisted the urge to tell Mary that he wanted her to be with him, to move back to Maple Falls and be together. He wanted to tell her so badly that he still regrets not letting her know his true feelings years ago before she started dating Alex. But what would that change now? She *was* with Alex, and she didn't live here. What would even come of telling her how he felt? He didn't even know if the feelings would be reciprocated.

"Would you like another glass of wine?" he asked as he walked to the kitchen to grab the rest of the bottle.

Mary reached for the same blanket she covered up with earlier. "Would it be too much trouble to make a pot of coffee? I'm starting to get a little sleepy, and I think it would warm me up wonderfully after our cold, brisk walk to your shop." She wasn't quite sure how the night would go with her having to stay. She was hoping he would snap out of his funk caused by Lauren's sudden appearance and enjoy her company once again. Unsure of how he felt about her staying over, caffeine seemed to be a quick solution to that answer, at least for the next few hours.

"No problem at all," he said. "Do you take anything in your coffee? I have a few different flavored creamers and sugar I can bring out." He placed a bowl of creamers and sugar on a tray and carried it out to the coffee table.

Mary leaned forward, sifting through the small glass bowl, deciding on hazelnut. "These little containers are so cute," she said, "just like the kind you'd find at a restaurant." She pulled back the tab and poured it into her mug.

"That's because they are," Will said with a chuckle. "Someone I used to know worked in a restaurant and brought me a huge bag of them after I complained about not being able to find them in the store." He dug through, choosing an Irish cream. He scooped a spoonful of sugar in his mug and returned the spoon to the tray.

"A variety pack would be amazing," Mary said in agreement. "I hate buying creamer at the store. By the time

I get through the box, I'm so sick of having the same flavor every day." She wrapped her hands around her mug and sat back, breathing in the aroma. "I love the smell of hazelnut. It reminds me of the last fall I lived here and working at my parents' shop. I used to make myself one every day."

Maybe we can invent that someday. Variety pack mini creamers. Your parents could stock it for us as our first retail space." He took a small sip and rested the mug on his knee.

"That sounds like a well thought-out business plan," Mary added. "I never had many options for cream or sugar unless I was at the shop. My mom always yells at me when I put anything in my coffee. She insisted that if your coffee was good quality, as theirs was, there was no need for cream or sugar." Mary laughed, rolling her eyes.

Will placed his coffee mug on the table and walked over to the fire to stoke it up a bit, since it began to go out. He reached under the wood holder and grabbed a few pieces of newspaper, wrinkling them up and placing them between the hot logs, hoping to ignite it again. He grabbed the poker and shifted the logs as the flames began to grow.

Mary sat in the chair and watched him, wondering if he was going to bring up Lauren, or if she would have to do it. Something about that woman put a bad taste in Mary's mouth. She really didn't have a leg to stand on since she was having her own issues with Alex, but she felt the urge to help Will through this. She wanted to help him move on from Lauren and to be happy again. She wasn't sure if she would ever be a part of his happiness, but it was definitely weighing on her mind — and her heart.

"So —," she started, "I ran into Lauren last week when Grace and I went out to dinner. She didn't say much, but I'm pretty sure she wasn't happy to see that I was back in town. I would imagine there is more to your story than what you've told me." She paused to see if she was hitting a nerve, but his expression was blank. "How did it come to what it is now? I thought you two were so happy, at least it appeared that way when I saw you last before my move."

Will sat back on the couch and took a sip of his coffee before saying anything, unsure of where to begin. "We were happy, for a long time," he shared, "but it seemed like almost overnight she decided she wasn't interested in our relationship anymore." He stared into the fire, watching the flames dance inside.

"When did all of this happen?" Mary asked, adjusting her blanket and tucking her arms inside.

"About a year ago; right before Christmas actually," Will said as he began to unload the story. "I was hoping to announce our engagement to our families on Christmas day." He cleared his throat, trying to swallow the lump that was forming. "I had the whole night planned out for her. I made reservations at a vineyard with a beautiful view that overlooked the lake. I even stashed the ring back in my shop, figuring it would be safe and she'd never run across it there. She never liked going back there, and I think she never really cared for my woodworking. To her, it was a child's hobby, not one of a grown man." He looked down at the floor.

The hair stood up on Mary's arms at his statement. "How could someone say or think that about your work? You are very talented."

He half smiled, not sure whether to believe her or not. "Do you need more coffee?" he added, hoping for a break in the conversation. He walked into the kitchen to grab the coffee pot and warmed up their mugs.

The fire was roaring now, the logs crackling, sending embers up the chimney. She looked over to him, the flames reflecting in his eyes. Taking a deep breath, he continued.

"I picked her up from work early that night, a few hours before sunset, so we would be able to watch it set over the lake during dinner. I knew there was something wrong when I picked her up, though. She was very standoffish and not talking much. I chalked it up as a bad day at work."

Mary couldn't believe the day he planned for her, putting so much thought into every little detail. She could tell that even after a whole year had passed, he still had a hard time talking about it. Part of her felt bad for bringing it up again, but she hoped it was doing him good talking about it.

"If you don't want to talk about it anymore," Mary said reassuringly, "I completely understand." She tried to guess what he was thinking, but he was a tough read.

He shook his head. "No, its fine. I just haven't really told many people about it. I just assumed that the few I told would get it in the mouths of someone who would spread it all over town for me. Once the town started getting wind of our split, I didn't feel it necessary to talk about it anymore. I got the occasional whispers for a while from passersby as I walked past them, but no one ever asked me questions." He stood again. "Are you hungry? I don't have much, but I'm good at getting creative in the kitchen."

"Sure, I could go for a snack. Can I help you?" Mary tossed the blanket on the arm of the chair and followed him into the kitchen.

"I'm never one to turn down help in the kitchen," he chuckled. "I'm a decent cook, but I'm always open for suggestions."

Mary admired the dark cabinets and granite counter tops, assuming they were both part of the renovation work that he had done. Will opened up a few of the cupboards and placed some boxes on the center island, lining them up in ascending order. His phone began to ring in the living room, but he ignored it, focusing on the task at hand.

"Are you sure you don't want to get that?" she asked.

"Nope. Everyone I want to talk to right now is in my kitchen." He smiled and opened the refrigerator.

Mary shrugged it off. "What do we have to work with?" she asked, checking out the counter. "I'm pretty good, too, at putting random things from the fridge together and making a meal. Alex is hardly ever home for a meal, so cooking for one is my specialty. And by cooking, I mean making a snack dinner of ten different things."

He laughed. "That's my favorite kind of dinner."

After about twenty minutes and a pile of dishes later, they had one of the best snack dinners ever created — a bowl of spaghetti noodles with butter and pepper, crackers and sliced cheese, and three varieties of cookies.

"Not too bad. We make a great team in the kitchen, if I do say so myself," Mary said, carrying two plates into the living room. She placed them on the coffee table and walked to the mantel to admire the photos lined up on top.

"Definitely not my first choice for our first meal together at my house," Will said, "but it will have to do." He placed two bowls of noodles next to the plates.

Mary raised her eyebrows. "So, you're saying you're hoping for a second meal?" She made him blush, something that was not easy to do. "Tell me who all of these people are up here."

He joined her by the fire as he pointed out the people. "That is a photo of my grandparents, taken at their sixtieth wedding anniversary." He pointed to the next and went right down the line. "These are my parents, that is my sister and her husband with their kids, and that's —," he paused, walking away from the mantel. "That one is me and Lauren. I'm not even sure why that's still up there." He turned back to the mantel and took the photo in his hand and walked to the desk in the hallway, placing it in one of the drawers, slamming it closed.

"Please don't feel like you have to put that away

because I'm here," she added, feeling bad that he had to revisit that feeling again. She watched as he mulled it over.

"No," he admitted, "I've been meaning to take that down for a while now. I just keep forgetting. She's moved on, so it's about time I do the same."

He sat back down on the couch and picked up his bowl of noodles. She joined him, back in her chair as they ate in silence for a while. The sound of his phone ringing broke the silence as he glanced at the screen.

"Maybe you should answer that," Mary said with concern. "I think someone is really trying to reach you."

He shook his head in disagreement. "It's no one important; they can just leave a message." He continued eating, letting the call go. She wasn't sure who it was, but she had her suspicions.

"Do you think she's really getting married?" Mary asked. She tried to think of another subject to talk about, but for some reason she couldn't move on from talking about Lauren and his relationship with her.

"Maybe — she does have a boyfriend, or at least she did," Will added seemingly uninterested. "I'm not really sure if they are still together, but it seems like they are. She said she met him one night when he came in to eat at her work, and they really hit it off — her words, not mine."

Mary huffed. "I can't believe she'd give up on such a great man like you for a man she just met. If I had someone like you in my life, I'd hang on to them with everything I had." She paused, realizing what she just said.

He half smiled. "Well, you don't ever have to worry

about that, because you have Alex. Do you think he'll propose soon? New year, new engagement perhaps?" He scraped up the last few noodles out of his bowl and placed it back on the table.

Mary was hoping Alex wouldn't be a topic of conversation tonight. It wasn't something she had planned to bring up, but since he did and had been so open with her, she felt it was only right to be honest with him. She took a drink and sighed, trying to decide where to begin.

Chapter Sixteen

Will carried the empty dishes back to the kitchen and placed them in the sink. He could feel himself finally relaxing, letting the tension release from his shoulders. He'd been so good about avoiding Lauren over the past year, but now it seemed as though she was wiggling her way back into his life. Six months ago, he may have allowed her to do just that, but after the past week, he realized there was so much more out there for him rather than reliving his past again.

There was an amazing woman sitting right there in his living room, one he hoped to crack and find out where she stood with Alex. He would never want to stand between two people who were meant to be together, but if there was any chance at all for the two of them, he needed to find out before it was too late.

"I know it wasn't a fancy meal," Will said as he came back to the living room, "but I hope it at least filled you up. Do you want me to make some more coffee?"

Mary shook her head. "No, thank you. I think I've had enough coffee to stay awake for a week." She took a deep breath, finally ready to talk about her relationship. "I thought Alex and I would have been engaged by now. It was kind of his promise to me when I agreed to move away with him, but now, two years later, I'm not so sure that it'll ever happen. To be honest, I'm not even sure that's what I want anymore."

Will was taken aback, not expecting her to say that.

"His job seems to be his only priority right now," Mary continued to pour out the story, "and I'm afraid I don't see that changing any time soon." She turned and watched the flames fade again.

"I thought I heard somewhere that he's working on a new development or something?" Will said, trying not to be too nosey. He was trying to remember the gossip he'd heard, but the rumors around Maple Falls were about as accurate as playing the game of telephone when they were younger.

"Yes," Mary added, "he's signing a contract on a new condo development, and they'll be breaking ground sometime after the first of the year. He'll be heading up the project, so I anticipate him to be even more scarce. I knew his job is what brought us there, but there has to be a balance somewhere." She wasn't sure what it was about

Will, but she felt like she could lay all of her cards out on the table without any judgment from him. She wasn't worried about hearing *I told you so* come out of his mouth like she was with the rest of her family. He felt safe to her.

"Is there anyone else in his company that he can delegate different parts to so he can be home more?" he asked, a confused look on his face.

Mary shrugged, and added, "I don't know all of the details yet, as most of this has unfolded while I've been here. Maybe if he returned my calls, I would know more. Or perhaps I could ask his new assistant *Trish*," she said sarcastically under her breath, but loud enough for Will to hear her.

"Not a fan of her, I take it?" Will said, totally understanding considering his own past situation with Lauren.

She sat up straight in her chair. "I mean, who goes to work on Christmas day to help her boss? Who cares if she just moved to town and doesn't know anybody? I was in that same position, and I'm doing just fine. She shouldn't have been there with him, plain and simple. He shouldn't have been there either, for that matter." She was now in a fit of rage and tried to dial it back a little, fearful of scaring Will.

Luckily, they were saved again by his phone. He grabbed it off the end table. Lauren again. He let it go to voicemail. After three calls, you would think she would get the clue that he was not interested in hearing what she had to say. He looked up at Mary, wondering if she'd noticed.

"Wrong number?" she asked. "You can answer it if you want; I'm just sitting here whining in your ear anyway. I'm sure whoever was calling had far more interesting things to say than I do." She was hoping he would tell her who called, her curiosity getting the best of her.

"I really don't think that would be the case," Will replied, trying not to let on who it was that called. "It wasn't anyone I wanted to talk to, besides, you were on a roll." He loved to tease her. "Can I get you some water?" He seemed to have a hard time sitting still and relaxing, like he had the constant urge to wait on her hand and foot while she was there.

"Can I ask you where the bathroom is?" Mary said, needing a quick break.

He pointed down the hall as he went to the kitchen to get her a glass of water. The hallway was filled with more photos hanging on the wall. Most were of his family from over the years. Mary stopped to admire how cute he looked as a little boy. A couple pictures of he and Lauren still hung there. After hearing how it all ended between them, she wasn't surprised to see them all still there. It wasn't *his* decision, and he wasn't ready for the relationship to be over. Mary found the bathroom at the end of the hall, doing a quick teeth and hair check to be sure she didn't have any pieces of pepper or noodles stuck between her teeth and that her hair looked okay.

Back in the living room, she found him staring out the

front window.

"I set your glass of water on the end table by the chair," he said, still looking outside.

"Everything alright?" Mary asked with concern.

He sighed. "It's fine. The calls earlier were from Lauren. I thought after sending her to voicemail over and over, she would get the hint I was upset, but I guess not." He wasn't sure why he felt the need to tell her who called, but Mary wasn't someone he wanted to hide things from.

Mary felt that by her being there, it had only made things worse for him. Maybe if she'd just had him take her home, Lauren wouldn't have been so angry at him. "I'm sorry, I feel like this is all my fault," Mary said apologetically. "I shouldn't have let her see me — or maybe I shouldn't have been here at all." Her voice trailed off.

He turned to look at her, holding her glance. "I wanted you here with me tonight. Don't worry about her, she'll get over it." He moved closer to her, his heart beat increasing.

She, too, began to move in closer to him, and just then his phone began to ring again. She closed her eyes and dropped her head.

"Maybe you should just answer it," Mary said somewhat frustrated, "or she may never stop calling." As much as she didn't want him to talk with Lauren, she wanted more for the interruptions to end.

He marched over to the coffee table and grabbed his phone. "Hello?" he shouted.

"Is this William Roberts?" the woman on the other end

asked.

He pulled the phone away from his ear to check the number and answered, "Yes, this is. Who is this?"

There was a short pause on the other end, chatter in the background. "This is the Maple Falls Hospital calling. Lauren Ridgeway was brought in a few minutes ago after being involved in a car accident." He could hear papers being shuffled around and wondered how it is that they used her cell phone. "You are listed as her emergency contact on her cell phone. I know the roads aren't great right now, but if you could try to make it in as soon as possible, I think that would be a good idea."

He had a sudden sinking feeling in the pit of his stomach as he asked, "Is she okay?" He waited for the nurse to answer as the world around him seemed to have stopped. "Hello?"

"She is still being checked out by one of our doctors, so I don't have that information for you at this time." He could hear her fingers moving quickly on the computer keyboard, the sound almost pounding in his ear.

"I'll be there as soon as I can," Will said. He hung up the phone and sat slowly on the couch, holding the coffee table unsure whether or not his legs were going to give out.

"Is everything alright? Who was on the phone?" Mary sat next to him on the couch, placing a hand on his knee.

He rubbed his temples, as he responded, "That was the hospital. Lauren was in a car accident."

"Is she okay?" Mary asked, her heart pounding now,

too. She wanted to ask why they called him instead of her family, but it was not the time.

"I don't know. The nurse didn't seem to know much, but asked me to come in right away."

Mary stood from the couch. "I'll go with you — what do we need to do?"

He stood up, but he was still in a fog, unsure of what to do next. Mary knew he wasn't thinking clearly and took over. She walked around the house turning off all the lights, leaving a lamp on in the living room in case they were back later on. She pulled their jackets, hats, and mittens out of the closet and handed his over.

"Do you want me to drive, or are you okay to?" She waited for him to snap out of it.

"No, I'm fine," he said. "We'll take my truck because it'll do better out on the roads." He reached for his keys on the key rack, and they rushed out the door.

The drive to the hospital was completely silent. Mary learned her lesson on breaking silence, choosing not to do so this time. Some of the major roads had been plowed, but all of the side streets were covered in several inches of snow. The snow was so deep in several areas, that Will had to use the four-wheel drive to get through the deep drifts, only getting stuck once or twice.

The hospital was fairly quiet at this hour, not many people out and about due to the snow. Mary thought to herself, if Lauren would have had the sense to go home rather than make the stop at Will's, this whole thing would not be occurring. They walked to the front desk where a woman sat, her glasses slid down to the tip of her nose.

"May I help you?" she asked, looking back and forth at them both.

Will couldn't find the words right away as they caught in his throat. Mary knew it was a good idea to come with him, even if he may not have thought it was.

"He was called about a patient that was brought in from a car accident — Lauren Ridgeway," Mary explained as Will stood there with a blank stare.

The woman pushed her glasses back up her nose and read the chart she had on the desk in front of her. "Are you both family?"

Mary looked to Will, but he said nothing. "No, he is listed as Lauren's emergency contact — William Roberts." She peered over the desk to see if she could see anything on the nurse's chart.

The nurse set the chart down and clicked on her computer. "I'm afraid her chart hasn't been updated just yet. Please have a seat in the waiting area, and I'll let you know when you can go back and see her." She motioned them to the empty chairs on the other side of the room.

Mary placed her hand on Will's back and led him over to a chair. The waiting area smelled of hand sanitizer and band-aids. Neither of them were a bad smell on their own, but the two together made her stomach turn. A doctor was being paged over the intercom as he finally sat down, the crackling sound overhead snapping him back to reality.

"Why are we just waiting here?" Will said, obviously frustrated, but concerned. "Shouldn't we go back and see how she's doing?" He looked confused, looking to Mary for the answers.

She shook her head. "Didn't you hear what the nurse just said? She's checking on her chart and will let us know when we can go back." She looked back over to the desk, but the nurse had disappeared. "Maybe it's not a good idea that I go back with you. I'm sure I'm the last person she wants to see."

Will bit his lip, clutching to the sleeve of her jacket. "I can't go back there by myself. I'm not good with situations like these."

The nurse walked through the door accompanied by what looked to be a doctor. He was dressed in all white with baby blue covers on his shoes. Will swallowed hard as they got closer, dreading what may come out of their mouths.

"Are you William Roberts?" the doctor asked.

Will shot a look to Mary, blinking hard before answering him. "Ye — yes, I'm William."

"Please come with me so we can sit down and talk about Lauren's condition."

Will's body stiffened, suddenly losing the ability to use his appendages. Mary grabbed his hand and squeezed it gently.

"Would it be alright if I came, too?" Mary asked.

The doctor turned back and nodded. Once she got him

upright, they followed the doctor to a small room just inside a large set of double doors. The smell of band-aids intensified on the other side, causing Mary to clear her throat. The walls were bare and painted bright white. A fluorescent light dangled above, similar to one you would find in an interrogation room. Was that what was about to happen? Was the accident somehow their fault? The doctor closed the door behind him and sat down, flipping through Lauren's chart he brought in with him.

"What is your relation to the patient?" he asked them.

Knowing how he was moments earlier in the waiting room, Mary spoke for the both of them. "I'm a friend, and he is her emergency contact. They used to date."

She wasn't sure she should have said that, but she assumed it may have been important information somehow.

"I see," he said, his face lacking expression. "It seems as though your friend was driving in the storm tonight and went off the road, hitting a tree just outside of town. A resident living nearby saw headlights in the snow and found her in the car."

Will's heart sank, an overwhelming feeling of guilt washing over him. He stared at the doctor, not wanting to miss a word he said.

"I examined her and ran a few tests, and at this point, we know she has a concussion as a result of head trauma from the accident and some minor bumps and bruises. She's very lucky someone found her, or it could have been a lot worse, considering the weather conditions out there."

Will sat back in his chair, wiping his hands across his eyes, down his face. Mary placed her hand on his shoulder, relieved at the news.

"When can we see her?" Will asked anxiously.

The doctor closed his file. "Very soon, Mr. Roberts. She was just regaining consciousness before you got here. We'll be keeping her at least for the night for observation. They are getting her settled into a room for the night, and after that, a nurse will take you back."

"Thank you, doctor," Will said, standing up to shake his hand.

"My pleasure. A nurse will come and get you shortly."

Chapter
Seventeen

The beeping sound of steady beats from the heart monitors in patients' rooms rang out through the cracked open doors as Will and Mary were lead down a long white hallway to Lauren's room. They followed in step behind a nurse carrying a stack of charts tucked in her arm. Halfway down the hall, she stopped, motioning them to Lauren's room.

"She was awake when I was in there a few minutes ago, but don't be surprised if she dozes off here and there," the nurse instructed. "Take your time, and I'll be back in a bit to check her vitals again." She walked toward the desk at the end of the hall, leaving the two of them standing outside her door.

Mary cleared her throat. "I think I'll wait in the hall,"

she said with a shaky voice. "She might get upset if she sees that I'm here with you."

Will nodded in agreement. "I suppose you're right, but she may not be too crazy to see me here either." He began pacing the hallway. "What do I even say to her? A few hours ago, I kicked her out of my house and told her I didn't want to speak to her." He clasped his hands together, resting them against his forehead.

"Just go in there, and make sure she is doing okay. Ask her if she needs anything," Mary suggested. "Don't bring up what happened earlier unless she does. There's a good chance she may not even remember going to your house. If she bumped her head at all, the details of the night might be a bit foggy."

As he pushed the door open slowly, it made a creaking sound. The walls of her hospital room were pale, but bright from the fluorescent lighting. A white board on the wall listed all of Lauren's information, including his name and contact information on the bottom. He was still puzzled as to why the hospital called him, or why he was her emergency contact person anyway. She had a lot of family nearby, and it would have made more sense to call them.

He took a few steps forward, unsure if she was awake or not, her head tilted to the side. As he approached the bedside, a small monitor beeped next to him as he heard the soft breaths of her sleeping. He was relieved she was okay and breathing, but still unsure of what to say to her.

He pulled a chair over to the side of the bed and sat,

watching as the pressure cuff filled with air. It made a loud buzzing sound as it filled, sure to wake her, but if not the noise, the intense squeezing sensation on her arm would. He held his breath as it finished filling and started letting out small puffs of air. She moved her head upright and opened her eyes, squinting at the bright lights. Pain swirled through her temples as she tried to get her bearings.

"Will? What are you doing here?" she asked with a confused look on her face.

"The hospital called me to tell me you were in a car accident," he explained. "How are you feeling?"

She looked at him with an empty stare. "My head is pounding," she said, pressing her fingers against her temples.

"Do you want me to call the nurse? Or I could just go get her; I saw her sitting at a desk down at the end of the hall." He sat up in his chair, ready to run down there at the word go.

She shook her head slightly, trying to fight the dizziness and headache. "No, they'll come check on me soon." She reached for the remote on the bed, elevating herself a few inches.

Will stood to help her adjust her pillows, still wondering if she remembered what happened before her accident. He could see she was in pain and wasn't sure bringing it up would help the situation. Angering her again right after a car accident while she was trying to rest seemed counterproductive.

"Can I get you some water?" he asked, spotting a tray near the bed.

She nodded.

He poured her a glass, his hands shaking as his nerves began to take over his body. He couldn't move past the fact that he felt this was partially his fault. If he would have just let her come inside the house and explain whatever it was that she came there to tell him, she wouldn't be lying in this bed right now. He wished the whole thing would never have happened — that she had never come to his house at all. He handed the glass to her, helping her steady it in her weak hands.

"You never told me why you were here," she said again, taking a small sip of water.

He exhaled slowly. "I was still on your emergency contact list. I assume that since I answered the call, they stopped with me and chose not to call anyone else." He took the glass from her and held it. "I can call your family if you'd like. I'm sure they'd come down here in a hurry to take care of you."

"I think the nurse already did," she muttered softly, pointing to the water glass. "Would you help me take another sip of water?"

He stood and bent over the bed, placing the cup against her lips.

A nurse approached Mary in the hall before entering Lauren's room. "You can go in and see your friend if you'd like. You don't need to stay in the hallway."

Friend. She cringed at the word. More like enemy, but

Mary did feel bad about Lauren being involved in a car accident and ending up in the hospital. "My friend is in there with her now. I don't want to interrupt them, so I'm fine waiting out here."

The nurse shrugged and carried on with her rounds. Mary was curious how things were going inside. She didn't hear any yelling, so she took that as a good start. She pinched the bridge of her nose, taking a deep breath. Against her better judgment, she stood and peeked through the cracked door. There he was, sitting bedside to the woman he used to love, and maybe still does. She watched him as he helped her drink her water and sit on the edge of the bed, taking her hand. She couldn't make out what he was saying, but knew it must have been something sweet. That was just the kind of person Will was.

Maybe she shouldn't have come with him, Mary thought. She dropped her shoulders with this sinking feeling in her stomach. She didn't want to come between them if they were supposed to be back together. Seeing how Will reacted in the room with Lauren, Mary thought it verified that he still has feelings for her. She was still with Alex, anyway, so who was she to think that she could begin to have feelings for another man? It wasn't the kind of person she was, and Will wasn't the kind of person to turn away from someone in need, especially someone he loved or still loves.

After quite some time passed, and seeing no signs of Will coming out, Mary walked to the nurses' desk. Three of them sat in the chairs, wheeling back and forth to monitors and answering phone calls. She stood by patiently until one of them was free.

"May I help you, ma'am?" one of them asked, still writing something on a chart.

"I was wondering if there was a phone I could use," Mary asked politely. "My cell phone isn't getting a signal in here."

"If you go down the hall about half way," the nurse instructed, "there is a small waiting room on your left. There's a phone in there you may use." She pointed down the hall and went back to her charting.

Mary walked back down the same hall from where she initially came, as she looked back still seeing no signs of Will exiting Lauren's room. She found the waiting room and picked up the receiver. She had two choices; call her mother to come pick her up, or call a cab. Uncertain of the road conditions still, she settled on a cab. They answered on the second ring, not busy at this time of the morning. They told her it would be a half an hour, she said that would be fine, and hung up the phone. Returning to the nurses' station, she stood quietly again until someone noticed her.

"May I help you?" the nurse asked, a different one than before.

Mary cleared her throat. "I was wondering if you could let my friend know that I went home to get some rest. He's visiting Lauren Ridgeway in room 304," she said, pointing down the hall. "I would tell him myself, but I don't want to interrupt them." She sighed, thinking back to what she saw earlier.

"Sure, ma'am, I'll make a note, and be sure he gets it."

Before Mary could thank her, she was already on another phone call. She had to pass by Lauren's room one more time on the way out. The door was still slightly ajar, so she peeked in. There they were, both sound asleep. He was still sitting in his chair, his head resting next to her on the bed. Mary thought to herself, he belonged there with Lauren, not her. She probably had no business being there to begin with. Her life was waiting for her back at home with Alex, not here in the hospital. She suddenly felt very tired. She stepped back out of the room, pulled her hat on, and walked to the exit to wait for her cab.

The sun was just starting to peek up over the horizon as the cab driver pulled into her parents' driveway. She settled her tab with him and climbed out, standing on the front step for a few minutes before going inside. The wind was blustery, but she was so numb from the whole recent experience that she hardly felt a thing. She knew the second she walked in through the door, her mother would bombard her with more questions than she'd have answers for. She wasn't in the mood to talk about it — any of it. She knew she'd have to tell her about Lauren and could already hear her mother scold her for going out in the storm.

She cocked her head from side to side, trying to loosen her stiff muscles before she opened the door. Just as she pushed her key into the lock, the door swung open.

"Mary!" her mother exclaimed. "Where have you been? Why did you take a cab home? Where is Will?"

There it was, the immediate question spew that she was anticipating.

"I'm fine, mom. You called me a thousand times to check in, so you should have known that." Mary pushed her way inside past her mother and took off her jacket.

"I knew you were alright last night, but that was yesterday," her mother continued. "I hadn't heard from you yet this morning." Linda sat in her chair in the living room and waited for Mary to join her.

"My phone battery was dying, and I wasn't getting a good signal, so I was saving what battery life I had left." She knew if she didn't tell her mother about the accident, she would surely hear it through the town rumor mill shortly, so it was probably best it came from her.

Linda sat at the edge of her chair. "You never answered my question," her mother reminded her.

Mary's eyes widened. "Which one? You threw about twenty of them at me the second you opened the door."

"I'm sorry, I'm your mother, and I was worried about you. You'll understand some day when you have children of your own," Linda explained. "Why did you take a cab home?"

Well, now was as good a time as any to tell her. Mary figured if she told her mother everything now, she could go up to take a nap and not be hounded when she woke up.

"I was at Will's house most of the night, but then there was an accident, and we had to leave."

Before Mary could explain any further, Linda jumped out of her chair. "Oh, my goodness, I knew something bad was going to happen. I knew you never should have left the house yesterday."

Mary held her hands up in front of her, trying to reassure her, "Mom, calm down, I'm fine."

Linda walked back to her chair and sat slowly. "Is it Will? Is he hurt? Is that why he didn't bring you home?" Again, with the twenty questions.

"Mom!" Mary shouted. "If you stop asking me a million questions, maybe I can finish my story, and you will have the answers. You need to stop interrupting me." It wasn't like her to be so short with her mother, but she hadn't slept, and her mind was moving in a hundred different directions.

Linda nodded slowly, making a zipper motion with her fingers across her mouth.

"Thank you," Mary said. "Like I was saying, there was an accident, so Will and I had to drive over to the hospital."

She could see her mother's eyes widen, but she kept her promise and didn't interrupt.

Mary continued. "Earlier in the day, when we were picking up our dresses, we ran into Lauren, his ex, at the bridal shop. Needless to say, she was not happy to see him there, especially with me. After we left, she showed up at his front door during the worst part of the storm. Long story short, he didn't give her the time of day and asked her to leave."

She paused a moment to be sure her mother was still following.

"Well when she left, with the treacherous weather conditions, she somehow went off the road resulting in the car accident. Will was still listed as her emergency contact on Lauren's cell phone, so the hospital called him to come to right away. He fired up his pickup truck and we drove, very slowly and careful, mind you, to the hospital."

Linda nodded along, smiling at the *very slowly and careful* part.

"He went in to her room to see how she was doing while I waited in the hall. He never came back out, so I left a note at the nurses' station and took a cab home."

Her mother sat there, unsure if the story was over or not.

"You can talk now," Mary told her, laughing a little under her breath.

"Is Lauren alright?" Linda asked.

Mary shrugged. "The doctor said she suffered a concussion and some bumps and bruises, but otherwise seemed okay. I never went in the room with him, so I don't know much."

Linda stood from her chair and sat next to Mary, wrapping her arm around her shoulder as Mary rested her head on her mother's shoulder.

"I'm glad you weren't hurt," her mother responded, "and I'm sure Will appreciated you being there with him."

Mary wasn't so sure. He never came back out to see her, probably forgot that she was even waiting out in the hall for him. Her eyes began filling with a burning sensation as she checked her watch.

"It's been a long day," Mary said yawning, "would you mind if I went upstairs to take a nap for a few hours?"

Linda smiled. "Of course not, dear. I'm just so happy that you're home."

Mary hugged her mother and went up to her room. As she closed her bedroom door, her cell phone began to ring. Hoping it was Will calling, she pulled it out of her pocket quickly.

It was Alex.

She didn't have the energy to talk to him at that moment. Her head and her heart were at odds with each other. She didn't know what she was feeling anymore. The only feeling she could identify was tired. She placed her phone on the night stand and crawled into bed. Within minutes, she was sound asleep.

Chapter
Eighteen

Mary woke later that afternoon, groggy and confused, not sure of what day it was. Rolling over, she checked her phone, seeing several missed calls, texts, and voicemails from Ali inquiring about the status of her dress. She huffed. That's what she got for asking if there was anything else to help with — a worried bride and the errand runner. As she was about to return Ali's call to ensure her that her dress was just fine, she sat straight up in bed, remembered the dresses were still in Will's car at his house.

She banged her fist against her forehead. Calling Will, or Ali for that matter, was not at all what she wanted to do at that moment. She flung the covers back and sprang up, hearing a nice hot shower calling her name. Just as she stepped foot on the floor, her cell phone began to ring.

Ali was calling again.

Having not had coffee or a shower yet, Mary wasn't quite ready for the wrath of her sister. She placed the phone on the counter in the bathroom as she turned on the shower.

It began to ring again.

Grabbing it off the counter and clenching her jaw, she answered abruptly.

"What, Ali?" she shouted, louder than she intended.

"Mary? It's Alex. Is everything alright?"

Great, she thought. That'll teach her to make sure she looks at her phone before answering next time.

"Mary, are you there?" he asked when she didn't answer.

"Sorry, yes I'm here," Mary said with a big sigh. "I thought you were Ali calling me for the billionth time today about wedding stuff." Mary began pacing the room, wanting nothing more than to throw her phone out the window and soak under the hot shower.

"Oh. I don't have a lot of time," Alex continued, "but Trish said she saw on the news that Maple Falls got a big snow storm."

Mary stopped pacing. She wasn't sure if she should be happy he called to check on her, or annoyed that the only reason he even knew what was going on was because his assistant told him. Trish had to have heard a little about Mary if she knew where she was from. Maple Falls isn't exactly a big spot on the map.

"Yes, we did," Mary said a bit exasperated. "I'm glad your assistant is keeping you up to date on the news. Is that in her job description, too?" she scoffed.

Alex mumbled something under his breath. "Listen, I've been really busy since you left and haven't had two seconds to sit down and watch television. I know you love to sit and do that all day, but some of us don't get that luxury."

Mary could hear the loud clicking sounds of a keyboard and another phone ringing in the background. "If you need to go and answer that, you can," she said.

"No, Trish will answer it," Alex said sarcastically. "That actually *is* part of her job description, in case you were wondering."

Of course, Trish was there. The simple mention of her name made Mary's blood boil. He knew exactly how to push her buttons; he had perfected it in the last few months. Part of her wondered if he did it on purpose, or maybe it was just part of his daily routine. Either way, she had little patience for it today.

"Was there a reason you were calling?" Mary asked impatiently. "It seems like you already knew about the snow. Were you just calling for me to confirm it for you or something?" Her tone was very short with him, hoping he'd get annoyed and let her go, but so far, no such luck.

"I just wanted to know how much snow you got and if you got snowed in or not," Alex answered — annoyed with her a little now, too.

"We got over a foot," Mary answered, "but on the way

home this morning, the drifts along some of the buildings around town were much higher than that." Her chest tightened as she realized what she'd just said.

"On your way home?" Alex said with curiosity in his voice. "Where were you this morning during that blizzard?" The typing in the background stopped.

Now was her chance to tell him all she'd done while she's been home. This was her chance to tell him about the feelings she was having for Will and how her feelings had changed for him. Suddenly, Mary realized what she was thinking and stopped herself as the vision of Will and Lauren from the hospital flashed back in her mind. Telling Alex about Will would complicate things and serve no good purpose. Will was probably already back together with Lauren, and it was sure to be a moot point.

"The weatherman said Maple Falls would only get a dusting at best, so I —." Mary was cut off mid sentence by Trish interrupting him.

Alex covered the phone and had a side conversation with Trish, the sound of his hand making a scratching sound in Mary's ear.

"Mary," Alex returned and said, "I have to take this call on the other line. I'll call you later."

He hung up the phone before Mary had the chance to tell him she wouldn't be able to talk later. Maybe it was for the best. This way, he'd likely get her voicemail, and she could avoid the conversation she needed to have with him for a while longer.

Linda knocked at the bathroom door, peeking her head

in so Mary could hear her over the sound of the running water. "I was just coming up to make sure you were awake. Did you sleep well?" she shouted.

"Yes, thank you for letting me nap," Mary answered. "I would have been a train wreck if I hadn't." She was still a train wreck, she thought, but at least a well rested one.

"I wanted to let you know that Will stopped by an hour or so ago," her mother replied.

Mary's heart stopped as she paused her lathering. "He did? What did he want?" She pulled back the corner of the shower curtain so she could hear better. Maybe he wasn't back with Lauren after all.

"He brought by the dresses that were left in his car," Linda said. "He told me that Ali was very specific with how you should handle her dress, and that leaving it in a frozen car was probably not on her list of approved situations."

Mary laughed under her breath. "Isn't that the truth," Mary chuckled. "She left me a bunch of text messages about it, but I haven't returned them yet."

"Not to worry, dear," Linda assured her. "I've already talked to Ali and told her that her dress was hanging in the guest room safe and sound. It may not have been at the time she called, but that'll just stay our little secret."

Mary's mother always stuck up for her, especially when it came to her sisters. "Thank you," she said. "I'll be down in a few minutes. Is there any coffee?"

Linda smiled. "I just brewed a fresh pot before I came upstairs. See you down there shortly."

After a long steamy shower, Mary spent the rest of the afternoon with her mother, as they gave each other manicures and painted each other's fingernails. Before leaving on her trip home, Mary packed in her suitcase every shade of red nail polish she owned, hoping that at least one of them would match her dress. Of the eleven bottles she packed, she and Linda narrowed it down to two that matched the dress almost perfectly. In true mother-daughter fashion, Mary knew the best way to pick which of the two bottles of nail polish they'd use.

"Pick a hand," Mary told her mother, hiding them both behind her back.

Linda tapped her left arm, revealing the Crazy for Crimson bottle. "Well that's one way to decide. That used to be one of your favorite games growing up. That, and hide-something-and-find-it. A Bradford family original." Linda smiled at the memory.

"That was the best game! And I love how creative we got for the name," Mary laughed.

Mary shook the bottle and began painting her mother's fingernails. "Do you want me to paint your toenails, too? Are you wearing open or closed toe shoes?"

Linda cocked her head to one side. "Mary, it's December, and there is over a foot of snow on the ground. Do you really think I'd wear open toe shoes?" She couldn't help but chuckle at the thought.

"You never know, mom," Mary chuckled, too. "I'm wearing open toe. My plan was to wear cute boots under my dress until we get to the church," she explained. She painted the second coat on Linda's nails and started on her own. "Can you believe Ali is getting married tomorrow? It feels like she's still in junior high to me — dorky little sister with braces and bangs that started halfway back on her head. Makes me feel old, and frankly, a little jealous that my baby sister beat me to the altar."

Linda sat back in her chair. "It makes *you* feel old? How do you think I feel? I gave birth to her. To me, it feels like she should be off to her first day of kindergarten, carrying her lunch box in her chubby little hand."

"You're right, mom," Mary agreed. "You are a lot older than me."

They burst out laughing at the same time. "I'd whack you in the arm if I knew it wouldn't mess up my nails," Linda said through her tears of laughter.

Mary backed away slightly. "Just to be clear, I'm laughing with you, not at you."

"Sure, you are," Linda said skeptically.

Once Mary's nails were dry, she went upstairs to put together everything she needed for tomorrow. She bought Ali a special gift before coming home, and she wanted to give it to her at the rehearsal dinner, so she wrapped it up and set it aside. She wasn't able to see the dress before coming home, so in true Mary fashion, she packed every fancy necklace, bracelet, and earrings she owned into a travel jewelry case she bought for the trip. Having come home without one last time, it took what seemed like forever to untangle them.

She laid the necklaces across the bed and settled on a silver teardrop one that would go perfectly with the neckline of the dress. When she bought new jewelry, she tended to buy all of the matching pieces to go along with it. That way, once she chose the necklace, the rest of the decisions were made for her. She found the matching pieces and placed the remaining pieces back inside the jewelry case.

Linda knocked on the door. "Mary, if you are going to ride with us, we will be leaving in about thirty minutes."

"Mom, I don't have a rental car, remember. Don't leave without me," Mary said, rushing in to the bathroom to fix her hair.

"I know that, dear," her mother answered, "but I wasn't sure if Will was picking you up or if you had another ride. See you downstairs when you're ready," she shouted through the door.

Will. How had Mary forgotten that he would be at the rehearsal dinner tonight? Obviously, he was in the wedding, too. Her hands began to clam up at the thought of seeing him. Would he be mad at her for leaving the hospital without telling him? What if he was still there and couldn't come tonight? Just what she needed, more unanswered questions swirling around in her brain.

Mary finished her hair and touched up her makeup. Initially not planning on wearing much makeup, she changed her mind once she remembered Will would likely be there. She pulled her dress from the closet and stepped into it, pulling her cardigan on over it to keep warm. The wind was rattling the windows as it whipped by, sure to mess her hair up the moment she stepped foot outside. After picking out one of the five purses she brought along, she grabbed Ali's gift and headed into the hall. Stopping just before the stairwell, she thought about texting Will to see if he would be there, but the vision she kept seeing play on a loop in her mind appeared again.

No, she told herself, and tossed her phone into her purse.

The drive to the venue was smooth as the plows already made several passes through town to clear the roads. Mary could hear small chunks of salt spinning up under the car as the wheels turned. Most of the curbs were covered in snow, making it hard to see any cross traffic. They drove past the coffee shop and noticed the city had already plowed the sidewalks and cleared the drifts that blew against the doors.

Traffic came to a stop as they allowed a couple to cross the street near the vacant building she was telling Will about. Mary quickly pulled a pen and paper out of her purse and jotted down the number for the real estate agent on the building. It was probably going to be a wasted effort, seeing that Lauren was never a fan of his woodworking, but Mary was going to try anyway.

Every time there was a big snow storm, the lines in the parking lots disappear — clearly the case tonight. It's not like people don't know how to line up cars together. It was as though they needed the lines to survive. Roger found a spot to park between two other cars whose drivers appeared to remember how to park, and he pulled his car into place.

"Are you sure you don't want me to drop you ladies off at the door? You look so nice, I'd hate for the wind to mess anything up," Roger offered, always thinking of others first.

"I'm fine walking, and the parking lot doesn't look too slippery," Mary said, thankful she decided on the lower heels.

"I'm wearing flats, so I'm fine walking," Linda said as she pushed open the car door. The wind gust blew right into the car, blowing her hair back and the bottom of her dress up to her knees.

Roger hurried around to her side of the car and took her hand, helping her out. With his daughter on one arm and his wife on the other, he walked into the building proud, happy to be joining his entire family again tonight. He was trying not to get too comfortable having Mary around, but he was also going to enjoy every minute of having her there. He would never admit it to her, making her feel guilty, but he missed her living close by.

The air inside was almost hot, a far cry from the dropping temperature outside. The hostess greeted them at the door and brought them to the room Ali had made reservations for, the special dining room for the dinner. The woman pulled open the French doors, and it took Mary's breath away. The walls were draped from floor to ceiling in white twinkle lights wrapped in tulle, and the tables were covered in dark crimson red linens. The bright white place settings popped against the dark red color. Dark crimson red napkin rings were placed around the cloth napkins and placed beside the plate with a name tent resting on top.

The wedding party was placed at a special table near the front of the room, stretching from one end to the other. Next to each of their place settings lay a small red gift box, tied with iridescent ribbon. Mary did a lap around the room before finding her seat. Most of the guests were close family and friends, but some she hadn't seen yet since being home.

Mary was going to make sure not to stay in one place too long while she was there to avoid the *"why aren't you married yet?"* questions. It was almost as though she should place a sticker on her dress that read "Yes I'm older than Ali, and no, I'm not married yet." Being that she was surrounded by her closest family, there wasn't a need, but for the wedding tomorrow, it might be something she would half consider.

The rest of the wedding party trickled in through the doors, each of them escorted back by the hostess to ensure their privacy. Mary hung out in the corner by the head table with a straight shot of the doors. All of the bridesmaids had arrived, and most of the groomsmen. She looked around the room counting heads. There was one still missing.

Will wasn't there.

She reached in her purse to see if he had tried calling her, but he hadn't. She thought about asking Ali, but she didn't want to bother the bride. She tucked her phone away and grabbed a glass of wine from a waiter walking around the room, returning to her spot in the corner.

"Why are you hiding all the way over here? The rest of us are talking about a plan for tomorrow if you want to join us," Susie told her.

Mary hesitated, glancing at the door as it opened again. Still not him.

"Come on, quit being antisocial." Susie grabbed hold of her sister's arm and pulled her to the other side of the room where the rest of the bridesmaids were gathered.

"You look pretty tonight, Mary," Cora said as she tried to keep an eye on Lily, hoping she wouldn't trip the waiter she was circling. "Did everything go alright with the dress pick-up?"

Another conversation Mary dreaded. It was like groundhog's day with her conversations lately.

Clang, clang, clang, clang. Saved by the bell as Ali tapped her champagne glass to get everyone's attention.

"We'd like to get started, so if everyone could find their seat, the meal will be served." Ali grabbed Zach's hand and led the way to the head table.

As Mary tried to see through the large moving crowd, there was still no Will in sight. If he were just a guest, no one would notice, but having an empty chair at the head table would certainly not go unnoticed. The wait staff circled the room in an orderly fashion, weaving in and out around tables, but never bumping into each other. It was impressive to Mary watching from a distance, wondering how many times they'd practiced.

A side salad arrived first, followed by a steaming plate of roasted chicken breast, fresh green beans, and a baked potato. The waiter placed a small basket of fresh dinner rolls on each table. She could smell the dough, still warm from the oven. She reached for her fork, and took a bite of her salad when suddenly the doors opened again. Will had finally arrived. Mary's immediate response was to look at Ali, questioning whether or not he notified her of his tardiness ahead of time. Ali looked fairly calm, almost relieved, when she spotted him.

He pulled his arms out of his coat as he walked straight toward Ali, whispering something at both her and Zach, and quickly took his seat. The way the tables were arranged, Mary and Will sat with five other people in between them making it impossible to communicate. She was having a hard time focusing on her meal, wondering why he was late and where he'd been. She looked down the table at him, but he was already digging into his salad — eating quickly as though he hadn't eaten all day.

Mary pushed the food around her plate, her appetite fading. She'd hardly eaten all day either, but nothing seemed to taste good tonight. When the meal was finished, a waiter came by and took their plates, followed closely by another who served the dessert. Though chicken and green beans didn't do it for Mary, strawberry cheesecake definitely did.

Chapter
Nineteen

After the tables had been cleared and the after-dinner coffee had been served, the Pastor took his place near the side of the room to begin the rehearsal. The large fireplace was used as the altar to know where everyone would be standing tomorrow. Molly, Lily, and Jack practiced walking down the aisle first.

Jack carried the ring pillow, nervously watching everyone stare at him. Molly had been worried all week about how many petals to drop with each handful, but her nerves seemed to be calm tonight while pretending to drop them along the way. Lily was probably the most confident person in the wedding party to walk down the aisle. She almost thrived on being the center of attention, even if only for a few minutes.

Susie and Mary were both Ali's maid and matron of honor. Ali tried to decide who to choose, but ultimately chose them both. Susie walked down the aisle with Grant who also stood as Zach's best man. Mary watched them walk down before her, while her palms were pooling in sweat. She ran her hands down the sides of her dress, trying to keep herself in control.

As the others were halfway down the make-shift aisle, it was her turn. Mary turned to face Will who was calmly waiting for her as if he wasn't nervous to see her at all. To Mary, it appeared for him that nothing had happened that morning to change things between them. Was she the only one who noticed?

She walked towards him, having to tell her brain to pick up each foot as she moved forward. Right foot, left foot — repeat. She was thankful she had to wrap her arm in his, or she may never have made it down to the altar. Even though the room was silent as the others present watched the wedding party do the walk through, Mary felt as though the questions screaming in her head filled the room with plenty of noise. Questions she was dying to ask Will, but she didn't want to interrupt the rehearsal.

Will kept his head straight, focusing on the people in front of them. When they reached the front, they parted ways without a single glance at each other. The tension in her body was impossible to ignore. Her muscles began to ache as she stood next to Susie, waiting for the rest of the wedding party to make their way to the front.

Cora and Brad followed next, with Katie and her

husband bringing up the end. As the wedding party stood by to watch, Roger and Ali appeared in the doorway together. They exchanged a look, one with so much emotion that no words were needed. The pride Roger felt as her father walking Ali down the aisle was evident, his face glowing. Mary looked at Zach, who she could see was getting choked up, trying to blink back the tears.

It was really happening. Tomorrow Mary would be the lone sister, the last single one in the family. She was so happy for Ali and Zach, but at the same time, so confused in her own life. Mary's relationship with Alex was waning, and the feelings she had for him were fading. She knew in her heart she wanted to be with Will, but he may have already given his heart to someone else — again.

As Roger and Ali walked down the aisle, Mary looked across at Will, hoping to catch a small glimpse of hope. Maybe, just maybe everything they both felt earlier wasn't gone, but Will kept his focus on the bride. Mary was sure that he had feelings for her; she didn't think she was imagining that. What was going through his mind? Mary was over there, picturing herself and Will walking down the aisle, but for all she knew, he was over there picturing himself with Lauren. Her stomach dropped at the thought.

The Pastor ran through the whole ceremony and everything went smoothly. The ceremony was fairly simple, and everyone felt comfortable with their roles by the time they wrapped it up. The Pastor said his good-byes and left the family to gather together for the rest of the evening. When everyone was back in their seats, Ali and

Zach each gave a short speech, saving their big speeches for the reception tomorrow.

As Ali placed the microphone down on the table, Mary knew it was time to make her move. She couldn't keep playing her situation over and over again in her mind. Her head was pounding, and if she didn't approach Will now and get these questions out in the open, she was likely going to explode.

Ali walked over to speak with her bridesmaids and flower girls. "Ladies, if you would, please join me over at the small table in the corner. I have a little something I'd like to give each of you."

Mary threw her head back, the pounding sensation increasing. She looked over to the men as they all stood and followed Zach to the opposite corner. The women and flower girls gathered around the table together as Ali handed each of them a small gift box wrapped in dark crimson red wrapping. Together, they lifted the lid to reveal a necklace, bracelet, and earring set — the stones alternating what appeared to be diamonds and rubies.

Mary gasped, "Ali, these are beautiful," she said, lifting the necklace out of the box. "I wish I would have known sooner about these. I could have saved myself a lot of time, packing all of the jewelry I brought from home. This is so much more beautiful than anything I brought with me." She ran her fingers along the stones, the facets catching the light off the chandelier above.

"I'm glad you like them," Ali said, "but just so you know, those aren't real diamonds. I love you ladies, but I do have an entire wedding to pay for."

The women laughed. Cora and Susie leaned down to help the young girls. Each of them received a necklace similar to the women's, but on a smaller scale. They each embraced Ali. Mary thought to herself that Ali was so put together and calm, her nervousness, if she had any, was not showing at all. The final details were all taken care of, and Ali could finally just allow herself to be excited and enjoy the evening. She was ready to wake up tomorrow and marry Zach, the love of her life.

Linda walked over and joined them, admiring their beautiful jewelry. Ali reached into her bag and pulled out one more box, handing it over to Linda.

"I think there might be one more gift inside here for someone special," Ali told her.

Linda lifted the lid off. "Ali, it's beautiful," she said, pulling out the necklace inside. The chain was gold and delicate, holding a small charm on the bottom that read "mother of the bride" with two small gemstones above it.

"The stones in the charm are our birthstones," Ali explained.

Linda wasn't as good at saying the words that she wanted to, but she didn't have any trouble showing her emotions. She wrapped her arms around Ali and squeezed tight. "I love you, Ali," she whispered, her voice soft. She stood back and looked at her. "I better make sure I have enough Kleenex in my purse for tomorrow. If I'm already this much of an emotional wreck at the rehearsal, I can't imagine how I'll be at the ceremony."

Everyone laughed, nodding in agreement.

"I think I'll grab a few boxes of tissue to bring along," Susie said, dabbing the corner of her eyes.

"Enough of the tears, already. This is supposed to be a happy time," Mary said, breaking up the emotions. She gave her sisters each a big hug and said her good-byes. "I just have to get my jacket, and I'm ready to head for home."

Linda nodded. "I just have to grab your father, and we are ready, too."

Mary turned to look at the guys, but they were already finished. They were always better in these situations, showing little or no emotion, just eager to get home to fill their new flasks they'd just received as their gift for the wedding. She peeked around the crowds that began to gather as couples were leaving, but Will was nowhere in sight. Mary walked to the head table to grab her jacket and looked over at his chair. Empty. His coat was gone, and so was he. Even though she wanted to talk to him tonight, it was probably better that she didn't. The last thing she wanted to do was make things more awkward between them before the wedding.

Roger went out first and warmed the car for Linda and Mary. He pulled up to the curb so Linda wouldn't fall on the ice in the parking lot and so that Mary's dress wouldn't be a victim of the wind again. Mary opened the passenger door for her mother, grabbing it tightly with her hand, as the wind tried to take it away. Climbing in the back seat, she placed her purse on her lap and closed her eyes. She was having second thoughts, wishing she would have spoken with Will. Why didn't she just talk to him when she was walking down the aisle? She should have at least told him she needed to talk to him, then maybe he wouldn't have left so quickly. She shook her head. Will was probably already on his way back to the hospital to see Lauren.

"That was a beautiful rehearsal, don't you think so, Mary?" Linda asked, bringing Mary's mind back to the present.

"Yes, it really was. I'm excited for Ali and Zach," she replied. She really was excited for them, but decided to leave the insanely jealous part out of it. She had two men in her life, sort of, and there was a really good chance that she could lose them both, if she hadn't already. Then what would she do?

Mary's phone began to vibrate in her purse, startling her. She pulled it out, expecting it to be Alex. It wasn't. It was Will. She bit her lip, trying to decide on whether or not to answer it. Roger and Linda were discussing the weather in the front seat, so she wasn't missing out on anything. She took a deep breath and answered the call.

"Hello?" she said softly, not wanting to get her parents' attention.

"Hi, it's Will. I wasn't sure if you'd answer my call or not," he started, "but I didn't get the chance to talk to you tonight, so I thought I'd try this way."

Mary leaned her head back against the head rest, bracing herself for him to tell her he was back with Lauren.

She could feel it coming in the tone of his voice. "Yeah, it was busy in there tonight," she said.

"I just left the parking lot a few minutes ago, and I was wondering if you'd want to meet up for a quick drink?"

Mary was silent, replaying what he just said in her mind before answering. It wasn't what she thought he was going to say, and it threw her off. Maybe he wasn't going to see Lauren tonight. Or on second thought, maybe he wanted to tell her in person instead of over the phone about his getting back together with Lauren. Her stomach did flips as she thought about it.

"Mary, are you still there?" Will asked.

She cleared her throat. "Yes, sorry, I'm still here. Where do you want to meet? I can see if my parents can drop me on their way home."

He told her the name of the place he picked and hung up the phone. She held her hand on her phone for a long moment, wondering if she should have answered at all. At least with the unknown, she thought there could still be a chance with him. But now, once he told her face to face that there was nothing between them and that he wanted to be with Lauren, there would be no going back. She'd have to accept it and move on — with or without Alex.

"Was that Alex calling, dear?" Linda asked from the front seat.

They had noticed her phone call. "Oh — no, it was Will." She tried to be nonchalant about it, but her shaky voice gave her away.

"Is everything alright? Why would he be calling if you

just saw him a few minutes ago?" Linda wondered.

"Actually, he was wondering if I wanted to meet him for a quick drink tonight," Mary explained. "Dad, would you be able to drop me off on your way through town?"

Roger nodded, keeping his eye on the road. "No problem," he said.

A few minutes later they pulled up in front of the restaurant. Mary climbed out of the back seat and walked to her mother's window.

"Do you need a ride home? We can wait up for you to call if you need," Linda offered.

"I think I'll be okay. If Will can't bring me home, I'm happy to take a cab." Mary waved and walked toward the restaurant.

Mary spotted Will as soon as she walked through the door. He was sitting on the bench near the hostess, playing on his phone and didn't see her come in. She stood there for a moment and watched him, trying to calm her nerves enough to get through one drink with him and to resist the urge to run back out the door. He hadn't seen her yet, so at this point she could still pull it off.

As she took a step forward, he looked up. Their eyes met, and it was like it was two days ago — before the accident and before Lauren had come back into his life. It was still there, somewhere deep inside of him, she could feel it and see it in his eyes, the way he looked at her.

He stood from the bench and met her halfway. "I'm glad you could make it on such short notice," he said.

Mary nodded. "Well, you did interrupt my big plans of sitting on the couch all night, but I figured I could pencil you in." She went back to her go-to humor when she was uncomfortable.

"I put our name on the list for a seat in the bar. I figured you wouldn't be hungry after just eating that huge meal at the rehearsal." Will walked to the podium to let them know his party had arrived.

He must not have noticed her pushing her food around on the plate earlier. Her appetite was non-existent, while his was clearly unaffected. They followed the hostess to a high-top table in the bar. The lights were dim, giving off a red glow from above. He pulled out her chair and helped her up.

"So, what did you think about tonight?" he wondered. He wasn't sure what to say first, relying on small talk.

Mary flipped open the drink menu. "It went good, I think tomorrow should go well." She kept her answers short and sweet, not wanting to give up too much of how she was feeling. She was never one to be able to hide her feelings well, so the dim lights were a blessing.

"Zach seemed pretty relaxed about tomorrow. How was Ali? Did she hand out strict schedules you are all supposed to follow?" he joked.

Mary laughed under her breath. "She was definitely precise on how she wanted tomorrow to go, but she was very nice about it." The waiter came by and took their orders. "I cannot, however, guarantee that she'll be that nice about it tomorrow. Especially if someone doesn't follow it correctly."

Their drinks arrived just in time. Mary was hoping the wine would help her to relax a little.

"I'm glad I'm on the groom's side, then," Will said, laughing.

Mary took a sip of her wine. "I better stick to just one of these tonight. I wouldn't want to be hung over on her wedding day," she said. "I don't think drinking excessively and being hung over is on the list of approved activities."

Will laughed. "If I were you, I'd turn your phone on vibrate before going to bed so she can't bother you about it."

"I think she is staying at my parents' house tonight, actually. I wouldn't be surprised if she pops her head in and checks that I'm home by a decent time," she said. "If she knew I was going out tonight, I have no doubt she would have given me a curfew."

Will's eyes widened. "She means business." He flagged down the waiter and ordered another beer. Mary passed on a refill, sticking with her original plan.

There was still the elephant in the room, but not just a regular elephant. It was a giant, pink elephant doing back flips around the room. She didn't want to be the first person to bring it up. If she brought it up, then they would be forced to address it, but if she ignored it completely, it may never come up. Will placed his empty beer glass at the edge of table and exhaled loudly. *Here it comes*, she thought. She took a deep breath in and held it, bracing herself.

"There's a reason I asked you here tonight," Will started, "but I'm not sure where to begin." He tapped his fingers on the top of the table. "I feel like we need to clear the air about the Lauren situation."

Mary closed her eyes, waiting for the words to come out of his mouth and hit her in the face like a ton of bricks. "You don't have to explain, Will," she blurted out. "You two have a long history, so it makes sense that you two would end up back together."

Will was taken aback. "Is that why you think I brought you here? To tell you that Lauren and I are back together?" He couldn't believe what came out of her mouth. No wonder she'd been acting so strange tonight.

"Isn't it?" Mary asked, feeling perhaps a little relieved that she was wrong.

"No, not at all. Lauren and I are not back together. What gave you that idea?" He sat up and rested his elbows on the table.

"I — I saw the two of you, in the room together at the hospital. I thought —," her voice trailed off.

He reached across the table and placed his hand on top of hers. "I was feeling a lot of different emotions when I first got there, I'll admit that. I felt guilty that it was all my fault, thinking if I wouldn't have told her to leave that it never would have happened." He took a drink. "But all of that aside, I never once thought about getting back together with her."

Mary couldn't believe what he was saying. She let him continue.

"I found out that she is not engaged and she was just there with her girlfriends trying on dresses for fun. She asked about us, too," he said.

Mary suddenly began to feel light-headed. "What did you tell her?"

"Well, when I noticed you had left, I wasn't sure how you were feeling, so I didn't tell her anything. I wasn't sure there was anything to tell at that point."

He had a point, Mary thought. She had left him there, assuming one thing, when, as it turned out, was actually something totally different.

She rubbed her temples. "I'm sorry I left without letting you know, but I didn't want to interrupt you two, and I didn't think it was a good idea for her to see me there," she explained.

"I understand," he said. He rubbed her hand with his thumb gently, sending chills down her body.

How could she have been so wrong about what she saw? She knew what kind of person Will was, and she felt bad for having doubted him. If anyone should be upset about getting mixed signals, it should be Will. Here Mary was, flirting with one man while still in a relationship with another. It was so out of character for her to be like this, and she was afraid she was in too deep to go back. She wasn't even sure she wanted to go back. Eventually, she knew that she had to face Alex, one way or another, but she was dreading even the thought of it.

"Is Alex flying in for the wedding tomorrow?"

Mary shook her head. "No. He had many opportunities to come home for Christmas or the wedding, but he chose work instead. I guess I'll be the pathetic and lonely sister that attends her sister's wedding alone."

"So, if it makes you pathetic to attend a wedding alone, does that mean I'm pathetic, too?" he joked. He took the last sip of his beer and set it aside. "I suppose we could go together and be less pathetic, if you don't think Alex would mind."

Mary thought about it, finishing her wine. "He had his chance to be my date, and since he passed, he doesn't get a say in me bringing another one," she said.

Will's face lit up. "Shall we?" he asked, standing from the table, offering his arm.

Mary slid her arm through his. "Practicing for tomorrow?" she teased.

"Well, I wouldn't want to do it wrong and ruin the day for the bride," he said, as they left the restaurant and walked to his car. He opened her door and helped her inside.

"You definitely have the gentleman part down, that's for sure," she replied. "I think tomorrow is going to be a great day."

"I am definitely looking forward to it," he said as he closed her door.

Chapter
Twenty

Mary could sense the mood in the house through the closed door when she woke in the morning. The sounds were muffled, but there was no mistake about the number of people that were arriving downstairs. Linda volunteered her house for the place where the women would get ready — hair, makeup, and dresses.

She hired one of the town's stylists and makeup artists to come to the house for a more intimate setting, hoping to keep the stress level down for Ali. That way, everything they would need would be in one place. The limo would pick them all up, and they'd ride together to the church. It kept with the style of Ali's schedule for the day, and if everyone was together, no one would show up late.

Mary rolled over and checked her phone for missed

calls. Nothing. She hadn't heard from Alex since the snowstorm hit a couple days ago. She assumed he was busy with work, or perhaps still on the phone call he had to take that was more important than she was. She sat at the edge of the bed, still lethargic from waking, and slid on her slippers. She was certain to be missed if she didn't get downstairs soon. As Mary approached the landing, she quickly got a sense of the chaotic scene unfolding in front of her before proceeding.

"Finally, you grace us with your presence," Susie shouted, spotting her first.

Mary didn't want Susie to make a big deal out of her coming downstairs. She'd hoped to sneak into the kitchen for a cup of coffee before she was discovered. When Susie was out of sight, she made a mad dash for the kitchen while everyone else hurried to the dining room.

"Good morning, Mary," her father greeted, turning on the coffee bean grinder.

"Morning, dad," she replied. She squinted at the sound of the grinder, pulsing in her temples for a few seconds after he shut it off. "How long until the next pot is ready? I could use a few."

Roger chuckled. "A few pots or cups?"

"I'll start with cups and go from there." Mary walked to the counter and poured her sugar and creamer in a mug and sat at the island until the coffee was brewed, ready to take claim on the first cup.

He poured the grounds in the filter and started the next pot. "You've missed a lot of excitement already this morning," he told her. "The hair stylist got lost looking for the house, and the makeup lady is running late. Luckily, I don't need to use either of those services today," he joked, running his hands along the sides of his head.

"I'm sure they could throw some grease in there for you and give you a pompadour," Mary teased. "A special hair style for a special occasion."

Roger grabbed some strands on the top of his head. "I don't think I have enough on top anymore for a style like that," he said. "But I do admire your optimism."

Mary missed her morning coffee chats with her dad. She spent many mornings at that exact counter, shooting the breeze with him, covering anything from sports to local gossip they'd heard at the shop. Some conversations got deep, but for the most part, it was kept light. Mary felt it was the perfect way to start the day.

She tended to do the same with her mother, only she saved those conversations for the evenings. Roger would disappear to the office and work on inventory or something related to the coffee shop, and she and her mother would chat in the living room next to the fire. Those memories were still so vivid. Now, with Alex gone all the time, the only people in her apartment she talked to during her morning coffee were the people on television. She'd turn on the news or a talk show and reply to them. It was a one-sided conversation, but it was still a form of communication in her eyes.

"I'm glad I missed the drama so far. It's not how I like to start my mornings," Mary told her dad.

She spoke too soon. No sooner had she stopped talking, Ali flew into the kitchen.

"Mary!" she said in a flurry, "you're next for makeup. Susie is just finishing up, so when she moves over to hair, you're up." Ali flew back out just as quickly, leaving Mary's mouth wide open.

"Perhaps there is still time to be in on some drama," Mary told her dad. She carried her empty mug over to him and held it out. "You better fill it all the way up. I have a feeling I'm going to need every drop." She held her hands tight around it, protecting it from the people rushing in and out of the room.

"Mary, you're next in the makeup chair," Ali shouted. "Susie just finished."

Ali had just told her the same thing mere minutes ago, but instead of bringing it up to her, she simply smiled and nodded. Mary climbed up in the chair, trying to balance her coffee.

"Do you mind doing my lips last so I can enjoy at least half of this before I have to leave?" Mary asked the makeup person.

The woman doing the makeup shook her head and immediately started dabbing Mary's face with something cold and wet from a glass bottle.

"Susie!" Ali shouted. "You're next for hair. Where do you think you're going?"

Susie stopped in her tracks and turned on her heels. "If it's okay with you, dear sister, I would like permission to have a bathroom break." Susie came off a little more sarcastic than she probably should have, but Mary laughed anyway. Ali shot a look toward Mary as she took an innocent drink of coffee, rolling her eyes at the makeup lady.

"Would you mind keeping your eyes closed so I can get your makeup on?" the woman demanded.

"Tough room this morning," Mary whispered under her breath.

"Yes, you can go to the bathroom," Ali said. "Just be sure to not mess up your makeup, and come right back when you're done."

Before Susie could reply, Ali stomped off to get after the next person to keep the ball rolling. Susie saluted Ali behind her back and marched off down the hall.

Zach wasn't nearly as strict when it came to his groomsmen getting ready. He stayed at his apartment while the others got ready at their own homes. A limo was supposed to pick each of them up by a scheduled time, so as long as they were all ready by then, that was good enough for Zach.

Will walked to his closet and grabbed his garment bag and carried it to his bed. He laid out each of the pieces, making sure not to miss anything. He was hoping to impress Mary by showing up put together with every thread in place. He stood in front of the mirror and fixed his tie three times before getting it right. It wasn't something he was used to wearing, but he learned back in high school on the off chance he ever had to dress up. It was just like riding a bike, though. Once he started tying it, it all came rushing back to him. It was the length that needed work — too short, then too long.

He accepted his third attempt and walked away from the mirror, knowing he could stand there all day playing around to make it just right. With his luck, someone would probably adjust it for him anyway when he got to the church, so he stopped.

Back in the kitchen, his mail stared at him again, piling higher each day. He sifted through it and found the letter he'd received last week. Will read through it again, still trying to decide what to do with the offer he was given. Mary had so many great ideas for him when the two of them were talking at his house the other day. He had planned on showing the letter to her to get her opinion on it, but their night was cut short. She seemed to believe in him more than anyone else had at that point, and he valued her opinion. He folded the letter back up and placed it back in the envelope.

He tapped the letter against his palm, wanting so badly to talk to her more about it. Taking a risk, he tucked the letter into the inside pocket of his tuxedo jacket and padded his chest. If there was any time he was able to be alone with her tonight, he'd show it to her.

Will nervously paced the room. His mind was spinning in so many directions and none of them made any sense. It felt like someone threw him into a blender with the lid off, and he spun around inside with his thoughts all jumbled together. He needed to clear his head and try to make sense of it all, one thing at a time. Once the wedding was over, he was determined to finally make some much needed decisions about his life. If he was finally going to tell Mary how he felt, he had to do it tonight, before it was too late and she left town again.

He continued to pace through the kitchen, and just then, the doorbell rang. He pushed his wallet into his back pocket and grabbed his keys off the counter by the door.

"Good morning, Mr. Roberts. I'm here to bring you to the wedding," the limo driver said, smiling.

Will took a deep breath, locking the door behind him. "Here goes nothing," he whispered as he walked toward the limo.

Two tubes of mascara, three cans of hair spray, and a countless number of bobby pins later, the women were just about ready to leave for the church. The wind was howling past the windows as they strapped on their shoes to leave, each one nervous that a hair incident was imminent. Linda finished tying up the back of Ali's dress just as the limo arrived. Susie ran around the room picking up all of the remaining hair supplies and stuffed them into a pouch she'd brought along, ready to help fix any hair or makeup disaster that came their way.

"I can't believe how windy it is outside today," Ali

complained. "Of all days, it has to be windy on my wedding day."

"I'm sure Mother Nature had it in for you and was holding off on the wind until today," Mary teased. The look on Ali's face made Mary think she went a little too far with her sarcasm.

Cora opened the door just as the limo driver was about to ring the doorbell. Ali recognized his voice right away.

"Otis! I'm so glad to see you," Ali shouted from the living room. "It wouldn't be the same if you weren't part of our day."

"It's nice to see you again, Mr. Frost," Linda greeted.

"Please, call me Otis," he replied. "You ladies all look stunning. I can escort each of you outside when you're ready. I have the limo running and the heat on, and freshly poured mimosas for anyone who would like one." Otis was so thoughtful. Ali couldn't have imagined any other limo driver taking her to the ceremony. He played such a big part in her engagement, he almost felt like one of the family to her.

One by one, Otis helped the women out to the limo, holding onto them so nobody slipped. Lily and Molly were running around with red cheeks, so the cold air would likely not affect them at all. Linda saw the hair dresser and makeup artist out the door, locking it behind her.

"Mother of the bride, as stunning as ever," Otis told Linda.

"You're so kind," she said, blushing a little.

Otis closed the door tight and climbed into the front

seat. The partition was down, as per Ali's request allowing him to feel a part of the fun.

"Do we have everyone?" he asked.

Ali looked around, counting heads. "I think we're ready to roll, Otis."

Ali sat back in her seat across the back of the limo. As Otis backed out of the driveway, Ali took in a deep breath. She'd been waiting for this day for over a year. Even though so much time had passed, it seemed like just yesterday that Otis was picking her up from her apartment, taking her around Maple Falls on a crazy scavenger hunt to find Zach. She'd watched the slide show of that special day that was given to her countless number of times, wanting to remember every part of it.

Today was going to be another one of those days where she wanted to cherish each moment, in order to remember every part of it for years to come. Of all the advice she'd been given from others, that of slowing down to enjoy the day was the one she'd heard most.

"Girls, are you excited to drop flower petals for Ali to walk on?" Mary asked. "Auntie Ali told you how many to drop each time, right?"

Molly's eyes widened.

"Very funny, Mary," Ali said. "Girls, you drop as many as you want." She smiled at them both. Molly seemed a little on edge, while Lily didn't seem fazed one bit by her comment.

"This is it, Ali," Susie shouted. "Are you sure you're ready for all of this? In a few short hours, you're going to be somebody's wife. I can't believe my younger sister is getting married. Well — one of my younger sisters at least." Susie elbowed Mary playfully in the ribs.

"Yeah, yeah. Maybe I just was holding out and saving the best for last," Mary joked back.

"Or you've already waited too long, and you are just that much closer to becoming a crazy cat lady," Ali teased.

Mary had to laugh. "Nice, I'll give you credit for that comeback. Who knows, maybe this time next year, I'll be the one getting married. With only myself left, I have a good chance." Mary knew saying it out loud wouldn't make it come true, but she was determined not to give up hope. She still had to figure things out with Alex before she could do anything. But for today, she was going to enjoy her date with Will, two friends making each other feel less lonely by not showing up dateless to a wedding.

Ten minutes later, Otis pulled up in front of the church. The men's limo had already arrived, and they were inside waiting. Cora and Katie went inside first to make sure Zach was tucked away in the groom's room so he wouldn't see Ali before the ceremony. Mary and Susie helped carry the train of Ali's dress, not wanting it to snag on the small patches of ice placed along the sidewalk. Linda hurried the girls inside to get them started on an activity while they waited for the ceremony to start.

"I thought you'd never get here," Grace, Mary's friend, shouted as they piled into the bride's room. "I have everything set out that you might need in case of a dress or hair emergency." Ali asked Grace to be her personal attendant for the wedding. Since she surprised everyone by coming home unannounced, it was the perfect job for her so she would feel included. Growing up, Ali thought of Grace as another sister, so it meant the world to Ali that Grace could share in her special day, too.

"You're a lifesaver, Grace," Ali said, taking a seat in one of the chairs. "That wind today is no joke." She checked her hair in the mirror, only seeming to have one curl come loose. Grace sorted through the emergency kit she'd prepared and pulled out a few bobby pins, fixing Ali's stray curl in no time. "How much time do we have?" Ali asked.

Linda checked her watch and compared it to the schedule Ali had typed and taped to the wall inside each room. "According to your schedule, we have about fifteen minutes until you walk down the aisle," Linda told her. "Girls, we'll get you lined up in about ten so you are ready to go when the music starts."

Just like clockwork, exactly ten minutes later, the wedding party began gathering near the double doors. As the men lined up, Mary finally spotted Will. As she looked at him, to her, it was as though there was nobody else in the room. She'd already seen him in his tuxedo a few days earlier, but something was different this time. Something she couldn't quite put her finger on.

"Ms. Bradford," Will said, holding out his arm for her to take. "Are you ready for this?"

Mary nodded. She wasn't sure if he meant for her sister to get married, or the friendly date they'd made the night before. Either way, she was more than ready to get their date started.

Grace stood in the back, in charge of straightening Ali's train before she walked down the aisle. As the music began, the doors opened, and the three little ones began their journey down the aisle. It was much longer than the one they'd practiced on last night, but Ali had no doubt that Lily would keep the other two in line.

Katie and her husband walked next, followed by Cora and Brad. As Mary and Will approached the doors, waiting for the signal to begin, he gave her one last look, squeezing her hand with his. No words were exchanged, but she felt as though so much was said with that one gesture. She nodded at him as they began walking to altar.

As the wedding march began, those in attendance stood as Ali and her father appeared in the doorway ready to make their way down the aisle. Mary watched Zach, never seeing him so happy as he watched his soon-to-be bride walk toward him. Roger kissed Ali's cheek through her veil as he put her hand in Zach's. Both Roger and Ali blinked back their tears as she left her father's side and walked with Zach to the altar.

The wedding march ended, and the Pastor asked, "Who gives this woman to this man?"

"Her mother and I do," Roger replied. He then took a seat next to Linda and grabbed her hand. "Our daughter looks so beautiful," he whispered to her. At that moment, seeing all three of his beautiful daughters standing up there together, he couldn't be happier.

Linda began digging in her purse, trying to find the tissues she'd packed earlier. Roger reached into his pocket and handed over his handkerchief like the well-mannered gentleman he was. He always seemed to know what Linda needed, sometimes even before she knew herself. She squeezed his hand gently, dabbing her eyes and leaned her head down on his shoulder.

Chapter
Twenty-One

The ceremony was even more beautiful than Mary could have imagined. She couldn't take her eyes off of her sister. Zach's mother Carol and Ali's mother Linda were chosen for scripture readings, their voices poised and elegant. Ali and Zach chose to write their own vows, and there wasn't a dry eye in the house. When the ceremony was over, the wedding guests lined the stairs outside of the church, congratulating the bride and groom with tossing birdseed in the air.

The wedding party split up into two groups to ride over to the reception at the hotel. Pairing up, all of the couples rode together — all except Mary and Will. Neither of them was sure of exactly how exactly it happened, but they each ended up in a different limo. They all crowded into the seats as the volume inside the limos increased from all of the excitement.

Mary reached into her purse to text Will just as her phone began to vibrate — he beat her to it. She pulled her phone out and read his text. *"You looked beautiful up there. I hope you will save me a dance."* Heat rushed to her cheeks as she looked around to see if anyone else noticed, but they didn't. *"Of course!"* she replied. After pressing send, she realized she probably shouldn't have included the exclamation point, but at this point she had nothing to lose. She was all in, and she was going to enjoy herself tonight and see where the night took her. She hadn't heard from Alex in a few days, so she decided to give him a quick call. She tried calling him a few times while still in the limo, but it went straight to voicemail.

The wedding guests began piling into the hotel ballroom. The wedding party was instructed to wait inside the limos until further instructions were given by Ali or Zach — which, of course, meant that it would be Ali giving the instructions to Zach to pass along to the rest of them. Although he was the groom, his involvement was minimal. He didn't think Ali intentionally kept him in the dark during the planning process, but he wanted to be sure this day was perfect for her. If that meant she planned everything down to the last detail, even down to the number of forks placed next to each plate, then he'd allow her to do so.

Lily was beginning to bounce off the walls of the limo by the time they were given the okay to exit. She was so excited for the dance floor to open and had no problem letting each and every person in the limo know that fact numerous times. Lily and the others in the limo in which she rode exited first and gathered in the foyer of the hotel, followed by the second limo, as they coupled back up again for the DJ to announce their arrival.

The DJ announced each couple of the wedding party as they entered the ballroom, making their way to the head table located near the back of the dance floor. The crowd cheered and whistled as Zach and Ali made their entrance, hand in hand, gliding across the dance floor.

"I'm proud to announce, for the very first time, Mr. and Mrs. Zachary Reiter," the DJ shouted into the microphone.

They made their way to the head table and took their seats. The large group of people near the bar began taking their seats, too, as the waiters weaved around the tables placing dinner salads at every place setting. The round tables were covered in white linens, christened with bright crimson red poinsettia's as centerpieces. The chairs were draped in matching white slip covers with large crimson red bows tied to the back of each one. Quiet music was playing in the background for the dinner, calming the noise of the loud voices that was beginning to take over the room. Not even two bites into their salads, one of the guests began clanging their fork against their drink glass. Playing along, Zach and Ali stood and pleased the crowd with a kiss.

Mary kicked off her shoes under the table and wiggled

her toes, releasing the pinching feeling that began to build up. She tried to choose the most comfortable pair of dress shoes she could, but having worn bare feet around her house for so long, her feet were out of practice and a little swollen, too. Another waiter came along with a bottle of wine, offering a glass to everyone at the head table. Normally not a huge drinker, Mary opted in, assuring herself she would need a few drinks to survive the rest of the evening. If not to calm her nerves for the dance she'd promised to Will, it would surely be for all of those distant aunts and cousins who were sure to dig into her business and ask where her ring was. Fortunately, she'd gotten very good about biting her tongue these days.

The dinner was delivered immediately after the salad, keeping right on schedule with Ali's vision. Though Ali would never admit it, Mary caught her several times checking her watch to be sure time was being kept. Susie suggested hiring a wedding planner to keep up on all of that, but Ali insisted she would take care of it.

For Mary, it seemed that the wine was going down quickly, almost as though there was a hole in her glass. The waiters continued to circle the room, offering refills to anyone — including Mary — whose glass was half empty or more. She didn't have a rental car, so she decided to relax and not worry about how much she had to drink for the night. Having enough courage to face folks in the room *was* a concern, so the drinks would help her relax a bit. As the waiter filled up her glass again, she smiled and took a sip before he barely cleared the bottle from it. She tried to look down the table at Will, but he was facing away from her talking to Grant.

Ali leaned over at Mary and Susie. "I can't believe this actually happened," she said in disbelief. "All of the planning and stress was all worth it to see this room filled tonight with everyone we care about." The three sisters glanced around the room, smiling at everyone who came to join them tonight.

The kids were assigned to sit at Roger and Linda's table. Ali thought ahead and placed a small basket of activities on one of the empty chairs for them to do during dinner at their table. Molly and Lily seemed to be eating their meal, but from what she could tell, Jack had taken one bite of his dinner roll and lost interest.

When their speeches were finished, Zach and Ali stood from the table as the DJ came back on the microphone. "I would like you all to turn your attention to the dance floor as the new couple share their first dance as husband and wife," he announced.

Zach grabbed Ali's hand and led her to the dance floor near the brightly lit Christmas tree. The dance floor was lined with large pots of amaryllis, making a statement as they stood tall and graceful. The lights dimmed as a small spotlight found the newlyweds in the middle of the dance floor. The song they chose for their first dance was an instrumental version of Silent Night. It wasn't the traditional wedding song most would have suggested, but the two of them thought it was perfect. As they danced next to the Christmas tree, listening to that beautiful song, they stared into each other's eyes feeling as though there was no one else in the room.

They each chose a more traditional song for the mother and father dances. Roger looked so calm out there, enjoying every minute dancing with Ali. His face lit up as they talked softly to each other. Mary watched them with envy, wanting so badly to be able to share that moment with her father. She could see how happy he was for Ali, and Mary wanted him to feel that for her. She wanted to make him proud, but she was afraid she would never get the chance — not with Alex, anyway. She sighed as her mind switched over to him. She still hadn't heard from him and she was beginning to get concerned.

The parents' song ended and the wedding party was called onto the dance floor for a group dance. None of them were warned of this in advance, and the guests in the room could sense the hesitation from several of them. Playing it safe, Mary stopped by the kids' table on the way and grabbed them, using them as her dance partners instead of facing Will just yet. When they were all out there, the music began, a loud fun dance song that the kids took to right away.

The men stood near each other, shuffling their feet from side to side, completely embarrassed at being out there. Zach, on the other hand, had no fear and was having the time of his life on the dance floor. The rest of the wedding party took turns dancing with the kids, taking hold of their hands and twirling in circles. Mary's cheeks were aching from laughing so hard. Ali started a train, and being good sports, the men joined in taking up the end of the line and Will being the caboose.

Mary caught his eye for a short second as they weaved around the dance floor, making her stomach do flip flops. Technically, they were dancing together, but she still hoped for a much slower dance later in the night. When the song ended, the men raced to the bar, clearly uncomfortable for that kind of dancing so early in the night. The rest of the guests were welcomed onto the floor as the dance portion of the night began. Losing Will in the crowd when he made a b-line for the bar, Mary went back to the table and tried to call Alex again. Voicemail again.

She tossed her phone back into her purse, threw it on her chair, and decided enough was enough. She'd tried to contact him several times already, and she wasn't going to give him another thought. Not tonight. She was here with Will and her family, and she was determined to enjoy being with them. Doing a quick check of her teeth in the reflection of her butter knife, she made her way towards the bar where the rest of the wedding party had gathered.

She felt a light tap on her shoulder. As she turned around, there was Will, waiting with a fresh glass of wine in his hand for her. "So — were you privy to that information, or were you as surprised as the rest of us with that dance?" he joked.

Mary laughed. "No, I had no idea she was going to do that," she told him. "I'm not exactly the fast dance kind of person."

Will shook his head. "Me neither. Do you think I look

like one? It's probably a good thing she didn't tell us in advance, or I would have made myself scarce."

Mary looked around the room at all of the couples, still not quite feeling like they were one tonight. "If they ever slow this dance party down, I believe you still owe me a dance," she reminded him. "Unless the shuffling of feet you did out there earlier counted as our dance." She playfully hit him in the arm.

"What did I tell you about using the same arm every time?" he teased, rubbing his arm up and down. "And no, that most certainly wasn't our dance. I had something a little slower in mind."

She was thankful for the dimmed lights as her cheeks began to flush. She was hoping he'd say that.

"I wouldn't get too excited about it though. I've been told in the past that I have two left feet when I dance," he admitted. "I've always hated that analogy, but apparently I'm the poster child for it." He took a drink of his beer and turned to watch the crowd dancing around the center of the room. He scanned the dance floor, trying to find the perfect spot to share their first dance together.

In the far back corner, there was an empty spot where no one else was dancing, a shadow casting over it from the Christmas tree — the reflection of the colored twinkle lights dimly illuminating the floor.

"I'm sure you're a better dancer than you think." She wasn't sure she was much better, not being able to remember the last time she'd slow danced. It had to have been at her sister Susie's wedding, she thought, and it was with one of Grant's college buddies who was by far the most immature person at their wedding. At one point in the night, he danced circles around the room with his beer as his dance partner. He was barely of drinking age and it showed.

"I admire your optimism," he said with a laugh. "If we get a chance later on tonight, I brought something I wanted to show you the other day, but never got the chance." He patted his tuxedo pocket to be sure the letter was still inside.

"I'd love to see it, what ever it is. Sounds mysterious," she said, raising her eyebrows.

The song ended and all of the kids exited the dance floor as the next song began. Couples from around the room grabbed each other for the first slow dance of the night. Mary wiped her hands down the sides of her dress, trying to keep the clamminess at bay. The last thing she wanted was for him to take hold of her hand to bring her out on the dance floor and it is a nervous sweaty mess. Her heart began pounding so hard she could feel it in her ears as he turned toward her.

Will placed his beer glass down on a nearby table and put one hand behind his back, extending the other out to her. "May I have this dance?" he asked.

"It would be my pleasure," she said, linking her arm through his.

He led them back to the corner he spotted earlier, still vacant from other dancers. Butterflies filled her stomach as they joined their hands, his other resting on the small of her back. She placed her other hand gently on his shoulder, feeling his stiff muscles through his tuxedo coat. As they began moving around, swaying in sync with the music, she could feel his tight shoulders begin to loosen. After a few rounds, she was finally able to loosen her frame, becoming more relaxed as the song went on.

She leaned her head back slightly. "I think you are a great dancer. I also wanted to thank you for being my date tonight and saving poor lonely me from facing her sister's wedding alone." She looked at him briefly and then turned slightly away. "I'm sure there were many more noteworthy candidates lined up that you could have brought as your date, but I appreciate you putting up with me for the night." She leaned her head forward, resting her chin on his shoulder as they continued moving slowly around the dance floor.

Will cleared his throat. "I couldn't think of anyone else I would have rather taken as my date tonight," he said.

He stopped dancing and took a small step back, both of them standing there, face to face. Mary could feel the moment coming, that feeling right before someone was going to kiss you. Their eyes locked, and the music sounded so soft — like there was no other sound in the room, and everyone around them seemed to not exist in that moment. He began to lean in as she was ready to surrender to him. As her eyes slowly began to close, she was paused by a firm tap on her shoulder.

"Mind if I cut in?" a man's voice said.

Mary stiffened and spun around, her lips pressed

firmly together.
It was Alex.

Chapter
Twenty-Two

Mary woke the next morning in a fog, still replaying what happened the night before. One minute she was dancing with Will, something she'd waited a long time for, and the next Alex was cutting in. The look on Will's face kept flashing in her mind, and she couldn't forget it. He was probably more shocked than Mary was to see Alex there, but she's the one who had to do or say something. Thinking back on it now, the scene could have been handled so many other ways — better ways.

Alex has always had some form of control over Mary, and the sad part is she allowed that to happen. It was always as if her guilt got the best of her, and she felt she owed it to him to do what he said. She hadn't been completely truthful with him up until that point, but when he suddenly showed up like he did, she couldn't find the words to say in the moment. She should have told him off, lord knows there was enough liquid courage present, but she couldn't find it in herself to do it. Like a child that was in trouble, she just went with him and obeyed his orders.

Mary rubbed the sleep out of her eyes and sat upright, finding Alex still sound asleep next to her. She sat there for a long moment and watched him sleep. Part of her wanted to apologize for being with Will on the dance floor, arm in arm, and the other part of her wanted to push Alex off the bed. She decided to do neither. She swung her legs over the bed slowly, trying not to wake him. As her feet touched the floor, he began to stir, as if he knew she was trying to run away.

"Good morning, Mary. You sure looked surprised to see me last night," Alex said, leaning up on his side.

Mary pressed her lips together and nodded. "I'd say surprised is an understatement." She stood up and pulled on her robe, tying it around her waist. "What made you decide to show up last night? I thought you were too busy with clients all week."

"I was busy, but Brian took a few meetings for me, and I got another agent to take my clients out," he said, walking toward the bathroom. "I have to be back tomorrow though for a meeting about the new condos. Make sure your bags are all packed after breakfast so we won't be late to the airport. I have a quick meeting at my old office in town this morning with a past client, so I won't be around much."

Mary froze in her steps. So, there was more to him coming home than just being there for the wedding. Her flight home wasn't for another couple of days, and she had already made plans with her family. "I have my flight in a couple of days. I'm sure your flight is booked solid already, because of the holidays."

"I had my assistant book you a returning flight with me so you don't have to stay here longer. I'm sure you're ready to get back home with me," he shouted through the closed door.

It was probably a good thing he was in the other room and couldn't see her reaction. Her heart sunk at the thought of leaving early. As a matter of fact, it sunk at the thought of leaving period. She had so many decisions she had to make, and none of them were clear to her yet. The room started spinning at the thought of going back to that lonely place. She wasn't ready to leave and had no desire to discuss it further.

"I'm hungry, so I'll meet you downstairs when you're ready," Mary shouted through the door.

"The noise in the kitchen was already in full force. Since being home, she often wondered if her mother ever slept. It seemed like all she'd done since Mary returned is cook for the family and wash dishes. By this point, Mary would have thrown a package of paper plates on the counter, ordered carry-out, and called it a day. But not her mother. She was born to be a mother and was too nurturing to cheat by ordering take out. She loved nothing more than to cook for her family and be sure all of their needs were met far before her own.

"Good morning, Mary," Linda said. "There's fresh coffee brewed on the counter. I thought you might need a cup."

"Try a pot," Mary replied. "Is Ali here, yet?" Mary poured herself a cup and was pleasantly surprised to find the cream and sugar waiting for her. Her mother must be getting used to having her around again.

"Ali called and said she and Zach would be here in about ten minutes," Linda told her. "If you're hungry, there's a breakfast buffet in the dining room — eggs, toast, sausage, and bacon. If there is anything else you want, just let me know."

Mary peeked into the dining room at the spread. "That all sounds wonderful, but I think I'll wait until they arrive before eating."

Linda turned off the stove burner and carried another batch of scrambled eggs into the dining room. "Are you sure this is enough food for everyone?" Linda added. "Maybe I should whip up some pancakes or something."

"Mom, this is plenty of food," Mary said, knowing her mom was totally serious. "Besides, I'm probably going to stick with coffee for now. My appetite isn't very big this morning."

Linda turned around, pausing mid scoop. "Did everything go okay with Alex last night?" she asked. "I had no idea he was coming to the wedding."

Mary huffed. "That makes two of us. I don't think I've ever been more surprised in my life." She blew on her coffee and took a small sip. "And his timing couldn't have been much worse. Will and I were just about to —." Mary stopped in her tracks as Alex walked into the dining room.

"Good morning, everyone," Will said, trying to sound friendly and chipper. "I was hoping there would still be some coffee down here for me." He walked into the kitchen and helped himself to a cup.

"We'll be eating shortly once Ali and Zach arrive if you're hungry," Linda shouted from the dining room. Looking back to Mary, she continued, "I don't think you were finished with your story."

The doorbell rang, timed perfectly so she wouldn't have to continue with her story, fearing Alex would be eavesdropping. Mary ran to the door to open it for her sister. The volume increased immediately as the rest of the family rushed over, cheering for the newlyweds. Everyone except Alex.

Will paced around the center island of his kitchen. He'd never felt so many different emotions all at one time. Not even when Lauren dumped him last year. What was with everybody throwing curve balls at him from out of left field? Either he was completely naive, or he just had the worst luck when it came to women. He replayed their dance over and over again trying to figure out what happened. Mary told him that Alex wasn't coming home for the wedding, so what was he doing there? Will was too busy being caught like a deer in the headlights to even see her reaction. He wracked his brain, trying to remember if she was happy to see Alex or not. Was she as surprised as he was?

He turned on the coffee pot, needing as much as he could possibly consume. He tossed and turned all night, trying to figure out what would come next. Things with Mary seemed to be moving forward until the moment Alex showed up. It was like his life was frozen in that moment, and he didn't know how to proceed.

He picked up his phone to call her, but he didn't know if Alex was there with her, so he set it back down. Roger and Linda invited him over this morning for brunch, but now that Alex was in town, he wasn't sure if the invitation still stood. The last thing he wanted to do was make anyone uncomfortable, himself included.

He closed his eyes, thinking back to them dancing alone in the corner without a care in the world. He was finally going to have the moment he'd wanted with her since the moment she came home to Maple Falls. Then Alex happened. What made him decide to come home anyway? From the way she spoke of him, he treated her more like a roommate than a girlfriend. Will pressed his fingers against his temples, trying to lessen the pounding sensation going on.

After a large cup of coffee, he sat down in the chair in the living room, the same chair Mary had curled up in only a few nights earlier. He tried to figure out what his next move was, or if there was even a move to make.

When Lauren told him it was over, he just let her go without a fight. He never chased after her or fought for what he wanted at the time. He felt as though in the end, she wasn't really what he wanted. But Mary was different. His feelings for her were beyond anything he'd ever felt for Lauren. He wasn't going to make the same mistake again. He wasn't going to give up on Mary without a fight.

He stood from the chair and grabbed his keys. If she still had feelings for him, he had to find out now before it was too late. He reached for his cell phone on the counter and saw a missed text. It was from Lauren asking him to meet her for coffee. He took a deep breath and replied that he would meet her there. Mary would still be home for another couple of days, and he should probably take a little more time to act, not just react on his current emotions. He threw on his jacket and hopped in his truck to meet Lauren.

Ali and Zach started at the breakfast buffet, just as they had the night before at the wedding. They both looked so happy, yet completely exhausted at the same time. Mary sat down at the table with only a scoop of eggs and a half of a piece of toast. She pushed the eggs around on her plate, waiting to see where Alex was going to sit. She assumed he would sit next to her, but she was hoping someone else would beat him to it. No such luck.

When everyone had their food and was sitting down at

the table, Linda stood up. *Ting, ting, ting.* She tapped her glass gently with a spoon.

"I just wanted to take a moment to congratulate Ali and Zach again on the start of their new life together," Linda said. "We could not be any happier for you two and cannot wait to see what the future has in store for you. I'm so thankful our whole family was able to be together for the wedding and able to celebrate Christmas together. It meant the world to your father and me that you were all here with us. To the happy couple," she said, raising her glass in the air.

The rest of the table raised their glasses in a toast. Mary took a big gulp of her coffee, still trying to come out of the fog she was in. She looked over at Alex who hadn't lost his appetite at all over all of this.

Zach placed his napkin to the side and began to stand to say a few words, but was abruptly interrupted by Alex.

"Hello, everyone," Alex started, jumping to his feet. "I don't mean to cut you off, Zach, but I wanted to take a moment to congratulate the two of you and apologize for not being able to make it to the ceremony. I had a meeting yesterday that ran late, and I had to catch a later flight than planned. I'm thankful I was able to at least make it to part of the reception though. I'm glad I am able to have breakfast with you all and catch up a bit before Mary and I fly out this afternoon. So, congratulations to you both," he said, raising his glass in the air again.

It was like a bomb had been dropped in the middle of the dining room. The glares Mary was getting from her family were burning right through her. Not able to look them in the face, she glared over to Alex who obviously didn't get what he'd just done. Mary hadn't even agreed to go with him yet, and he just blurted out the news like it was no big deal.

Linda was the first to speak. "Well, is that so?" she said, trying to form more of a sentence, but failing with her words. She stared over at Mary who was still staring down at her plate.

"I can't believe you're leaving today!" Ali shouted across the table. The rest of table stared at her outburst. "I'm sorry, but she wasn't supposed to leave for a couple more days."

Mary knew Ali was right and felt terrible about the whole thing. She didn't want to go back with him, but what was the point in putting off the inevitable for two more days. She lived clear across the country now, and whether she left today or two days from now, she had to go back.

"I know you all may be surprised by her leaving," Alex said, "but I need her back home with me. I was generous enough to share her with you for the past week and a half, and I think that was plenty fair."

Mary squeezed her eyes shut, hoping to disappear from the table. She couldn't believe the words that were coming out of his mouth. What did he need her for anyway? He had his assistant to do everything for him, including booking Mary a flight back there early. The nerve of her — and him for that matter. He didn't even have the decency to ask her first. That was probably the part that bothered her the most.

"So that's it?" Ali said in disbelief. "You're just going to do what he says and leave with him this afternoon?" She stared at Mary hard, wanting her to feel every ounce of anger that was running through her.

Mary couldn't bring herself to say the words, but simply nodded. She knew how much she was disappointing her entire family, but didn't know how to change it. Things had gotten so messed up over the past week, and it felt like her life was spinning out of control.

Alex dropped his fork down on his empty plate, making a loud noise. "Thank you for the wonderful breakfast, Linda, but I'm afraid I have to get ready for a meeting at the real estate office this morning." He looked over at Mary who was still completely mortified, not saying a word. "I'll need a ride over, so would you mind taking me?"

Mary looked over at Linda and asked sheepishly, "Can I borrow your car for a little bit to take him?"

Linda nodded.

Mary and Alex excused themselves from the table and went upstairs to get ready while the rest of the family whispered behind them as they left the room. She could only imagine what they were saying about her. This wasn't the way her trip home was supposed to end. If she could have had things her way, it wouldn't end at all. She would tell him to go back alone, and she'd send for her things later, but she couldn't get the words out for some reason.

Something was holding her back. She didn't even feel like herself anymore, at least not when he was around her. For the past couple of weeks, she'd felt more like herself than she had in years. Why was she letting Alex control her the way he was? She used to be so driven and independent, and it feels as though he took that from her.

She walked into the bathroom and closed and locked the door. Leaning her hands on the sink, she stared at herself in the mirror. *"Where did you go?"* she whispered to herself. She didn't even know the person staring back at her. The person in the mirror was broken. She thought she had finally begun to find herself again, but the second Alex showed up, that restored feeling of confidence and drive faded quickly.

Knock, knock, knock. "Mary, are you almost finished? My meeting starts in fifteen minutes, and I can't be late. We should probably get going," Alex shouted through the door.

Where had she heard that before? The last time she was with him started the exact same way — him rushing her out the door to get to something that was only important to him.

"Okay," she said in a meek voice. "I'll be right out."

Ten minutes later, she dropped him off outside of the real estate office in town. He hadn't done much business there since they moved, but every once in a while, a client would request his services if he was available. He slammed the car door and rushed inside without even a good-bye or a thank you to her for driving him. She pulled away from the curb and drove aimlessly down Main Street, unsure of where to go next. Her family didn't seem very happy with her, so she was in no hurry to get back there.

As she approached the next block, she spotted Will's truck parked on the street in front of the restaurant. She knew she needed to talk to him before she left, but didn't know what she was going to say. How was she going to explain to him that she was not only going back home, but leaving in a few hours? She pulled into the parking lot to find a spot. A car was backing out near the entrance, so she turned on her signal and waited. The person was taking forever to back out, and Mary was getting impatient, losing her nerve to go inside with every passing second. She turned to the side and looked through the windows on the side of the restaurant.

There he was.

Will was sitting in a booth right next to the window. Mary leaned forward to see if he was dining alone or if there was someone on the other side. She could see his lips moving, so she figured he had to be talking to somebody. When the car finally pulled out of the parking spot, she pulled her car up a few inches for a better view. She recognized the profile right away. He was with Lauren. Mary quickly ducked in her seat as they stood from their booth and pulled through the parking lot to the other side before he could spot her. Turning the corner, she circled the block and came back around the front just as they were coming out the door. No one was behind her so she stopped the car and watched them, unable to take her eyes off him, even if she wanted to.

They stood near the front door for a few seconds and talked. As Mary was getting ready to pull away, she saw him lean into her and hug her, kissing her gently on the cheek. A knot formed in the pit of her stomach. She gripped the steering wheel hard making her knuckles turn white. Had he already moved on from Mary? Had Alex scared him away? Maybe it was best that she was leaving in a few hours. If he really wanted to see her, he would have come by for breakfast, but he didn't. Instead, he made a breakfast date with Lauren. In all fairness, Lauren still lived in Maple Falls, and Mary didn't.

Mary sunk down in her seat and drove past the restaurant without them noticing her and made her way back to her parents' house to pack her things. Alex was sure to call as soon as his meeting was over and want her to be ready to go. *This is for the best,* she said to herself. *I don't live here anymore.* She watched him as long as she could in the rearview mirror. She thought about sending him a text, telling him that she was leaving, but she didn't. At this point it would be best if she just left — so she did.

Chapter Twenty-Three

After Will left the restaurant, he felt a little more at ease. Oddly enough, seeing Lauren was exactly what he needed, and he was sure that she felt the same way in a sense. He decided to wait until later to go see Mary. Having Alex answer the door when he showed up didn't sound too appealing to him.

He drove back to his house and made the walk back to his wood shop. It was the one place in the world where he felt completely like himself, and no one could judge him. It was a place that he could let his creativity take over and not allow his mind to over think things. Right now, that is exactly what he needed. A mindless act to keep himself from falling apart.

He turned on the lights and walked to the heater. It

wasn't as cold in there as it was the other night, but it would help to take the chill out of the air. He made several laps around the room, hoping something would get his creative juices flowing. When he was anxious about anything, working with his hands seemed to help. Looking around at what he'd already made, he decided he wanted to make something special for Mary. Something to show her how he felt — but what? What if all of his work was wasted if she were to deny his gift? What if Alex wouldn't allow her to take it?

He pushed those thoughts aside and pulled open his tool chest. Resting next to it were the business plans he drew up a while back. He had shown them to Mary when she was there to get her opinion. The support for his business plan that she gave him in just that quick review was more than he'd ever gotten from anyone else.

He picked the plan up in his hands and paged through it, hoping to finally be able to make a decision. He was given a deadline that was looming, and he wasn't sure what the right decision was. Had Alex not shown up at the wedding, he was planning to show Mary the letter he'd gotten and had been carrying around with him. Will was sure she would have been able to help him make a decision.

He pulled out his chisel and a few smaller saws and set them down on his workbench. Pulling out one of his woodworking books, he paged through it to find an idea of what to make for her. His mind was blank. All he could think about was going over to see her and tell her how he felt. He wanted to tell her that she was making a mistake if she went back with Alex. The thought of losing her was beginning to consume him. His hands were trembling, and his breath was catching in his throat. What was he going to do?

He turned around, and there it was. The answer was sitting right in front of him. It was a risk, but no risk gets you no reward. Will ran out the door, raced to the driveway and climbed in his truck. It was now or never. He'd already known what *never* felt like, and this time around, that wasn't an option.

Linda paced around the house in a flurry, not wanting to believe what had just happened. Mary wasn't supposed to leave so soon, and it was tearing her up inside. When Linda was frustrated, she took it out on house work. Making her way upstairs, she tore the sheets off of Mary's bed to wash them, wadding them up into an angry ball and throwing them on the floor. Roger peeked his head into the room.

"Is everything okay in here?" he asked, watching her spin the fitted sheet around her arms.

"Why did he have to come back here anyway?" Linda blurted out. "We finally had our daughter back, and he had to swoop in here and take her away from us again." She ripped the pillowcases off the pillows and tossed them over by the sheets. "Am I the only one who is angry about this?" She squeezed the pillow against her chest.

"I think Ali shared similar feelings at breakfast," Roger said. He stayed back in the doorway, not wanting to end up like the sheets.

Linda huffed. "Aren't you upset about her leaving early?" She glared at him, trying to get him to see her side. "You know, I don't even think she loves him. She never straight out told me, but I think she was beginning to have feelings for someone else." She waved her finger through the air.

Roger stood there nodding, letting her get it all out. He learned over the many years of marriage, that sometimes it's better to nod and stay silent.

"He could have gone back home by himself," she continued. "Why did he need her to go back with him?" She began pacing the bedroom. "And did you hear what he said at breakfast? That he had *let* us have her long enough? Doesn't that sound odd to you?"

She didn't give him the chance to answer before continuing on her rant.

"And did you see how different she started acting once he showed up? It was like she was a completely different person."

Linda gathered the pile of bedding from the floor and carried it down the hall to the laundry room. He moved aside to let her out of the room and followed quietly behind her.

"I just don't understand any of it." She poured the soap into the washing machine and tossed the sheets in, pushing them down with her hands. She slammed the lid down and started the wash cycle. "Aren't you going to say anything?" She spun around to look at him as the doorbell rang downstairs.

Roger pointed towards the stairs. "Did you want me to get that?"

"That wasn't the answer I had in mind," she said, stomping to the stairway.

The bell rang again before Linda got to the door. She unlocked it and pulled it open as Roger caught up to her, waiting beside the door.

"Will," she said. "What are you doing here?"

"Hello," he said shyly. He cleared his throat that was suddenly as dry as the desert. "I was hoping to speak to Mary for a few minutes. If she's busy, I can just come back later." He tried to peer around Linda into the house, but he couldn't see anybody.

"Please, come inside." Linda motioned him in. "What do you have there?"

"Oh, this? It's just a gift I wanted to give to Mary. Would you mind if I bring it inside?"

"Please," she moved aside and held the door open for him. "You can put it here in the living room if you'd like."

Will picked up the gift for Mary and carried it inside. "I know it's an unusual gift, but there is a story behind it." He slipped his boots off and sat down on the couch. "Is Mary upstairs?"

Roger and Linda exchanged a look and sat down across from him.

"Well," Linda started, "she actually isn't home." She could see the confusion in his eyes and felt terrible having to be the one to tell him. "Have you talked to her at all today?"

Will shook his head. "No, not since the wedding last night."

Linda took a deep breath before continuing. "Mary flew back home with Alex this afternoon. He had to be back for a meeting in the morning, and he booked her a flight back with him early."

Will sat frozen, nodding slowly while he tried to process what Linda was saying. Once again, he was too late. He let her get away again. "Oh — I see." He didn't know what else to say. He felt like he was going to be sick. How could she leave without telling him? From what she had said to him before, she really didn't want to go back there.

Linda reached out and placed her hand on his. "I'm so sorry she didn't tell you she was leaving. We had no idea either until Alex sprung it on all of us at breakfast." She knew saying that probably wouldn't make things better, but she didn't want him to think they were all hiding it from him. The way Linda had seen Will and Mary interact in the last several days led her to believe that some pretty strong feelings were developing between them.

Will stood from the couch. "I'm sorry to have bothered you both. I'd better get going." He wanted nothing more than to run from there as quickly as possible.

"You're no bother, Will," Linda responded. "You know

you are welcome by here any time you want." She walked him to the door. "What would you like to do with this gift you brought for her?"

Will turned around and looked at the gift he brought. The one thing in his work shop she fell in love with. The one thing he was so excited to give to her — to see the look on her face when she saw it again. He shook his head and threw his hands up in the air.

"I guess I will leave it here for her," he said, sounding frustrated. "If she ever comes back to visit, you can tell her I left it here for her." He placed his hand on the door handle.

"Wait," Linda said. "Are you sure you want to do that?"

What he wanted was for her to be here and for them to be together. "If it's not a bother, that is what I'd like to do. Perhaps in the meantime, you can enjoy it until she visits again."

Will opened the door and showed himself out. Linda stood by the window, holding her hands against her chest and watched him back out of the driveway.

She turned to Roger. "I knew it."

Roger wrinkled his eyebrows. "You knew what?"

Linda walked back into the living room. "I knew he loved her," she said. She ran her hand along the top of the rocking chair Will brought. "Will is in love with Mary."

Alex marched through the airport pulling his carry-on behind him. Mary stayed behind him, not wanting to get in his way as he raced to the gate. She had half of mind to stop walking and see how long it took him to notice she wasn't behind him, but all that would get her was an angry seat partner for the long flight home. Mary could hear his phone begin to ring as he pulled it out of his pocket, not slowing down one bit. She slowed her pace even more, not wanting to hear him babble to whoever was on the other end of his call.

"Mary!" someone shouted from behind her. "Wait up!"

Mary stopped and turned around to find Grace running towards her. "What are you doing here?"

"I fly home today," Grace said. "I think the better question is what are *you* doing here? I thought your flight wasn't for a couple more days."

Mary turned and pointed to Alex, who was so far ahead of her that she had to squint to see him. "That was the plan, but he had another one apparently," she said, rolling her eyes. "It's a good thing I'm not a small child traveling with him, or I'd be completely lost."

Grace laughed, trying to lighten the mood. "I'm sorry. I tried to call you this morning so I could see you before I had to leave, but I just got your voicemail."

Mary sighed. "I'm not myself today. I don't even remember seeing a missed call from you. I've been avoiding my phone all day."

Mary and Grace walked together toward their gates, only three apart from each other. If it weren't for Grace,

Mary probably would have walked the other way. She filled Grace in on the walk about how her night had gone after the wedding and the bomb Alex dropped on her and her family that morning. She tried to play it off that she was alright with it all, but Grace knew better. They had only seen each other a few times over the past three years or so, but Grace could still read her like an open book. There was nothing Mary could get by her, and if she tried, she'd call her on it immediately.

Mary approached her gate to find Alex checking in at the desk with the airport employee. She stood back in the aisle, not wanting to leave Grace just yet and be stuck with him alone any longer than she had to.

"Alex seems like he'd be one of those annoying travelers. You know, the people you see in first class with a hot towel and a martini."

Mary laughed. "I can see him being that way," she agreed, "but honestly, I haven't traveled with him since we moved away. As a matter of fact, I think we were on different flights then, too." She hadn't realized it until now that they'd always taken separate trips.

"Is he flying first class?" Grace watched him as he pointed his finger at the employee as he spoke.

Mary shrugged. "I have no idea. As far as I know, we're in coach, but I suppose I could be wrong."

Alex finally turned around to see where Mary was and waved her over.

"Do you want me to wait here for you?" Grace offered. "My flight doesn't take off for two more hours."

"That's alright, we'll be boarding shortly, so I better get checked in." Mary put her hand in the air to let him know she was coming. She hated nothing more than to be rushed — something he seemed to be an expert in.

"I'm so glad you came home for Christmas. I don't know that I would have survived all of my trip home without you," Mary said, hugging her.

"I wish we could have spent more time together, but maybe I can fly out to see you soon. I'd love to see yours and Alex's new place." Grace held her hug for a few moments longer, not wanting to let go of her friend. "Call me anytime if you need to talk. You know that I would always be available for you — remember, it's earlier where I live."

They gave each other one more hug before Alex started walking toward them. Grace tiptoed away quickly, not wanting to speak to him.

"I've been trying to get your attention, Mary. I have to check us in, and they need you up there. Apparently, I can pay for your ticket, but I can't check you in." He walked back to the desk before she had a chance to answer him.

She wheeled her luggage to the check-in desk and stood behind Alex, waiting for further instructions.

"This is Mary Bradford," Alex said in a matter-of-fact manner. "Can you check us both in now?" Mary noticed that Alex was short with the woman, much like he is with most people he came in contact with.

"I'll just need to see your ID, miss," the woman said.

Mary smiled at the woman as she pulled her driver's

license out of her wallet, giving the woman a sympathetic look in an attempt to silently apologize for his rude behavior. The woman looked over at Alex, then back to Mary, returning an even more sympathetic look to her, knowing at least in the next hour, she would never have to see him again, unlike Mary.

"It looks like you requested two first-class seats on your flight today, but we only have one left." She looked at them back and forth, bracing herself for his reaction.

Mary opened her mouth to talk, but once again, he beat her to it.

"Well that's simple enough. I'll take the seat in first-class, and Ms. Bradford here can have the seat in coach." Alex didn't even flinch before answering for the both of them.

Too tired to argue about it, Mary half smiled and nodded. The woman handed her back her driver's license and turned around to find an empty seat. Lucky for Mary, there weren't two open seats next to each other. She sat next to an elderly couple reading the newspaper, while Alex — talking on his cell phone — took a seat next to another businessman. Mary pulled her cell phone out to text Grace and tell her what happened, and had to laugh at the situation. At this point in her day, if she didn't start laughing some of it off, she was sure to burst out in tears.

The woman started announcing boarding instructions over the loudspeaker, telling the first-class passengers that they could prepare to board first. Mary looked over at Alex who was scratching down notes on a legal pad he'd pulled out of his briefcase while he balanced his phone between his chin and shoulder. All of the other passengers in first-class boarded before he realized his section was called. Only when the woman began announcing the rest of the seats on the plane did he finally get up. Mary waited for him to come over to her before boarding, even though she wasn't sure there was a point, but he didn't. Not even a nod or a wave before he disappeared down the jet way.

When Mary's row was called, she walked to the back of the line and waited to board. As she stepped onto the plane, the first-class curtain had already been closed. One of the flight attendants was picking hot towels out of the warmer with a pair of tongs for the first-class passengers. She had no doubt that Alex was the one who requested some. Mary peered in as the flight attendant pulled the curtain back. Sure enough, she saw Alex's hand reach for a towel off her tray.

Mary found her seat and pulled out her cell phone before they were instructed to turn off their devices. She sent a quick text to Grace, confirming what she already knew, that Alex was a high maintenance traveler. Mary placed her neck pillow behind her head and closed her eyes, trying to relax before she was brought back to the life she had no desire to return to.

Chapter
Twenty-Four

Mary and Alex had been home for a full day, and life was already back to normal — or at least to the old normal she was used to before she went to Maple Falls. Alex was at work by six o'clock in the morning, leaving her to sit at home by herself again, hoping someone from one of the many job applications would call. Since it was still between the holidays, she knew the chances of that happening were slim. Today was New Year's Eve, and nobody would be at work — unless of course you were Alex Dawson.

She poured a cup of coffee and curled up on the couch, staring out the balcony window. She was supposed to still be home with her family today, planning to ring in the new year with them. They had planned a big party at her parents' house with drinks, dancing, and as many board games as they could tolerate. Instead, she was stuck home in her lonely apartment. She thought about asking Will to join them for the New Year's Eve party, too. Mary imagined how the night would have played out and what would have happened at midnight when the proverbial ball dropped. The thought brought a smile to her face — the first one she's had since arriving back at their apartment.

Mary was certain Will would have contacted her by now, but he hadn't. She checked her phone every couple of hours to see if she missed a call from him, but it never came. Maybe what she saw in that restaurant window was real. She went back to Alex, so he went back to Lauren. She knew the phone worked both ways, but now that she was halfway across the country, it seemed pointless to try. It didn't make sense for her to come between Lauren and Will again.

While staring at her phone, praying it would ring, it finally did and nearly made her leap off the couch.

"Hello?" she answered quickly, not even looking at who was calling first.

"Wow, that was fast. The phone didn't even ring on my end." Mary dropped her shoulders hearing Susie's voice on the other end. "You sounded a little anxious — is everything okay?"

Mary drew in a deep breath, trying to slow her rapid heart rate, and not sound too disappointed that it wasn't Will on the other end.

"Yes, I'm fine," Mary responded. "It was quiet in my apartment, and the ringing made me jump. What are you up to today?" Mary tried to sound nonchalant so her sister wouldn't ask any more questions.

"I was calling to check in with you since no one has heard from you since you left here so abruptly." Susie was using her mom voice with Mary. "What was that all about anyway? You're going to miss all the fun we have planned for tonight."

Mary's stomach ached at the thought of all she would miss. It seemed like all she did was miss fun things with her family since she left. "I guess I'll just have to play some board games by myself tonight," she joked.

"We had a slight change of plans," Susie told her. "Ali and Zach thought it would be fun to get all dressed up and go out on the town for New Year's this year. Mom and Dad didn't want to go and said they'd keep the kids. I think Lily is even sleeping over."

Mary was silent on the other end, trying to hide the insane jealousy she was feeling. That would have been the perfect redo for her and Will. What did it matter anyway? He was probably planning an unforgettable evening with Lauren, and she would be just as lonely tonight there as she was here.

"Hello? Mary, are you still there?"

Mary shook the thought out of her head. "Yes, sorry, I'm here. Listen, can I call you later? I need to run some errands, and Alex just walked in the door." She forced a smile in his direction, holding her finger up in the air.

"I guess so," Susie replied. "If I don't hear from you before we go out tonight, I'll call you from the limo so you can say hello to everyone."

"Yep, sounds good," Mary said and hung up the phone.

Alex opened the refrigerator and snapped open a can of soda. "Who was that on the phone?"

"It was Susie," Mary answered. "What are you doing home so early? I didn't expect to see you for another ten hours or so." She didn't hide her sarcasm in her statement. She pulled up a barstool and placed her cell phone on the counter, giving her a clear shot in case it rang again.

"I stopped home quick to tell you that you need to go out and buy a fancy dress for our New Year's Eve party tonight. Brian decided at the last minute to throw one over at Sunset's in the roof top ballroom, and you need to make sure you look nice." He took a sip out of the can and set it on the counter, waving his hands in the air. "Hello? Are you even listening to me? You get to dress up in a fancy dress and go to a party in a limo tonight, and you act like you aren't even interested in going."

Mary mentally skimmed her closet. "I think I already have a dress I can wear. I bought one back when you were supposed to take me to another fancy party with Brian, but it turned into a guy's night, and I never got to wear it, remember?" She looked down at her phone again.

"I guess that'll work," Alex said. "I have to run back to work for a few more hours, but I'll be back around five o'clock to change my clothes and pick you up. Do you think that will be enough time for you to look presentable?" He stood next to her, looking her up and down.

Apparently sweat pants and a slouchy over-sized T-shirt wasn't what he had in mind. She shook off his snide comment. "I believe I can be ready by five," she snapped back. "But, you have to promise me one thing first, otherwise I'm not going."

He cocked his head to the side and let out a loud sigh.

"You have to promise you won't ditch me tonight and hang out with your colleagues and leave me sitting alone at the table."

Alex threw his hands up in the air. "Here we go," he shouted. "I never ditch you when I take you places. It's not my fault that you lack social skills and choose not to talk to anybody when we're out together. It's a night out of the house, and I thought maybe you'd be a little more excited about it." He grabbed his soda can off the counter and started for the door.

"I'll be ready by five o'clock, and I'll set out a clean suit for you on the bed to change into when you get here." Mary felt almost robotic in her reply.

Alex slammed the door as Mary sat there, listening as the sound of his footsteps faded down the hall.

At exactly five o'clock, Alex marched through the front door. Mary was in the bathroom putting her earrings in that he gave her for Christmas last year. She stepped back and took one more look at herself in the mirror before going to find Alex.

"I hope you're ready to go," he yelled through the door as he walked into the bedroom.

Apparently, there was no need to go find him, he'd already found her. She took a deep breath and opened the bathroom door, bracing herself for criticism before she walked into the bedroom. Alex had more opinions on wardrobe than Mary ever heard in her life. He took twice as long to get ready and changed his outfit more times than she could count.

"I picked your black suit with a white shirt and red tie," she said, pointing to the bed. She bit her lower lip, waiting for his reply.

He walked toward the bed and paused, looking over every detail of the outfit that Mary chose. "Looks great," he said. "I should be ready in ten minutes."

Mary jerked her head back, her eyes wide. "Wow, I don't think you've ever before approved an outfit on the first try that I've chosen."

She didn't wait for a reply before she walked down the hall to the living room. Looking out the balcony door, the sun had already set and several of the balconies across the street were beginning to illuminate with twinkle lights. It made her think of all of the lights on the houses back in Maple Falls. She couldn't help but wonder what Will was up to tonight. Mary glanced up at the moon, hoping even for a second, that he may be looking at it too. Her family would be together shortly, but she wouldn't be there. Instead, she'd be starting another new year with nothing to show for the past one. Nothing had really changed in her life, and she didn't expect much change for this coming year either.

Alex came rushing down the hallway, fastening his cuff links along the way. "Are you sure this tie isn't too red?" he asked.

"It's the holidays, Alex," Mary said in a sarcastic manner. "I don't think there is such a thing as too red at Christmas."

He checked his reflection one more time in the mirror hanging on the wall by the front door. "But Christmas is over," he chimed back. "This tie needs to say Happy New Year, not Merry Christmas." He pulled on the knot and loosened it from his neck. "I'm going to see what other options I have."

Mary just nodded, knowing it was too good to be true that she succeeded on the first try with his clothes. The buzzer rang on the wall.

"Who is there?" Mary answered in the intercom.

"Your limo is ready downstairs, Miss," the driver replied.

"Thank you, we'll be right down." She shouted to Alex that it was time to go and that she didn't want to keep the driver waiting. For once, she was able to rush him out the door, and though she'd never admit it, she took a little pleasure in doing so.

The limo was parked right outside the front door with

the driver waiting alongside. "Good evening, sir," he said to Alex. The driver pulled open the door and helped Mary inside.

Having been in a limo crammed with half of a wedding party and impatient little girls, the inside of this one felt so lonely. It was cold and dark inside, much like the rest of her life. The driver climbed back into the front seat and leaned over to the partition.

"There is champagne chilling on the side table; please help yourself," he said. "We should arrive at your destination in about fifteen minutes."

He rolled the partition back up, giving them some privacy. Mary reached for a glass and filled it to the top, assuming she would need every drop of it to get her through the night. She offered a glass to Alex, but he waved his hand in the air. *More for me,* she thought.

The traffic was heavy this time of night, even more so on a holiday. There was more fancy dresses and tuxedos walking down the street than she'd ever seen in town. Everyone was out tonight, and she was thankful she didn't have to worry about driving around herself.

When they pulled up in front of Sunset's, the sidewalk was filled with men in tuxedos and women in shimmery dresses. Mary felt like they may be a bit under dressed, but even still, it was a major step up from her jeans and sweatshirt. She adjusted the cardigan she wore over her dress and waited for the driver to open the door. He was very polite, but he was no Otis. When the door opened, Alex climbed over her to step out first. The chauffeur offered his hand to help Mary out of the limo.

"Have a wonderful evening Mr. and Mrs. Dawson," he said, closing the back door.

Mary sighed at the comment, just not in the mood to correct him. By the time she crossed the sidewalk, Alex was already halfway through the front door. He stopped periodically to shake hands with several people, but as for waiting for her, it was the furthest thing on his mind. She clenched her toes in the tips of her heels and did a quick jog to try to catch up with him. She squeezed through the door behind another couple, hoping to catch him before he made it to the elevator.

The lobby was trimmed in dark wood and dimly lit chandeliers. In the corner of the room stood a large Christmas tree, trimmed in white lights, that stood nearly two stories tall. She followed along in the crowded group to the elevator, still trying to weave her way forward to Alex. She saw the top of his head walk on to one of the elevators to her left. She pushed through the crowd and stepped inside just before the metal doors closed. She was stuck between two larger men who smelled of stale smoke and whiskey. Apparently, she wasn't the only one who needed a drink on the way.

When the doors slid open, she nearly fell forward from the force of everyone pushing to get out. The ballroom was decorated beautifully with white linens on the tables stretching from wall to wall. Near the middle of the room was a shiny wooden dance floor. Her stomach sunk looking at it, thinking back to when she danced with Will a few nights ago. The room was so similar to Ali's wedding with poinsettias as centerpieces and another beautifully lit tree near the side of the dance floor.

"I'm going to get a drink," Alex said, finally noticing her. "Would you like anything?"

"I'd love a glass of chardonnay, please," she said. "I think I'll just walk with you so I don't lose you in this crowd again."

Alex led the way through the ballroom to one of the bars along the wall. A group of agents from his office were gathered near the bar.

"It's about time you showed up," Brian said to him, shaking his hand. He looked over to Mary. "Oh, you came, too?"

He looked surprised to see Mary there with him. Maybe Alex hadn't told him she came back early.

"I couldn't miss out on a fancy party like this," Mary responded, trying to sound authentic. "Thank you so much for inviting me." She stood awkwardly by, waiting for Alex to return with her wine. "Is your wife here?" she said, trying to add to the conversation.

Brian leaned back and looked around the room. "I think she's sitting over at the table," he said, pointing to the other side of the room. "We are sitting at table number three if you want to go find her. I think that's where all of the women are gathering."

Mary looked over at a few of them sitting there, knowing her chances of enjoying herself and fitting in were probably better off with them than staying with the men. None of them seemed too thrilled by her presence.

Massive chandeliers hung between the layers of tulle draped across the ceiling. As the live band played in the corner, a few couples had already found the dance floor. Mary weaved through the tables, careful not to bump into the white-gloved waiters carrying trays of appetizers around the room.

As Mary approached the table, Julie, Brian's wife, stood up to greet her, air-kissing her on both sides so as to not mess up her bright red lipstick. "I'm so glad you came," she said, taking a step back to give her a once over. "Alex said you were out of town and wasn't sure if you'd make it tonight."

"Thank you, I wasn't sure either," Mary responded, "but it worked out." She didn't feel like elaborating on the subject any further. "Would you mind if I join you? The men are all by the bar, and I got the feeling that I wasn't welcomed with them." She took a sip of her wine.

"Not at all, please join us," Julie said, motioning her to a chair. "Come, have a seat."

Mary pulled up a chair next to Julie, not recognizing the other woman that Julie was sitting with. She placed her clutch on the table and took another sip of wine.

"Mary, I'm sure you've met Trish already," Julie said.

Mary's heart stopped. She had never met Trish before now, but had heard her voice in the background of several phone calls with Alex. Her body felt numb as she tried to keep her composure. Mary straightened up in her chair, sitting tall as she put up a wall.

"I can honestly say I don't think we've met," Mary said.

Trish sat there staring at Mary as though she had three eyes. She could tell Trish was just as uncomfortable as Mary was sitting at the table.

"Oh, that's odd," Julie said. "I guess Alex must have hired her around the time you went out of town."

Mary nodded slowly, keeping her eye on Trish. "It's nice to finally put a face with the name." She was purposely cold and not interested in getting to know her any further.

Trish continued to watch her. "You look nothing like the photos I've seen of you."

Mary wasn't sure how to take that statement. As far as she knew, Alex wasn't the type to hang photos of anyone in his office. "I didn't think Alex had any photos of me hanging up in his office."

Trish laughed. "Oh, trust me, he doesn't."

Mary looked puzzled. "Then how would you know what I look like?"

Trish thought for a moment before answering. "Alex and I were on our way to a meeting a few days ago, and he spilled coffee down the front of his shirt," she explained. "He didn't want to show up with a huge stain on his shirt, so we made a detour to his apartment so he could change. While he was doing that, I was admiring the photos he had up on the mantel."

Mary mentally scanned the mantel, trying to remember what photos she had put up there. There weren't very many recent photos of them together, so she was certain they must be severely outdated.

"It was so nice of him to invite you up and not make you wait down in the car for him to change." Mary wrinkled her nose, annoyed at the fact that she'd been in their apartment while she was away.

Julie shot Mary a look, but said nothing. Instead, she shifted in her chair, thankful to be sitting between the two women, placing them just out of reach of each other. The men eventually joined them at the table and could sense the tension between them. The look on Alex's face was priceless as he looked from Trish to Mary. He loosened his tie a bit as he sat down next to Mary. She waited to see if he would introduce them, being that he never had, but he didn't even acknowledge Trish's presence. He kept his body slightly turned away from her, keeping his conversation going with Brian.

The waiters came by with salads and placed bottles of red and white wine on the table. Brian and Alex continued to discuss the plans for the condo development as the women quietly ate their salads. Mary talked a little to Julie, chiming in on the condo talk, but Trish never said a word. Mary wasn't sure what made the situation more uncomfortable — the fact that Trish was there, or the fact that Alex completely ignored her.

Chapter
Twenty-Five

The dinner dishes were being cleared from the table by the wait staff as the men went out on the terrace for an after-dinner cigar. The conversation for the men consisted of mostly real estate talk, the current market, and plans for the business in the next calendar year. Nothing that interested Mary in the slightest, so she was glad to see the men leave. She then excused herself from the table, feeling the daggers from Trish on her as she walked to the restroom. She pushed through the door and plopped onto one of the leather couches placed in a sitting area.

Reaching in her purse, she thought about calling home to see how her sisters' night was going, and noticed a missed call. It was from Will. Her heart felt like it was going to beat right out of her chest. She checked her voicemail, but he hadn't left one. Why would he have called and not left a message? Maybe he dialed her by accident and hung up immediately once he noticed his mistake.

As she was toying with the idea of calling him back, her phone started to ring, showing up as an incoming call.

"Hello? Will, is that you?"

"Will? No, its Ali," her sister said. "Why would you think I was Will?" she asked. "I thought you were out with Alex?"

Mary let out a sigh, slumping back on the couch. "Sorry, I missed a call from Will, and your number didn't show up when you called." She smiled as three women walked by and left the bathroom. "I am technically out with Alex, I guess. I haven't seen him much tonight, but he is in the same building that I am. Are you guys still out?" Mary tried to change the subject off of Alex as quickly as she could.

"Yes, we're all here, and we miss you so much. We decided to just hang out down at the bar until the New Year's ball drops. The fancy party fell through, but we all still dressed up. I'll send you a photo."

Mary could hardly hear Ali with the crowd noise in the background from the bar that they were at. She was happy to hear she was missed, considering they were furious with her leaving just a couple days ago. Trish pushed through the door and walked right by Mary as though she weren't even sitting there. Her text sound beeped as she removed the phone from her ear to check it. There they all were, all but her. The photo had everyone in it, minus her parents, everyone she cared about back home. Susie, Ali, Cora, Katie, and all of the special men in their lives. Mary's heart ached for home.

"Did you get the photo?" Ali shouted over the crowd.

"I did," Mary said, choking back tears. Oh, how she wished she was in that photo. "I miss you all so much. I wish I was there with you." The background noise seemed to be getting louder and harder for Ali to hear her. "It's really loud there; can I call you back a little later?" The sitting area was very quiet, and Mary already felt like she was shouting.

As soon as the call ended, the tears wouldn't hold back any more. They came rushing down her cheeks like she'd turned on the faucet, though she tried to blink them back in. They had been building for days now, and she couldn't hold them in any longer. Just then, the door from the restrooms opened as Mary tried to catch her breath, and she was face to face with Trish. She froze in her tracks and looked at Mary. Her face softened for a brief moment, and then her feeling badly for Mary disappeared as quickly as it appeared. She dropped her head and speed-walked out the other door.

Mary allowed Trish to see her being vulnerable, and she didn't even care. Anything she had left in her to get through the night was gone. She was mentally and emotionally exhausted and just wanted to get out of her dress and crawl into bed. She no longer wanted to be there at midnight, although seeing the look on Trish's face as she kissed Alex was somewhat tempting. She didn't feel like ringing in a new year with people she didn't even know and could care less about who she was. New Year's was supposed to be about hope and wishes for the new year, and there was no hope for her at the restaurant with these people.

She pulled herself together, wiped the tears off her cheeks, and cleaned away the mascara that pooled under her eyes before walking to the elevator. She paused for a short second, scanning the room for Alex, but didn't have the energy to find him. He was sure to still be out on the terrace, and it would take her longer to find him than it would to send him a text from the cab.

As she walked outside, the wind picked up and large snowflakes began swirling through the air. The doorman hailed her a cab and helped her inside. Once the feeling was back in her frozen hands, she pulled out her phone and sent Alex a message. *"Wasn't feeling well and decided to take a cab home. Enjoy the rest of your night out. -M."* She breathed a sigh of relief for no longer having to be at the party. She probably should never have agreed to go in the first place, but she didn't have anything better to do.

Her mind wandered back to Will and the call she missed from him earlier. She wanted so badly to call him back, but knew it would be best to wait until she got home and away from the cab driver and the sounds of the busy streets. She kept her phone in her hand the whole drive home, waiting for Alex to text back.

He didn't.

For all she knew, he hadn't even seen her message. He seemed to be enjoying himself with his colleagues, and completely unaware that she'd even left. She leaned her head to the side against the head rest, watching the snow fall out the window for the rest of the drive home.

Thirty minutes and three traffic jams later, the cab driver pulled up in front of her building. If there was any night of the year where you would get nowhere fast, it was tonight. The cab companies were working overtime, and the streets were flooded with them. Her ride home was comfortable, but a far cry from her limo ride earlier. The cab driver threw the car in park and hurried to her side of car to open the door for her. It wasn't normal cab driver behavior, so the gesture caught her off guard. He held out his hand and helped her out of the car.

"Thank you, you're very kind. How much do I owe you?" she asked, reaching for her wallet as the snow continued to blow by her.

"You're welcome, ma'am. I would have hated for you to get your pretty dress caught trying to get out," he replied. He had a kind smile, and his hair matched the color of the falling snow.

Mary settled up with him and thanked him again for his kindness.

"Happy New Year," he shouted as he slammed the back door.

Mary turned around as she pulled open the door to her apartment building. "Happy New Year to you, too."

She rushed through the doors as the warm air burned against her cold cheeks. The lobby was deserted except for and elderly man who just returned from walking his dog. She supposed there were other parties going on in the building, but for the most part, it was quiet. She placed her purse on the small table next to the chairs in the lobby and walked over to check her mail. She hadn't checked it since returning home and assumed Alex hadn't either.

Mary dropped hard into the chair, flipping through the stack of envelopes that were piled inside. Most of them were either bills or junk mail, but halfway through, one envelope caught her eye. She flipped it over and ripped it open, pulling out a one-page letter inside.

Dear Ms. Bradford,

We want to thank you for applying for the receptionist position at our company and for taking the time to do an interview with us. Unfortunately, with a large number of applicants who were more qualified, we have decided to move forward with the other candidates. We will keep your resume on file for a year in the case something else were to open.

Sincerely,
Brenda Vogel

How qualified do you have to be to answer a phone

and write down appointments? It looked like the new year was off to a rough start already. Mary stuffed the letter back into the envelope and walked to the elevator, even more ready to climb into bed. She reached into her clutch purse and pulled out her keys. As she got closer to the apartment door, she was startled to find a man napping on the floor next to her apartment. She approached him slowly, leaning down to see if she could get a look at his face, assuming he was a guest of someone in her building that partied too much and lost his way home. She crouched down next to him as her breath caught in her throat. She stood up quickly placing her hand over her mouth.

It was Will.

Mary stood frozen in the hallway, unsure of whether she should wake him or let him keep sleeping. She squeezed her eyes shut, blinking over and over again to make sure she was really seeing him there. Moments later, he began to wake up. She slowly backed away as he lifted his head, not wanting him to think that she'd been staring at him sleeping.

"Mary, you're here," he said, his voice raspy. He rubbed his eyes and shuffled to a more upright position.

"Yes, I'm here. I live here," she said, a little confused. "What are *you* doing here?"

Will pushed his arms against the floor and stood up, his head dizzy from getting up too fast. He cleared the frog out of his throat. "I went to see you the other day at your parents' house, but they said you had already left."

Mary unlocked the door and ushered him inside. "Please, make yourself comfortable on the couch. I'm going to change out of this dress and I'll put on some coffee." She unzipped her dress as she sped down the hall to change, still in shock that he was actually sitting in her living room. She slid on a pair of black yoga pants and a loose-fitting sweatshirt and walked back to the kitchen to make a pot of coffee.

She sat down next to him on the couch, leaving the middle seat open between them. "You went to see me at my parents' house? When?"

Will tried to think back through the last few days. So many thoughts had been running through his head that he didn't even know what day it was.

"I went there the afternoon you left town. Your parents let me inside and then told me Alex made you fly home with him early. Is that true?" He sat there waiting for her answer, needing to know if it was her idea or his.

"Mary nodded. "That is true," she said. "I wasn't supposed to leave until tomorrow, but he booked me an earlier flight, and I didn't really have a choice." She wanted so badly to tell him that she didn't want to go, but wanted to hear why he was there before she went any further. She stood from the couch and poured them each a cup of coffee.

"Thanks, I could use this right about now," he said, taking the mug from her hands.

"Why didn't you just call me instead of coming to the house?" She placed her mug on a coaster next to her.

Will sat there wondering what Mary must be thinking of him showing up at her door. "I had to see you in person. I guess I didn't factor in the thought that you would fly home early."

Mary felt a knot in the pit of her stomach. "I was going to tell you I was leaving, but then I saw you at the restaurant with Lauren and I didn't think you'd want to see me after what happened at the wedding."

Will jerked his head back. "You were at the restaurant? I didn't see you there."

Mary shook her head. "No, not exactly. I saw your truck parked outside, and when I pulled into the parking lot to go in and find you, that's when I saw you with Lauren."

His heart sank. He had no idea what she saw, but could already tell she had the wrong idea.

Mary continued. "I was afraid you'd see me in the parking lot, so I drove around the block, and when I came back around, I saw the two of you hugging good-bye." She shrugged. "I can't blame you for being with her. And, of course, for all you knew, I went back here to live the rest of my life with Alex."

He placed his hand on her knee. "It's not what you think," he explained. "Yes, I was hugging her good-bye, but that is the whole point."

Mary cocked her head to the side, not following.

"She asked me to meet her there for breakfast, and that's why I didn't make it to your parents' house." He scooted closer to her on the couch. "Lauren wanted to know once and for all if there was any chance of her and I getting back together."

Mary raised her eyebrows. "And? What did you say?"

"I said no," Will said with a swell in his heart. "I told her my heart belonged to someone else, and I had to let her go and follow my true feelings." He held his breath for a long second. "So, I did. I followed it all the way across the country to your doorstep."

Her stomach fluttered as she tried to swallow the lump that formed in her throat. "I had it all wrong," she admitted. "I'm so sorry."

He leaned over and wrapped his arms around her. "Don't be sorry. I'm sorry for not fighting for you harder while you were still there. I should have stood up to Alex when he showed up at the wedding and told him he had to leave, but I didn't know if it was my place."

She leaned her head against his shoulder, choking back the emotions she thought she'd already released. "You wanted to fight for me?" she asked.

He placed his hands on the sides of her arms and sat her up. "I wanted to fight for you two years ago, before you first moved away," he said. "And I wanted to fight for you last year when you came home for Ali's engagement party. I wasn't going to let you go a third time without finally fighting."

"So, you hopped on an airplane and showed up at my door? What if Alex would have answered the door?" She wiped her cheek with the back of her hand.

Will pressed his lips together. "I guess I hadn't thought

that far ahead." They both started laughing.

He held onto her hands, and really focused on her. "I'm not sure how you feel exactly, since he interrupted us at the wedding before we got to that part, but I'm not letting you go this time. I don't need your answer now, but I couldn't go one more day without telling you exactly how I felt."

She sat there next to him, still trying to process all of what he just told her. It was everything she had wanted to hear, and she felt like she should pinch herself to be sure it was real. Her phone chimed on the coffee table as she got up to refresh their coffee.

"Do you need to get that?" he asked.

"I wouldn't worry about it. It's probably just a drunk text from my sisters or something." She checked the time on the microwave and noticed it was nearly midnight.

Her phone chimed again.

She walked back into the living room and picked up her phone. "Oh no," she whispered.

"Is everything okay?" He stood from the couch and placed his hand on the small of her back.

"Yes, but its Alex. He said he's leaving the party early to come home and spend the new year with me." Mary regretted saying that the second the words left her lips. "I'm sorry, I shouldn't have said that."

"Its fine, Mary," Will responded. "The man is still your boyfriend. He would be crazy if he didn't want to come home to his beautiful girlfriend. I know I would."

Heat rushed to Mary's cheeks as she dropped her

head. "I'm not sure it's a good idea that you're here when he gets back. I'm not sure how I would explain to him that you flew halfway across the country." She gathered their mugs and carried them back to the kitchen in an effort to hide the fact that she had company.

Will's heart sunk. "I suppose you're right," he agreed. He watched as she rushed around the apartment, destroying any evidence that he had been there.

She felt like she was a teenager again, trying to sneak her friends out of the house before her parents got home and caught her. No matter how hard she tried to hide it, they always found out. She wasn't sure if it was neighborhood spies, or if they were just that good. She was praying that Alex wouldn't be as smart as they were.

Will walked to the front door as Mary closed the dishwasher, hiding their coffee mugs inside.

"I'm sorry to have to rush you out of here after you flew all this way to be here." She wrapped her arms across her stomach to keep the butterflies at bay. "Will you still be here in the morning?"

"My flight leaves tomorrow in the early afternoon," he said. "I didn't plan for a long trip on the off chance you had no interest in seeing me. The last thing I wanted was to be stuck here alone, feeling like a total loser for a week." He tried to laugh it off, not wanting to show her how disappointed he was that he had to leave.

Mary playfully hit him in the arm, purposely in the same one as she had all last week. "Why would you think I wouldn't want to see you?"

He didn't answer. "How about a late breakfast tomorrow before I go to the airport? There's a restaurant right down from my hotel that I saw on the way over here. I think it was called diner something?"

"Sal's diner?"

"Yes, that's it. See, I was close. Should we say ten o'clock?" He glanced at his watch to see how close to midnight it was. The last thing he wanted was for Alex to get off the elevator, and he was still standing in the doorway.

"That sound's perfect," Mary said with excitement. "I'm sure Alex will have a meeting or meet a client, blah, blah, blah. I'm sure it will be fine."

Will ran his hands down Mary's arms, resting her hands in his. "I'm looking forward to it. If anything changes, just give me a call." He gently kissed her on the cheek, resting his lips there for a few seconds. He said good-bye as he turned to walk toward the stairwell, not wanting to pass Alex in the elevator, when Mary called out to him.

"Happy New Year," she said.

"I have a feeling it will be," he said, and disappeared into the stairwell.

Chapter
Twenty-Six

Two hours later, Alex finally arrived back at their apartment. Mary was awoken suddenly by the sound of him fumbling his keys on the other side of the door. She whisked the hair out of her face and still half asleep, walked to the door to unlock it for him. Just as she reached for the door knob, he found the correct key and unlocked it himself.

"Mary," he said, startled by her standing there. "Why are you awake?" Alex was slurring his words as he stumbled into the kitchen, tripping on the leg of the dining room chair on the way. "Be careful, there's a chair in the way." He slapped his keys down on the counter and pulled his phone out of his suit coat pocket.

"I'll be careful," she said sarcastically. She walked back

into the living room to straighten the blanket she used to cover up with while trying to wait up for him. "So much for making it home by midnight, huh?" she said angrily. Mary watched him from across the room as he studied the buttons on his suit coat, trying his hardest to unbutton it. "Do you need some help with that?" she said thinking of how pathetic he looked in his attempt.

He looked at his watch, his head bobbing from side to side. "I almost made it on time," he mumbled. "I'll be right back. Stay right there." He pointed in her direction and then disappeared down the hall.

Mary stood silent in the living room, bracing herself for the sound of him knocking something over on his way — himself included, but all she heard was silence. She tiptoed down the hallway to the bedroom and peered around the door frame into the room, but all she could see were his dangling legs. He must have sat down to change his clothes and passed out. As annoyed as she was with him, she was thankful he had fallen asleep so she wouldn't have to try to deal with him this late at night.

She walked into the room when she was sure it was safe and lifted his feet up onto the bed, causing him to roll into place. She grabbed the quilt that was draped over the end of the bed and covered him up. Turning off the light, she closed the door behind her and headed back to her bed on the couch. Come morning, the couch would likely be her permanent sleeping spot, so she might as well get used to it.

Her eyes filled with a burning sensation as she rested

her head on her pillow, but they wouldn't close. She was focused in on the bright light of the moon shining in the balcony door, illuminating the flakes of snow still falling from the sky. Being on the seventh floor, she couldn't tell whether or not the snow was accumulating, but right now that was the least of her worries. If nothing else, the falling snow brought a sense of calm about her. There was something so peaceful about the light powder falling so gracefully from the sky that seemed so soothing to her.

As hard as she tried, she couldn't fall asleep. Her mind was running in a million different directions as she tried to weigh the positives and negatives about the decision she was about to make. She thought about both men, weighing one against the other. With respect for Will, one of the most positive things about him that came to mind almost immediately, was his kindness. He treated her like no other man ever had. If for some reason things didn't work out between the two of them, it would at least give her something with which to compare every other man in her future. Comparing Alex to Will at this point, Mary realized all she could see was negative with the way Alex treated her.

Another major positive concerning Will — he lived in Maple Falls, where her family lived as well. She knew she had hurt them when she left so abruptly, but they weren't the kind of people to hold grudges, especially when it came to family. Her list of negatives in this decision-making process wasn't nearly as long as her list of positives. Only one, really, came to mind — failure. How would people view her? If she moved back home, Mary thought people would think of her as a failure in her relationship and the town would be full of *"I told you so's."* That was probably the one thing Mary feared most, out of all the things that were about to change, the fear of being thought of as a failure was at the top of the list.

She moved away nearly two years ago, so maybe that wouldn't qualify as failure. She'd given their relationship nearly twenty-four months of her life, trying to see if it would work out for her, but it didn't. She was proud of herself for trying, but it was time to accept the fact that it wasn't working. Her feelings have changed so much toward the life she'd been living, and towards Alex. She was finally realizing that she needed to stand up to all of it. She truly believes that Will was brought back into her life to help her do so.

Mary laid awake for most of the night until her brain had exhausted all the possible scenarios that may take place in the morning, and she finally fell asleep.

Slam! Mary was once again woken with a startling noise, this time by the slamming sounds of kitchen cupboards as Alex opened and shut each one. Not exactly the way she liked to be woken up, but that was a risk she took by sleeping on the couch.

"Why can I never find anything in this kitchen?" he shouted. "Nothing in here is arranged with any rhyme or reason." He continued to open and slam the doors closed until Mary got off the couch to help him.

"Maybe if you ate here once in a while, you'd know where things were," she snapped.

Alex paused from slamming cupboards to give her an annoyed look.

"Is it necessary to slam every cupboard in the kitchen? What are you looking for?" She took a step back and waited for him to stop throwing a fit.

He stopped slamming the doors and leaned his elbows on the counter, rubbing his temples with the tips of his fingers. "I'm not feeling well, and I was trying to find some ibuprofen or tea, anything really. I'm freezing, I have the chills, and a headache the size of Texas." He never was one who took being ill very well.

"A little too much fun last night perhaps?" Mary said with a smirk.

Alex groaned. "No, it's not a hangover if that's what you're implying. I think I have the flu or something." He placed the back of his hand against his forehead. "How do I know if I have a fever?"

"Move," she said, slapping his hand out of the way. "You can't take your own temperature like that. Let me do it." She placed her hand against his forehead. "You feel a little warm. I'll go get the thermometer to double check." She walked to the bathroom, leaving Alex in the kitchen to whine alone.

Moments later, she returned with a thermometer in one hand, and a bottle of ibuprofen in the other.

"Open your mouth, and place this under your tongue," she ordered. She stood on her tip toes to be sure he got it all the way underneath. "Let me know when it beeps." She poured him a glass of water and set the bottle of medicine next to it for him to take when he was finished.

Alex crossed his arms and tapped his foot against the floor, impatiently waiting for the beep. "Great," he growled. "I do have a fever — a hundred and one to be exact." He set the thermometer on the counter and attempted to open the child-proof lid on the bottle. After three failed attempts, he handed it over to Mary, accepting defeat.

Mary opened it on the first try, placing three pills into his hand.

"Thanks," he said with a scowl. "I think I need to go lie back down. Can you make me some tea or something? I'm freezing, but coffee sounds awful." He dragged his feet in a pathetic manner down the hall to the bedroom.

Mary stood there and watched him, thinking how much of a baby he was being. She glanced at her watch and realized it was nearly quarter to ten. She hadn't showered or even gotten dressed yet. She flurried through the kitchen to find any kind of tea they had in the cupboard, filled a kettle of water on the stove, and dashed to the bathroom for a record timed shower.

The kettle was whistling in the kitchen by the time she turned off the shower. She wrapped a towel around her hair, patted her body dry, and threw on her robe. Making a cup of tea as quickly as possible, she carried it down the hall, careful not to spill and burn herself. That was the last thing she needed after a rough night. She placed the mug of tea on the nightstand within his reach and went to pick out something to wear. Grabbing a fresh pair of jeans from her dresser, she resisted the urge to pull a sweatshirt off the hanger. Instead, she opted for a soft pink sweater, something a little fancier than her usual attire.

In a panic, she looked at the clock on the nightstand. *How is it already past ten?* she thought to herself. Mary threw her robe on the floor in the closet and quickly pulled her clothes on. Grabbing a last-minute infinity scarf, she pulled it over her head and rushed to the bathroom for a little makeup.

Alex sat on the bed, watching her run around like a crazy person.

"I have to run a few errands this morning," Mary shouted from the bathroom, "so if there is anything you need while I'm out, I'll pick it up for you." She towel-dried her hair as best as she could and ran a quick brush through it. She put on a few swipes of eye shadow, ran her eyeliner over it and a few brush strokes of mascara to finish it off. She had never been a huge makeup person, but this would do for now.

"You're leaving?" Alex asked in a dramatic voice. "I was hoping you'd be home today. I'm really not feeling well, and what happens if I need something?" He gave her the eyes that she used to fall head over heels for once, but not anymore. Maybe he'd used them all up, but either way, she didn't feel the same as she did before.

"I think you'll be just fine," she assured him. "Your medicine should be kicking in any minute, and you have a hot cup of tea. All you have to do now is drink it and lie in bed and relax. Was there anything you wanted me to pick up for you while I'm out?" She waited impatiently for him to hem and haw as she stepped one foot into the hall, ready to dart out the door.

"I'm a little hungry," he said, trying to sit more upright. "Would it be too much trouble to ask you to make me a cup of soup before you go? My mom used to make it for me when I was younger, and it always helped. I think I saw a can in the cupboard this morning."

Mary sighed, knowing that was true. She was hoping he hadn't seen it and she could use that as an excuse to leave and pick some up. "Are you sure you want soup now? I think you should let the medicine kick in a little more and maybe take a little nap. I bet you'll feel much more like eating after that." She checked her watch, tilting her head to the ceiling and letting out a slow sigh.

Alex took a slow sip of his tea. "I'm really hungry now, but I'm afraid I don't have the energy to stand up in the kitchen to make it myself." He flashed her the look again. Even though it didn't make her fall for him again, it did cause great guilt deep in her stomach. All he wanted was for her to stay home and take care of him, and all she wanted was to run out the door to have breakfast with another man.

The guilt won over as she stood in front of the stove, stirring a can of soup into a pot. Checking her watch again, her heart sunk. She was already pretty late. Will was sure to think she was standing him up. If only he'd told her what time his flight left, maybe she would be able to calm her nerves. For all she knew, he was already at the airport, ready to fly out of her life again. There had to be a limit of how many times you can *lose* somebody before they don't come back again. Their entire relationship so far had been based on secrets and misunderstandings. She wanted so badly to put it all out in the open and move forward.

She placed the lid on the soup pot and reached for her cell phone on the counter. No missed calls from Will. Her stomach began to quiver at the thought of him leaving her again. Mary pulled up Will's number to text him so she could explain that she was running late, not standing him up.

"Had to take care of a few things this morning. Running a little behind. Hope to be there soon! What time does your flight leave?" She pressed send and tossed her phone back on the counter seconds before the pot boiled over.

She pulled the lid off and gave it one last stir before pouring it into a bowl, when she heard a strange ringing sound coming from the living room. She was familiar with the sounds that both Alex's and her phones made, and it was neither of those. She turned the burner off on the stove and walked into the living room, waiting for the sound to repeat.

Nearing the couch, she stood quietly and listened. It rang again. She ran her hands through the cracks of the couch, trying to see where the noise was coming from.

Then her hand hit something across the back. She wrapped her hand around it and pulled it out, her heart landing in the pit of her stomach. She now had an even bigger problem. The sound she was hearing was Will's cell phone.

The waitress stopped by the table several times to refill Will's coffee, but by the third time, he turned her down. Checking his watch, he got an uneasy feeling. After his conversation with Mary last night, he was certain this would finally be the meeting that wouldn't be interrupted. The moment when they would finally be able to lay it all out on the table and decide on their next move together. It wouldn't be so stressful if she was still living in Maple Falls, but she wasn't. And, of course, he was only visiting for less than twenty-four hours, so time was not on their side.

He finished the last of his coffee and asked the waitress for the tab. He waited for Mary before ordering food, so he ate nothing. It was probably for the best having no appetite left. He walked to the front, paid the tab and hailed a cab that was passing by outside.

"Where to on this wonderful day?" the cab driver asked.

If he only knew how far from wonderful his day really was, Will thought. "To the airport, I guess," he mumbled.

"You guess, or you know?" The cab driver was

attempting to make a joke, but Will was too preoccupied to notice.

"What did you say?" Will looked up, not hearing a word the driver had said.

"Oh, nothing," said the driver. "We should be to the airport shortly." He pulled out with the flow of traffic and headed toward the freeway.

Traffic was fairly light as they drove through town. Will leaned against the back seat, flicking a crumpled-up gum wrapper off the seat next to him. He zoned out for most of the ride, watching the pine tree shaped air freshener spin in circles that hung below the rear-view mirror, masking the odors of the half eaten to-go box sitting in the front passenger seat. Will rolled the window down, and his fingers stuck to the handle. He wiped his hand along the top of his jeans and decided not to touch anything else.

The driver screamed down the entrance ramp onto the freeway, the shocks squealing as the cab bounced up and down with every bump they hit. He passed by cars aggressively on the freeway, zooming in and out of lanes to get him there as quickly as possible. Will wanted to roll the window back up, but feared what his hand might stick to if he touched the handle again. Besides, if he cut off his fresh air supply, the driver's lunch would begin to linger to the back seat again.

In a record amount of time, the cab driver pulled up to the front of the airport. Only having packed a small carry-on, Will was able to bypass the curbside check-in. The automated glass doors opened as he stood in front of them, and he made his way to the security checkpoint.

He stepped on the back of his heels and removed his shoes as the line piled in behind him. The security guards moved the line through quickly, only pulling a few to the side for an extra check with the handheld device. He placed his shoes into a large gray bin and began emptying his pocket — his keys, some spare change, his wallet, and his —. Where was his cell phone?

He frantically began searching all of his pockets, trying to remember when he last used it. The line behind him was pushing him forward. He placed his duffel on the conveyor belt and walked through the body scanner. On the other side, he slipped his feet back into his shoes and gathered the rest of his belongings, carrying them to a nearby table.

He unzipped every zipper, looking in each pocket of his bag. It was nowhere to be found. He was praying he didn't leave it in the cab or at the restaurant. With not much time before his flight was scheduled to board, he had no choice but to go to his gate and figure something out later. He walked to the check-in desk and was greeted by a friendly woman.

"Good morning, sir," she said. "Are you checking in for your flight?"

"Yes, please," he said, pulling his driver's license out of his wallet.

"I'm sorry to tell you, sir, but due to some inclement weather in the flight path, your flight has been delayed."

He checked his watch. "Do you know how long it will be?"

The woman checked her computer. "I'm not sure on an exact time," she explained, "but it looks to be at least two hours, maybe more if the storm slows its pace."

That was all he needed to hear. He thanked her and pulled his duffel bag onto his shoulder as he jogged back through the terminal.

Chapter
Twenty-Seven

Mary grabbed the ladle and scooped the soup into a bowl, trying to steady her hand so she didn't spill as her nerves began to take over. Slipping on a pair of oven mitts, she carefully placed it onto a serving tray with some crackers and carried it to the bedroom for Alex.

"Here's the soup you requested," she told him. "It's boiling hot, so I'll leave it on the nightstand to cool for a little while."

Alex slowly turned his head in her direction and whispered thank you in the most dramatic fashion possible.

"I looked in the refrigerator and didn't see much else for you to eat. I'm going to run to the store while I'm out doing my errands and pick up some jello, crackers, more soup, and some popsicles." She stood next to the bed, praying he wasn't going to protest her leaving again.

"That sounds good, Mary, thank you." He half smiled and rolled back over.

She knew that he would likely not eat the soup and fall asleep like she told him to do in the first place. Of course, part of her felt better making it for him, even if it made her late to meet Will. She grabbed her purse, tossed Will's phone inside, and locked the apartment door on the way out, rushing down the hall to the elevator.

Four cars passed by her before she was able to pull out of the parking garage. The sound of the turn signal pulsed in her ears, ticking away each second, making her later and later. She turned in the direction of the restaurant, but after looking at the clock, she assumed he was likely gone already. She turned around the block and headed in the other direction, straight for the airport.

There was probably little to no chance she was going to find him there, but she had to try. Will hadn't given her any of his flight information that would have sped her along, but she wasn't going to let that stand in her way. She didn't know his gate, flight number, or which terminal he was in. Just thinking about it, made her chest begin to tighten. She felt so helpless.

She pulled onto the exit ramp and merged into the flow of traffic heading in to the airport. Thankfully, the parking lane there was far shorter than the drop-off lane, giving her a little extra hope. For all she knew, he could be in one of nearly twenty taxi cabs sitting in the drop-off line. She veered to the left and entered the parking ramp, pulling out a stamped ticket from the machine to lift the arm. Driving around in a circle for the first two levels, she finally found a small compact spot near the elevators. Mary threw the car in park, jumped out of the car, and slammed the door, listening for the honking sound that it locked behind her as she ran for the door.

The airport was extremely crowded — full of passengers fighting their way to the security lines, weaving back and forth through the roped off partitions. Children, unable to stand still while waiting in line, were running circles around their parents. Mary went straight to the monitors to try and find his flight. She scanned the long list that stretched across seven television screens, but none of them were flying to Maple Falls.

Her chin began to quiver as she came to the realization that he could have a connecting flight. She blinked her eyes hard, trying to focus on all of the flight numbers on the screen as they began to blend together. After scanning them one more time, she realized without having a flight number, it was impossible to know which one was his. She felt the room begin to spin as she turned around, trying to decide where to go next. The amount of people walking around in the ticket area was overwhelming.

She searched by the e-ticket terminals on her way to the ticketing counter. Mary chose the closest airline and got in line, shuffling her feet uncomfortably as she waited near the back. She wasn't even sure what she was getting in line for. She didn't have a ticket and was certain they wouldn't give her any information about the passengers.

She dropped her shoulders, feeling defeated, as tears balanced on the rim of her eyelids. However, she wasn't going to give up. Dabbing the corners with her sleeve, she tried to regain her composure. What if his flight already left? Will had no way of contacting her without his phone. She rubbed the back of her neck to release the tension that was taking over her body.

When she finally reached the front of the counter, her voice quivered as she tried to speak. "I know this may sound crazy, but I'm looking for a friend who was flying out today, and I was wondering if you could tell me if he left already."

The airline employee leaned her head down, looking at Mary over the top of her wire-rimmed glasses. "Was he flying on our airline, ma'am?"

Mary cleared her throat. "I'm not sure. Is there any way you could search for his name in your database?"

The woman shook her head back and forth. "Are you a passenger on the flight?"

What little patience Mary had left was wearing thin, ready to snap at the drop of a hat. "If I were on the flight, I would know the flight information. I just want to know if you have a flight going to Maple Falls this afternoon, and if there is a man by the name William Roberts on the flight." She leaned over the counter, hoping to intimidate the woman, but it wasn't working.

"I'm sorry, miss, but I'm not at liberty to release that kind of information." She looked past her to the next person in line, wanting Mary to move aside.

"Please, this is very important," Mary begged. "I don't have a ticket to get through the security checkpoint, so I have no way of checking to see if he is waiting at his gate."

The woman showed no sympathy for Mary. "Like I told you, I cannot give you that information. If you'd like to purchase a ticket, I'd be happy to help you with that."

Mary threw her head back. "Thanks for nothing," she said in a disgusted manner and walked away from the counter. She walked over to the closest wall she could find and leaned back against it, crouching down wrapping her arms around her knees. There was nothing left for her to do. She had no way of finding him — it was like trying to find the needle in this giant haystack.

Her heart ached as tears poured out of her eyes, unable to hold them in any longer. How did she get here? Her life had changed so much over the past few weeks. It felt as though someone had thrown it into a blender with the lid off, causing it to go in a million different directions. She'd been fighting the feelings in her heart on what she really wanted for so long. Now that she finally knew, it seemed as though something kept getting in the way.

Mary felt a light tapping on her shoulder. An elderly man was bent down next to her, resting his hand on her shoulder.

"Is everything okay, miss?" He reached into his jacket pocket and pulled out a tissue, handing it to her.

"Thank you," she said, wiping the wet streaks off of her cheeks. "Everything is a mess."

The man placed his hands under Mary's elbow and helped her to her feet. "There, there," he said with a sympathetic tone about his voice. "Can I buy you a cup of coffee? Something warm to drink might help a little."

She looked him in the eye, taken aback by his kindness to a complete stranger. Completely lost at that point, she simply nodded.

As they walked together, he talked to her about the weather, delayed flights, and many stories about his granddaughter that he was spending the holidays with. Anything he could do to get her mind off of whatever was troubling her, even if only for a moment. There was a small coffee shop near the security area that he led her to. By the time they got in line, she was almost calm again.

"Please, order whatever you'd like, miss. My treat," said the kindly gentleman.

Mary ordered the flavor of the day coffee, not in the mood for anything fancy. They handed it over the counter to her, and the warmth felt comforting around her hands. "Thank you, you're so kind," Mary responded, still not believing how kind he was to her.

He grinned. "I have a little unexpected time to kill, so your company is a welcomed surprise." He reached for his coffee and walked to a small table. "My flight home was delayed due to some bad weather somewhere between here and there."

"Delays are the worst," Mary said. "Where are you flying to?" She blew on her coffee, taking a small sip.

"I'm flying into Maple Falls, but I live about an hour

north of there."

Mary nearly spit her coffee across the table. "You're going to Maple Falls?" She sat straight up in her chair. "The man I've been looking for is flying there, too. It got delayed?" Her heart began to race at the thought that Will was still in the airport. "I tried to find it on the monitor, but I didn't see it."

"Sometimes when the flights get delayed, they disappear from the monitors while they are being updated. Bad timing, I suppose. Is your friend flying alone? I saw several young men sitting at the gate earlier."

"Yes, he was. His name is Will, and I was supposed to meet him for breakfast this morning before his flight, but I got delayed and didn't make it there in time. When I tried to call him, I discovered he'd lost his phone at my apartment, so I have no way of reaching him."

The man nodded, trying to follow along. "So, you got delayed this morning, and now he got delayed this afternoon." He laughed at the coincidence. "I'd say it's a sign."

Mary tilted her head to the side. "How so?"

"His flight got delayed to give you extra time to find him. If you weren't meant to, our plane would have taken off already. Twenty minutes ago, to be exact."

She looked around the crowded ticket area again from her table with renewed hope. "Do you suppose he's still by the gate, or do you think he came out?"

He shrugged. "I suppose he could have come back out. The only reason I did was so I could step outside and get some fresh air."

She sat there, listening to the barista shout out names on coffee orders. "Clara. Megan. Will." Mary's heart stopped. She jumped out of her chair and looked over at the counter. "Oh, my goodness," she whispered under her breath. "There he is." She stood on her tip toes and shouted, "Will!"

He took his coffee from the barista's hands, and as he turned to look in her direction, he nearly dropped it. He rushed over to her. "What are you doing here?" he said with a shocked look on his face.

The man stood from the table and joined them. "I see you've finally found him. I'll leave the two of you alone to talk," he said. "It was a pleasure meeting you, miss." He tipped his hat and made his way back over to the security checkpoint.

"Who was that?" Will asked.

"An angel," Mary said, waving as he turned to look back in her direction.

"What are you doing here?" he asked again. "When you didn't come to the restaurant, I thought you changed your mind."

"Everything is a mess," she sobbed, leaning into his chest.

Will wrapped his arms around her back, letting her have a moment before asking her a third time.

She lifted her head as she wiped her cheeks with the cuff of her jacket. "I woke up this morning and was getting ready to meet you, but then Alex needed soup. Then he fell asleep and didn't even eat it, and I was running late. When I tried to send you a message to let you know, I found your phone in my couch. I panicked because I didn't know how to reach you." Mary took a deep breath from rattling all of that out in one long sentence. She tried to calm down before speaking again, realizing she must be coming off as a crazy person, making no sense at all.

"So, you were running late because Alex needed soup?" He tried not to laugh, but he was trying to make sense of everything she just blurted out.

She took another deep breath. "Yes. I was sleeping on the couch. Alex woke me up from all the noise he was making in the kitchen, trying to find soup because he wasn't feeling well. He was having so much trouble, I thought I better help by fixing the soup for him. It took me a while to get the soup opened and heated, of course. I realized I was going to be late, so I tried to contact you, but you must have dropped your phone in my couch last night." She reached into her purse and handed the phone back to him.

"I realized I lost it when I got to the airport. I was worried I left it at the restaurant or lost it in one of the cabs I had been in." He checked his messages, and saw her text.

Mary continued. "When I realized you probably weren't at the restaurant anymore, I came straight here, hoping I would find you." She waved her arm at the crowd of people in the ticket area.

"And you actually thought you were going to?" Will added, knowing the almost impossible task with the crowd there. They both burst out laughing.

"Well, technically, I did," she teased. They walked to the table she was sitting at earlier and sat down. "How much time do you have?"

Will checked his watch. "About an hour, I think. I suppose they'll announce it over the intercom if it changes."

Mary set her coffee down on the table and reached for his hands. "There is something I've wanted to tell you for a while now, but for some reason, we keep getting interrupted."

"We have? I hadn't noticed," he joked.

"Last night you told me that you were all in, that you wanted to be with me, but you had to leave before I had the chance to tell you — I want to be with you, too. I've wanted to be with you almost from the start when I first saw you making that delivery at my parents' shop." She waited for a reaction before she continued, but he sat there quietly. "I want to move back home to Maple Falls and see where this takes us."

He sat there with a blank expression on his face. Mary waved her arm in front of him, trying to get him to come back from wherever he'd gone. A slow smile began to spread across his face.

"Do you mean that?" he said with excitement.

"Yes, I've never been more certain of anything in my life," she said. "I'm not happy here anymore. Honestly, I'm not sure I ever was. I didn't realize how much I missed home until this last trip. And seeing you brought out feelings I pushed away many years ago. Everything came rushing back all at once, and I didn't know how to handle any of it."

Will quietly listened.

"When Alex showed up unexpectedly at the wedding, I hadn't figured it all out yet, and at that point, leaving seemed like the easier answer. I had so many decisions I was faced with, and I was afraid to make any."

Will kept his eyes locked on hers, taking in everything she was saying. "This is a big decision to make," Will said, his eyes fixed on hers. "Are you sure you've had enough time to really think about it?"

Mary wasn't sure if he was trying to talk her out of it, or if he was happy with the decision she had made. She leaned across the table closer to him. "I want to come back home with you," she whispered.

Will leaned in the rest of the way to her and kissed her. "I've waited a long time to do that," he said. "You had something to tell me, now I have something I want to show you." He leaned down and reached into his duffel bag, pulling out an envelope. "I've been carrying this around for a week now, hoping to get the chance to show it to you, but again, we were always interrupted." He pulled the letter out and unfolded it, handing it across the table to her.

She placed it down on the table and read through it. "This company wants to buy your furniture?" she said with so much excitement, she could hardly contain herself.

Will beamed. "Well, they did, but I met with one of

them a couple days ago and we worked out something a little different. While I would supply them with a few select pieces to sell in their stores, they are also going to help me with opening my own store in Maple Falls."

Mary's face lit up. "Will, that's amazing! Are you going to do it?"

Will shrugged. "I haven't signed anything yet. I was hoping I could get your opinion first."

Mary thought about it for a moment. "Where do you want to be a year from now? What do you see yourself doing?"

Will pressed his lips together. "I think I can see myself running my own shop. And I see you there, running it with me."

Mary jumped up out of her seat. "Yes!" she shouted, causing several neighboring tables to look over at them. "Let's do it. I want to help you make your dream a reality."

He wrapped his arms around her, kissing her again, only this time a bit more passionately. "But what about your dreams?" he added.

"Do you want to know what my dream is?" She leaned back, looking him in the eye. "This. This right here is my dream." She leaned into him, listening to his heart racing in his chest. "Take me home," she whispered.

The intercom crackled overhead. "We are now boarding flight number five seven six to Maple Falls at gate three."

Will wrapped Mary's hands in his. "Where do we go

from here? I have a flight to catch, and you still live here."

"I need to go home and talk to Alex. After that, I want to come home." Her body felt weightless at the thought of making Maple Falls her home again.

Will embraced her one more time, kissing the top of her head. "I'll call you when my flight lands and we'll figure everything out. I hope your talk goes well with Alex."

Mary dreaded the thought of having to tell Alex she was leaving, but it shouldn't bother him too much. After all, how would he even miss her when he was never home for them to have a real relationship? She stood by the security area and watched Will until he disappeared into the crowd.

Her drive home was silent, no radio, no nothing, so silent it was almost deafening. She didn't want any distractions as she thought about how she would tell Alex it was over between them. As she pulled into the parking garage, she ran different lines through her head, still trying to figure out the best way to tell Alex everything. She locked her car and walked to the elevator. *Here goes nothing,* she thought.

The following week, Mary sat on the floor in her bedroom as she taped the last box shut. She pulled the end of the tape and smoothed it across the box with her hand. The past week was spent packing, doing name and address changes, and avoiding Alex. He was asleep when she returned from the airport that day, so she had to wait until later that night to talk to him. Mary explained to him that she still had feelings for him, but was no longer in love with him. Alex told her that he knew she wasn't happy there, but avoided the topic.

In the end, Mary left out the part about Will coming out there, figuring it wouldn't do anyone any good. He asked her if there was somebody else, but she avoided answering the question. The point she was trying to get across was that she was no longer happy with him or living where they did. She made the decision to go back to Maple Falls, regardless of Will being there. She realized that it was always going to be home to her and until she moved back, she wouldn't be happy with anything in her life.

Alex seemed to take it pretty well, admitting that maybe he did spend too much time away from home, but it wasn't something he was willing to change. He asked her if they could stay in touch as friends. She agreed, even though she knew the moment she left, she'd likely never hear from him again. Mary almost felt resentful thinking that Alex and Trish had a spark between them, but it wasn't really a concern of hers any more.

She carried the last box into the living room where she had been stacking them the whole week. The moving van was scheduled to arrive later that afternoon to drive her belongings back to Maple Falls. The day she made the phone call home to her parents to tell them the good news was very exciting for her. Mary held the phone away from her head as far as she could to help distance the joyous screams coming from the other end. Her parents agreed to let her stay with them when she came back as long as she helped out in the coffee shop a few days a week.

Two hours later, the movers arrived and began loading the truck with the boxes. There was minimal furniture, since most of it was Alex's. She decided to leave her furniture, because she didn't have anywhere to store it even if she did take it. Alex decided to come home for lunch to say good-bye to her. Coming home for lunch to spend time with her was something he never seemed to find time to do in the past two years living there. He weaved in through the door between the movers.

"I can't believe you're actually leaving," he said, looking around at the room as the boxes dwindled. "I was hoping I would catch you before you left." He walked into the kitchen as he sent a text on his phone, half listening to her as she answered.

"The movers are just about finished here, so when they leave, all I need to do is wait for my cab." She stared at him while he typed.

"Sorry," he apologized, "I have a lunch appointment, and they were just telling me what time they could meet." He set his phone down on the counter. "Are you sure you have everything? If you remember something you left behind, I suppose I could just mail it to you." He opened the cupboards, checking to see what all she had taken.

"I'm pretty sure I have everything. I went through the

apartment again this morning to double check." She watched him as he continued to open the kitchen cupboards. "I left you all of the dishes and most of the kitchen things. I really only took my clothes, some pictures, and a few other things I bought while living here. There really wasn't much here that was mine anyway." She glanced at her watch. "What time do you have to meet your lunch appointment? I don't want to keep you waiting."

"They are actually meeting me here to make it easier, but they won't be here for another ten minutes or so." He checked his phone, sending another text message.

The mover came into the apartment for the last box. "Ms. Bradford, this is the last box we need to load, so if you have a moment, we just need you to sign the papers downstairs, and we'll be on our way."

"That was fast," she said. "Please tell them I will be down in a few minutes." Mary turned back toward Alex. "Well, I guess this is good-bye," she said, trying to swallow the lump that was forming in her throat.

"I guess it is," he said. "I'm not really sure what to say. Have a nice life, I guess." Alex never was one to express him emotions very well. He was a man of few words when it came to sharing his emotions.

The buzzer on the wall sounded, breaking the awkward silence in the room. Mary walked over and pushed the button.

"I have a cab downstairs for Mary Bradford," the voice on the other end shouted.

"Thank you. I'll be right down." She looked back at Alex who was typing on his phone again. That was something she was not going to miss. "Take care of yourself, Alex. I'm sure I'll see you around Maple Falls the next time you come to visit."

"Yeah, I suppose you may," he answered, still typing.

Mary found the key to their apartment on her key ring and turned it around until it came off, and set it on the kitchen counter. "I won't be needing this anymore." She stood waiting for him to finish with his message to see if he would say good-bye or not. "Well, my cab is waiting so I better be going."

She moved in expecting a hug, and he reached out with one arm, patting her on the back, his phone still in the other hand. It was not the ideal good-bye hug, but from him, it was more than she thought she would get anyway. The fact that he came home for lunch to see her off should have been enough. In his eyes, it probably was. She walked to the door and turned back toward him one last time. "Good-bye, Alex," she said, and closed the door behind her.

Downstairs the cab was parked behind the moving truck near the front of the building. She met the movers, who were waiting in the front first, and then signed all of the documents.

"Will you be heading straight to Maple Falls from here?" Mary asked. "When should I expect you on the other side?" She signed the last form and handed the clipboard back to the driver.

"Yes, ma'am," the driver responded. "We will be leaving straight from here and will meet you at your house in about three days." He checked the forms to be sure all of the information was listed. "When we are about a half an hour out, we'll call the number you listed on the paperwork and let you know we are almost there." He shook her hand and crawled into the driver's seat. "Have a safe trip home, miss, and we'll see you in a few days."

As the truck drove away, she took one last look up at her apartment, trusting she wasn't making a huge mistake by leaving. She knew Alex would be fine there by himself. He certainly never showed much emotion about her leaving, so she was sure he'd be fine without her. The cab driver met her at the back and helped her place her bags in the trunk. He opened the back door and helped her inside as another cab was pulling up behind them.

As the driver climbed into the front, Mary took one last look back at the building as he pulled away from the curb. There it was, the sign she was waiting for, telling her that she was making the right decision. The person who climbed out of the other cab, was none other than Trish, Alex's lunch client. She didn't see Mary climb into the cab, but Mary saw her, and that was enough for her to know in her heart that she was making the right decision. She watched Trish walk until she disappeared into the building.

Mary shook it off, knowing that it was no longer a concern of hers. She reached into her purse and took out her phone to text Will. *"The moving truck just left, and I'm on*

my way to the airport. I'll call you before I board. I love you.
~M."

She placed her phone back into her purse and leaned back in her seat, smiling as the driver made his way to the airport. She had such a feeling of freedom as they drove further and further away from her old life. She was beginning a new chapter in her life, and with that new beginning, she felt a wonderful sense of love and excitement at the same time. She was ready — ready to go *home.*

ABOUT THE AUTHOR

Shannon Graupman lives in rural Minnesota with her husband and four children. When she's not running her family to dance, t-ball, and driving the carpool, Shannon enjoys reading, crocheting, and coffee. And of course, writing.

Shannon loves connecting with readers at
www.shannongraupman.com